TRUST

Colin Green

2QT Limited (Publishing)

First Edition published 2018 by
2QT Limited (Publishing)
Settle, North Yorkshire BD24 9RH United Kingdom

This is a work of fiction and any resemblance to any person living or dead is purely coincidental. The place names mentioned may exist but have no connection with the events in this book

Cover Design by Hilary Pitt
Printed in Great Britain by IngramSpark UK

Cover photographs copyright Chris Lishman Photography

A CIP catalogue record for the paperback format book is available from the British Library
ISBN 978-1-912014-98-9

I would like to dedicate TRUST to all those people who give freely of their own time in working tirelessly within amateur sports clubs, providing enjoyment and pleasure to so many people.
Please remember these dedicated few carry out their duties for absolutely nothing.

Acknowledgements

To Ruth for her love, total support and encouragement throughout the process of writing and finishing TRUST.
To Marge for her time, assistance, and always constructive criticism. Without their help this book would never have been written.

Morpeth RFC and Morpeth Golf Club for permission to obtain cover photographs.

Chris Lishman Photography.

John Scurfield for the aerial views supplied of the 17th hole.

Thanks to Josh, Tom and Loren for the fantastic birthday picture which proved the inspiration for the front cover.

1

Nina

It was absolutely freezing walking around the trading estate on the outskirts of Parton. The country was suffering another one of those very cold spells when February showed the world that winter was far from over. Not only was it exceptionally cold but the county of Parton was also notorious for spells of freezing fog that descended like a huge grey, heavy duvet and embraced the area. Tonight's weather reduced visibility to no more than thirty yards.

Nina was dressed for work and not the weather. She was wearing a short red miniskirt, seamed black stockings and bright-red high heels. The top half of her small, slim figure was covered with a black see-through blouse, which partially hid the tramlines on her arms, a result of self-harming, as well as drug taking. A short imitation-fur coat gave any potential punters a full view of her long legs. The coat was only a token effort to keep her warm. Her hair was short and self-dyed purple.

Nina had been a pretty girl but the ravages of her relatively short life had taken their toll and her beauty had all but disappeared. She was becoming noticeably thinner by the day. Taken into care at birth, her mother a heroin addict, Nina was pregnant at fourteen and fell into soft drugs shortly afterwards. She had continued with this life and within five years was dependent on heroin.

Nina had a younger sister. After ten years or so of separation, they had met fleetingly at their mother's third wedding. The wedding invitation was a complete surprise to Nina and she wondered how on earth her mother had located her. With her itinerant lifestyle, sleeping at various rental properties with other drug addicts, she was not easy to find.

After such a long time Nina was overjoyed to meet up with her sister, but her pleasure was short lived. Across the room she recognised the voice of her uncle Ron, who had abused her some years previously. She could no more tell her mother about the abuse now than she could the day it happened.

'Hi, Nina, as lovely as ever,' Uncle Ron said enthusiastically, as he started walking towards her. Recognition of that voice hit Nina like a thunderbolt and was followed by immediate paralysis. She could not move, let alone speak. Her abuser acknowledged the effect of his presence and withdrew from pursuing his former prey.

Now, standing on the street, staying warm was not a problem for the twenty-eight-year-old sex worker; she never felt the temperature after another hit. Her pimp, Dunc Travis, had dropped her at this location, one that had been well chosen away from any nosy members of the public. There was little CCTV coverage in the area and any cameras that were actually working protected a particular property, not the roads surrounding them. Neither would the cameras have picked up much movement in the gloomy fog.

Parton was the only city in the county of Parton. It was the hub of the county, housing all of the main administration centres as well as the Crown Court and maximum-security prison. The trading estate that Nina patrolled was well away from the hustle and bustle of the city centre.

She had scored with a punter in the early evening then

scored again almost straightaway, with the money she earned going immediately on her next heroin hit. Now, with her eyes staring and pupils dilated, she was trying to stay upright on the slippery pavement, hoping for another pick-up before trying to find somewhere to sleep.

Travis observed her from a safe distance. He had a couple of girls working tonight but Nina was proving increasingly difficult and time-consuming because of her escalating heroin addiction. Travis was nobody's fool; he had carved out a successful illegal career for himself. He had a dozen or so girls of many different nationalities on his books, able to fulfil most sexual needs. The girls caused him few problems – apart from Nina.

Brought up in a background of low-level drug dealing, he had diversified into pimping – it brought him more money and less hassle. His success had allowed him to purchase his Uncle Joe's garage when Joe suddenly passed away. He used the forecourt to operate a hand car-washing business. Dunc never got his hands dirty and never touched a bucket or a wet rag, but the business kept his employees and his drug contacts happy. It earned him pocket money and gave a legal front to his main business. He had a small office at the car wash from where he could operate his illegal but efficient enterprise.

His business profile was to change in an instant as Nina slid away from him along the icy, frost-bound pavement.

***

Peter Roberson, the recently appointed local Police and Crime Commissioner, had just left the reception for the opening of the new leisure centre. That was another photo shoot in the bag that would appear in the local press and show, yet again, that he was Mr Community for the people of Parton. Roberson had immense confidence in his own ability, to the point of arrogance.

The Police and Crime Commissioner (PCC) was a relatively new role that had replaced the old police authorities. Roberson's appointment had taken place when the force was in a state of flux. Recruitment had been suspended temporarily and a decision made to use former employees on short-term contracts to sustain operational commitments.

Parton Constabulary faced the normal problems of modern policing. It had to balance resources between tackling the extremes of terrorism as well as dealing with emerging local scrap-metal crime, which was increasing because of the current high cost of that particular product. The force was stretched in every direction; the day-to-day tasks of drug-related crime, youth disorder and protecting vulnerable people remained constant. Roberson had made it known publicly that his priorities were resource management and protecting the vulnerable.

Pete Roberson was extremely ambitious; a good showing in this role and then a Member of Parliament, that was his ambition. He was a man with a mission and in a hurry to get there. However, his position was not helped by the Temporary Chief Constable, Alan Conting, whom he thought was weak.

Roberson looked around nervously as he approached his car. He knew full well that the last drink had been one too many. It was purely due to him having a flirty conversation with Detective Inspector Sue Dalton from the Parton Constabulary, currently off-duty, who had received an invite through her swimming membership.

That extra drink had been an undoubted success; it allowed him to get her phone number – and, as far as Roberson was concerned, the anticipation of a little bit more. He got into his black Lexus knowing that he was over the legal drink-driving limit, pressed the automatic ignition pad and set off.

Roberson had one thing on his mind. He wasn't thinking of his recent meeting with Dalton, he was thinking of the trading estate and the goods on offer. He had been there before. It was seedy and base, providing cheap sex, which was just what Roberson liked. He simply couldn't help himself. More importantly, it was safe pick-up point for someone as high profile as the PCC.

He thought the fog was getting worse as he negotiated the final set of traffic lights and made his way to the entrance of the trading estate. Then, just as he turned right and began accelerating away from the junction, Nina appeared from out of nowhere in her red-leather miniskirt and red high heels. She staggered and slipped from the icy footpath. As she fell, her head and shoulders arrowed towards the road.

Roberson braked automatically but his reflexes were slightly impaired by that final drink. The angle of Nina's descent meant that she couldn't break her fall and she collided with the front nearside wheels of Roberson's Lexus. It was a classic case of being at the wrong place at the wrong time, for both Roberson and Nina.

There was negligible damage to the Lexus but the same couldn't be said for Nina's head and shoulders. She died instantly.

Roberson, an unfit and overweight forty-eight year old, levered himself out of his car. He looked around and saw absolutely nothing, not even Dunc Travis videoing the whole episode on his smartphone.

Roberson, shivering both from fear and the cold, stared into the gloom, his lifetime ambitions disappearing into the mist. Then he made a split-second decision, based totally on the fact that there were no apparent witnesses to this tragedy, either physical or technical. He turned on his heel, levered himself back into the driver's seat and drove away.

Dunc Travis finished his recording and replayed it. He ignored Nina's prone body lying on the road; this was more important. He'd got it all neatly recorded, all the evidence he would ever need.

Such was Travis's attention to detail, he had researched

the observation points from which he could monitor his girls' meetings; even in bad weather, he always had an unobscured view of a pick-up. Travis noted the full details of the punter and, most importantly, his or her vehicle registration despite any adverse weather conditions. Dunc Travis knew exactly who had driven over Nina. Ninety-nine per cent of the Parton public knew Peter Roberson; his name and face featured regularly in every local publication.

Travis was the second person at the scene to make an immediate decision. He pulled up his car and took a couple of bags from the boot. With some difficulty, he wrapped up Nina's slight corpse before lifting it into the boot. Thank goodness for her drug habit and associated weight loss. He used some de-icer to wash small fragments of her skull down a nearby drain.

He knew exactly what he had to do now: he needed some help to dispose of the body. He made a quick phone call to Stanislav Zenden, his tried and trusted deputy, who was the foreman of the car wash. Stan asked no questions, he simply agreed to cycle out to where Travis kept his small fishing boat at the west side of the marina and meet him in fifteen minutes.

Travis drove out to Parton West Marina, purposefully choosing a route to avoid any traffic camera coverage. His little fishing vessel was his hobby. It was berthed on that side of the marina, known locally as the 'cheap side', where there was no need for any security or cameras. The east side of the marina was the place to be; it was well known, not only in the area but nationally. It was an exclusive and sought-after berth, far too exclusive for Travis's small boat.

Duncan Travis thoughts started drifting. One day he would have a luxury boat, the envy of everyone, and berth it in the Parton East Marina. To afford an apartment or a berth at that location meant a great deal to the locals. Everyone who was anyone hung out there. Some of the professional footballers with struggling championship side Parton Rovers had purchased quayside apartments.

None of this was a concern for Travis as Stan cycled up alongside him. The two of them easily managed to transport Nina's body from the back of Travis's car down the short flight of steps on the harbour wall and then onto the small boat. Stan padlocked his precious bike to an unlit lamp post not covered by any cameras. No questions at all, just quiet obedience from Stan – despite the obvious package on board. The little fishing boat was soon heading out to sea with three passengers – but only two of them were alive.

Some twenty minutes later, there were just two people on board as Travis's boat headed back to the deserted Parton West Marina. Nina's body had been deposited some three miles offshore; with the assistance of some of Dunc's fishing weights, it would not re-emerge. Stan had operated the controls in the small cabin whilst Travis dumped the body.

'Keep it still,' shouted Travis, as he caught a glimpse of Stan seemingly preoccupied with his phone rather than the boat controls.

***

Roberson was standing at the window of his apartment overlooking Parton East Marina with a very large gin and tonic in his shaking hand. Gone was his arrogance and confidence; he was petrified. A couple of hours earlier life had been good: he'd been chatting up Sue Dalton; he was in a role that, for the time being, satisfied his exceptionally large ego.

He looked out again at the panoramic view. The freezing fog was beginning to lift and far ahead in the distance he saw the lights of a small fishing boat, no doubt returning from yet another long, hard fishing shift in the unforgiving cold of the North Sea. The vessel was obviously heading back for its West Marina berth.

If there was one matter that both Travis and Roberson

would have agreed on that night, it was that it was highly unlikely that Nina's absence would be reported. Travis knew for a fact that most of her peers would think they were a lot better off without her.

Roberson was still shaking as his phone pinged. He flicked the phone screen and saw that there was a message. Everyone in Parton knew his contact details; he'd posted them far and wide during his many media campaigns. That was Pete Roberson's way; he was Mr Publicity.

When he opened it, he saw that it was a video.

The video relayed the night's earlier incident. Clearly, despite the fog, it showed Nina's death, her body on the road, and his own actions at the scene. His car disappearing into the gloomy night, the number plate clearly visible. There was a chilling message: 'I will be in touch.'

Roberson dropped his gin and tonic. The glass smashed into pieces on the hard floor.

***

Dunc Travis was still smiling to himself after he pressed the send button. He had converted Roberson's mobile number into one of his favourites.

Let the new life begin, he thought.

2

Chilter and Wrightson

Twelve months later

It was on a clear, dry and very cold February morning that Geoff Sutton stood alone on the seventeenth tee of Parton Golf Club. The seventeenth was a short par three, approximately 130 yards in length when playing off the yellow tee markers. The green was surrounded by bunkers, with a small stream guarding the largest bunker immediately in front of the putting area.

Geoff hated this hole; it had not been made any easier by the recent introduction of the small white out-of-bounds posts on the right side of the fairway. These ensured that the penalty of a bad shot increased and the target appeared even smaller. If that wasn't enough, bushes and trees were anticipating the renowned Sutton hook. Sutton's plight was increased as this Saturday's competition was a Texas scramble with the rules requiring each of the four-person team to take the first shot at each of the par threes. This was Sutton's last opportunity; 'the team' had performed admirably, creating even greater pressure on the fifty-nine-year-old former Detective Chief Inspector, now employed as a part-time police civilian.

The north-westerly breeze strengthened as he addressed

the ball with his recently purchased six iron, which the golf club professional had promised him 'would make all the difference'.

His team mates, Roger Strong, Pete McIntyre and Stew Grant, all looked on nervously. Winning the Saturday winter competition would give them a prize of £20 each. Despite their increasing years, Geoff and his mates, who had a lifetime of proud sporting achievements to call on, remained fiercely competitive.

Geoff looked at the ball; it now looked smaller, perched on his small plastic red tee. He was panicking. A combination of wanting to win and not letting his mates down was creating havoc. He was numb from the waist down, a feeling similar to that from the epidural that had been administered during his hip-replacement surgery two years previously.

His swing seemed reasonable but the connection of club on ball felt like a domestic iron hitting a small rock. The sound of a brick hitting concrete seemed to resonate as Sutton made contact. The ball climbed to about six inches in height, certainly no higher, before racing parallel to the ground and plummeting into the stream a hundred yards from the tee box.

Nobody said anything, nobody dare say anything; any thought of winning had literally gone downstream. Nothing that his team mates could say would have made it any better in the immediate aftermath of the tee shot.

The silence continued until about ten minutes later when they approached the eighteenth green. Roger turned to Geoff. 'Unlucky, Sutton,' he said, in a very poor attempt at being sensitive to his lifelong friend.

'Bugger off!' came the immediate response from Sutton. 'Another crap shot. I bloody hate that hole,' he stated, in total frustration.

'Yes, you're right. Crap shot,' Pete said. He made the comment confidently; he had known Sutton since their rugby-playing schooldays.

Pete, Stew and Roger had been in the same successful schoolboy rugby team as Sutton. Whilst their lives had taken various twists and turns, they had remained intensely loyal to each other. In later life golf offered them the same competitive environment that rugby had once supplied, even if their respective physical limitations were heading over the horizon at an increasing pace.

The clubhouse, recently renovated, gave the four friends welcome respite from the biting cold. As in most amateur sports clubs, it was crammed with honours boards, trophies and photographs of past captains and administrators, without whose efforts the club would not still exist.

Emotions calmed as Stew paid for the drinks and food – three pints of Guinness with accompanying crispy bacon sandwiches. Sutton had his usual coffee and homemade shortbread biscuit. It was the same order week in, week out.

'Who's in at scrum half for Tony?' Pete asked, as thoughts turned to Upper Parton's first team fixture that afternoon. Upper Parton RFC was the focal point of their existence.

Geoff, Stew, Roger and Pete were lifelong members, former players who now performed various roles within the club. Roger still held the purse strings as treasurer, a role that befitted the former financial advisor. Geoff chaired discipline, a role he hated with a vengeance. Within the mini-junior section of the club, it often involved the parents more than their children. Pete had responsibility for ground maintenance, whilst Stew completed the match reports for the club website and local press, a role he enjoyed with some relish. It allowed him to court favour with a couple of free pints, as people sought to influence his weekly releases on the Upper Parton RFC website and the *Parton Weekly*, a publication dedicated to sport in the county. Needless to say, none of the four knew who was Tony's replacement at scrum half.

It was the same simple ritual every winter Saturday: early golf; quick lunch; down to the club; watch the rugby, and then, very importantly, a few beers around 'their table' to complete the day.

***

As the four of them continued their conversation about how things might have been on the golf course, Detective Constable Mike Chilter was leaving home, a very ordinary three-bedroom semi on the outskirts of Parton city centre. He pressed the key fob to unlock the car door, activating the hazard warning lights and allowing him access to his Silver Vauxhall Astra. He had deliberately chosen this vehicle as it would never attract attention and was essential for the covert nature of his work.

Chilter was a well-qualified, level-one informant handler, highly trained in this dark and unsung world. Obviously his own vehicle would never be utilised in any meeting with a source; Chilter took the cautious, but necessary, view that if there was ever a compromise and a source became hostile, he could protect himself and his family. It always made him smile when he saw newly appointed Area Command detectives running around in their own cars with personalised number plates. To his mind they were either being paid too much or were asking for trouble.

Chilter's appearance was similarly unassuming: black trainers, denim jeans, with a plain dark-blue overcoat bereft of any designer labels or badges. He looked like what he was, no more, no less, a very ordinary thirty-five year old, of medium height and weight with a mode of dress deliberately chosen not to attract attention.

Often his work involved meetings with significant criminals, as they alone had the necessary contacts and trust among their peers to provide their handlers with crucial information. They were well paid for their efforts.

The most critical aspect of his work was whether he could ever trust the untrustworthy. The danger of the informant using the handler, as opposed to the other way around, was the graveyard for many detectives.

Each registered informant was provided with a pseudonym. The force had a duty of care, so false names were an absolute necessity in order to protect their identity. The informants' real names and personal details were only known to those who had an operational need. It was imperative that the informants' true identities remained a closely guarded secret.

Chilter made the twenty-five-minute journey to Parton city-centre police station. As with most commutes, he was on automatic pilot. He parked his vehicle at the rear of the station in the dedicated bays reserved for the Confidential Unit and entered the building via the keypad-coded doors.

Just as he entered the barren office, his encrypted and secure work mobile buzzed in his pocket. At the end of the line was Billy Spitz, the pseudonym for his informant, confirming the time and location of their forthcoming meeting. As required, Chilter contacted Detective Inspector Sue Dalton, his supervisor and informant controller, to gain the necessary authorisation to allow the meeting to take place.

'Where is the venue, Mike?'

'Unit lock-up. I'm picking him up in Cranston Lane. No CCTV.'

'Confirming you have Linda as co-handler?'

'Confirmed, boss.'

'Authorised 2.30pm. Let me have an update sometime over the weekend.' It was a complacent comment she would subsequently regret, born out of her experience and the reliability of the two handlers. Dalton usually requested an immediate update when they returned from their meeting.

Chilter enjoyed working for Dalton; she was an experienced controller, demanding and straightforward.

He looked around the depressing office that was his current posting. Drawn blinds, allowing little or no natural light, covered all the windows. Due to the covert nature of their work, this was necessary. There were four workstations for the DCs, one for the Detective Sergeant; Dalton, as Detective Inspector, had a small office in recognition of her role and responsibilities.

In the corner of the room, diagonally across and furthest away from the entrance, was a small microwave and electric kettle where a few unwashed mugs congregated. Each was emblazoned if not with the names of football teams then with 'Greatest Mum' or 'Greatest Dad', usually smeared with coffee stains. Both the kettle and microwave displayed the tell-tale labels of the last health and safety inspection. The clear-desk policy was rigorously enforced by Dalton, ensuring a limited degree of tidiness.

The unit was small and had been reduced by the recent austerity measures, yet the eight trained informant handlers, a Detective Sergeant and DI Dalton were still able to provide regular gems of intelligence. It was the most cost-effective policing tool in the force, despite the significant risks involved.

Chilter's attention was distracted by the faint noise of the keypad being activated as Linda Wrightson made her entrance into the office. 'Bloody Saturday meets,' she stated to no one in particular as she walked past Chilter almost as if he didn't exist. She made her way to the kettle in a similar action to a 'do not pass go' movement on a Monopoly board.

Wrightson was the only other level-one trained informant handler in the unit; she and Chilter were responsible for the recruitment and subsequent handling of 'Billy Spitz'.

The handlers worked in pairs. Wrightson and Chilter dealt with the most high-profile informants in recognition of their training and experience, as well as the significant personal and organisational risk.

Chilter noted Wrightson's appearance as she went to fill the kettle. In her early forties, medium height and build with shoulder-length brown hair, she was wearing a plain, dark-blue baggy sweater and black denim jeans with practical flat brown shoes. A dark brown overcoat hung over her right arm.

They had worked together for the past two years and Chilter never ceased to be amazed by how easily Wrightson obtained information. It was obvious that the informants enjoyed talking to her far more than him. She was like an agony aunt, never interrupting, always listening keenly and offering support, feigning a genuine interest in their welfare despite being fully aware that often the individual concerned was involved in serious criminal activity. When Wrightson did interrupt or question, it was always in an attempt to ascertain the truth behind the rhetoric, seeking both provenance and motive.

'Coffee, Mike?' Wrightson asked, as she flicked the kettle switch.

'Please,' said Chilter. He started to go through the paperwork required for the meet.

Without looking at the scruffy notice Blu-Tacked onto the wall adjacent to the kettle that listed the beverage requirements of the entire unit, Linda Wrightson made Chilter his customary black coffee.

'Been in touch with the boss?' Linda asked, seeking confirmation that today's meeting had received the authority they needed.

'Yep, sorted. Just need to count the money.'

Due to the amount of money – £2000 – that would be paid to Billy Spitz, Dalton had previously briefed and sought authority from Assistant Chief Constable Bob Harries about the operation. The ACC knew the real identity of the informant; but this was restricted to himself, Sue Dalton, Mike Chilter and Linda Wrightson.

The fewer who knew lessened the risk of compromise.

Linda and Mike checked and rechecked the money then signed the required receipt in advance, their names appearing underneath 'Billy Spitz' and a gap for the informant to sign with his pseudonym when the moment arrived for payment. Whilst a payment such as this would normally be made in the presence of a supervisor, Dalton had sought permission from ACC Harries for the two experienced handlers to carry out the payment alone. This was a request from Billy Spitz, who wished only to deal with his two handlers.

Dalton was amazed that the ACC had conceded to the request; after her few dealings with Harries, she viewed him as an ambitious officer who had not yet seen his last promotion. She thought that any operational matter that had him as Gold Commander would be completely risk averse.

Linda handed Mike his green-and-yellow Parton Rovers Football Club mug then they counted the money between mouthfuls of some exceptionally cheap, and not too tasteful, coffee. They split the money, £1000 each, to carry to the meeting. If they were stopped by some young and enthusiastic Constable or had an accident, £1000 would raise half the suspicion that double the amount would.

At 4pm they left the dimly-lit Confidential Unit to go out into the clear winter sunshine, their eyes squinting against the light. They walked across the courtyard, a distance of some thirty metres, to the lock-up garage. Chilter blew on his hands, white vapour showing between his fingers, before hitting yet another keypad with the relevant code. His efforts were greeted with a short buzzing noise indicating incorrect numbers.

'Bugger,' he said under his breath. He re-entered the code, this time taking a great deal more care and attention. All the locks associated with the unit had a 'three strikes and you're out' restriction, which became acutely embarrassing, particularly at the beginning of the month when all codes were changed at the same time.

When they were safely inside the garage, they viewed their plain white Bedford van. 'What reg did you give him?' Linda asked, referring to the number plates.

'VE62 WFX,' Chilter replied. They rummaged through

the rack of ghost registration plates held securely in the garage safe, before finding the relevant match and fixing them onto the front and rear of the vehicle.

Mike unlocked the vehicle as Linda pulled back the sliding side door on the near side of the vehicle, which accessed the van's storage space. What should have been an empty space had been converted into a comfortable seating area that would easily house four people and had a facility to record any meetings that took place. This area was screened off from the cab, which could accommodate the driver and a maximum of two front-seat passengers.

It was 4.30pm as Linda Wrightson and Mike Chilter exited the Confidential Unit courtyard in the plain white Bedford van. Mike was driving, Linda hidden from view in the rear converted seating area.

The meeting with Billy Spitz was as they had arranged.

What they did not know was that the journey and meeting would be life-changing both for Geoff Sutton and the two detectives.

3

Upper Parton Rugby Club

As the game moved into the last quarter, Upper Parton RFC were leading 10–7 against Hudgate in a closely contested league match. 'Move it,' shouted Sutton from his position immediately behind the posts, furthest away from the clubhouse. This was the hallowed ground where he and his mates always stood.

His advice was completely ignored and Parton's fly half kicked for the corner, hoping to gain position just outside Hudgate's twenty-two-metre line. 'Another bloody wrong option,' was Sutton's interpretation of what was a well-executed kick as he turned to Stew Grant.

Geoff, Stew, Roger and Pete always knew better than the current players. They believed their advice had gained in wisdom as they grew older. They certainly shouted louder than they had a few years previously.

***

You could not get a more scenic place to play rugby than Upper Parton; at least, that was the view of Sutton and his close friends. The first and second team pitches were set in glorious countryside on the outskirts of the city.

It was one of a number of community rugby clubs in the area. Parton Hornets, the only fully professional outfit, were really on the up and up thanks to significant investment coupled with excellent management and coaching. They had reached the dizzy heights of the premiership, with qualification into next season's European Champions Cup a distinct possibility.

You entered Upper Parton RFC via a short driveway from the main road. This thoroughfare passed the local comprehensive school, which provided strong links to the rugby club, giving it a thriving youth section that was the bedrock of the club's consistent performance.

At the end of the driveway there was an inadequate car park on the left and the recently built, state-of-the-art changing rooms on the right. The club badge was proudly displayed above the main entrance door to the changing rooms. Teams exited this door and made their way across the car park to access the pitches through a small gap in a wooden fence that surrounded the first team pitch. The fence not only acted as a barrier for spectators but also displayed the billboards of the club's many sponsors. A player walking or running through this gap entered the first team pitch to be confronted by the proud H-shaped statue that constituted the rugby posts. Not that they were gleaming white in colour, more of a flaky grey.

State-of-the-art changing rooms meant that due to health and safety issues the former glorious cracked-tiled, red-hot baths, which the Sutton era players had enjoyed, were like some relic from a David Attenborough documentary. They had all been replaced with rows upon rows of boring, silver-plated showerheads.

Sutton's mind was far from Attenborough documentaries as the game moved into injury time with Upper Parton desperately defending the last play of the game and a three-point advantage.

'Get him down!' shouted Roger. 'Legs, legs, get his bloody legs!' His shriek was reminiscent of an adolescent at a boy-band concert.

Despite what they honestly thought was good advice being bellowed from their vantage point, it was to no avail. Hudgate's right winger dived over in the corner for an unconverted five-point try, sealing a 12–10 win for his side. Upper Parton secured a losing bonus point, adding to their league tally and maintaining mid-table mediocrity.

The final whistle saw the Famous Four, Sutton, Strong, McIntyre and Grant, make their way in a line back across the first team pitch. It was similar to a scene from an old spaghetti western. Their dark silhouettes stood out against a watery winter sky and the backdrop of the small picnic area with its raised forest walks, located immediately behind the pitch.

It really was becoming very cold, the light fading and the ground beneath them starting to crunch slightly as the night's frost began its shift. The cold was insignificant to the four men as they made their way towards the warmth of the clubhouse.

Sutton's mind began to wander as he thought of past Saturdays when he'd had to dash back to work or couldn't have a couple of pints when he was performing the on-call role of the force's senior detective. This was a nightmare task that could see you called out to all manner of incidents across the county on any weekend you were rostered.

The immortal words of the Duty Supervisor in the Control Room rang in his ear, 'Boss, I am just making you aware of this incident,' meaning that DCI Sutton's name had appeared on the computerised incident log. Not now, though; those days had gone. Now he could enjoy a cup of tea with a pork-and-stuffing roll, a few beers, some excellent chat and, most importantly, no interruptions.

The four men left the grassed area opposite the first team pitch and turned left as they approached the changing rooms. They walked the twenty yards or so to the clubhouse entrance doors. The clubhouse was a typical rugby venue design, reminiscent of an airplane hanger. Its aim was to accommodate as many people as possible, enabling them to drink vast quantities of beer and, on occasion, host functions to supplement the club's running costs.

Sutton, McIntyre, Strong and Stew Grant gathered around their table. They always went to the same place immediately opposite the bar, a circular table where they could sit on their own personalised high chairs. Behind the table was a wall emblazoned with photographs of club personalities and teams, past and present. That wall was replicated, in terms of decor and pictures, throughout the clubhouse. In that respect, Upper Parton RFC was like every other rugby club in the country.

Ask any of the team's followers and they would tell you where the four men gathered – and they would never dare to invade the area. There had been the odd occasion when uneducated spectators from the opposition infiltrated the men's territory but those instances were few and far between.

It was Roger Strong's turn to get the teas and rolls. 'Pickle with mine,' shouted Pete McIntyre.

'Brown sauce for me, Strongy,' shouted Stew Grant.

Roger Strong joined the back of the tea queue and was served via an old-fashioned hatch where the kitchens were located. The other three made their way to their table and chairs. Sitting down was now becoming a necessity for them, due to the morning's golf and a couple of hours standing around watching the rugby.

'Took your bloody time,' said Sutton as Roger Strong approached wearing his blue Upper Parton RFC V-neck sweater with a blue-and-white club scarf and customary blue-denim jeans.

Roger continued his struggle with four mugs of tea, pork-and-stuffing rolls and a free bowl of chips that he'd managed to blag. All the items were strategically placed on a well-worn tray. 'Bugger off,' he replied. 'Your turn next week.'

'Where's the vinegar, Strongy?' chirped Stew. He was wearing a very smart waistcoat, again in the customary

Upper Parton RFC colours, over a well-ironed white shirt. He was, by some margin, the best dressed of the four friends – and he knew it. Stew repeatedly advised the other three on their inadequate attire.

This treatment happened every week to whoever was buying a round, whether it be the teas, rolls or beers. They would be the next item on the agenda when the first – and only – non-alcoholic drink had been finished. Dull and boring it may have seemed to an outsider, yet the four good friends were more than content.

The clubhouse was at its busiest immediately after the game, when both players and spectators gathered for the post-match inquest. The four continued their conversation about the game as they finished their tea.

'The standard of refereeing is crap,' McIntyre addressed the other three.

'That's not why we lost. It's about game management,' said Roger Strong, immediately regretting his comment as the other three burst out laughing.

Sutton, unable to hide a wide grin, said, 'You been watching the premiership punditry on BT or Sky again?'

The other three had rightly assumed that Roger had used a phrase, word perfect, by a so-called expert from a recently televised premiership or European game.

'Beers. I'll go,' said McIntyre, collecting ten pounds each from his mates to see them through the next hour.

'Like the Gobi desert around here,' said Roger Strong, giving back some of the grief he had received when completing his task as this week's tea and bread rolls monitor.

They continued their conversation whilst sipping their favourite tipple, a pint of hand-pulled bitter whose qualities were always part of their weekly discussions around the table. On the few occasions that it was not up to standard or, heaven forbid, the club had run out, the beer dominated all proceedings.

Sutton needed this time with his friends badly, having lost

his wife some fifteen years previously after a long battle with cancer. Their only daughter Maggie, unmarried and living in the south of the country, had a busy life of her own. He was sometimes lonely and this was one of the main reasons he was still working. He enjoyed being with people.

Social work seemed a good description of his current employment. His tasks now were fairly mundane – investigating unpaid speeding fines, taking witness statements for discipline matters on behalf of the force's Professional Standards Department, amongst other duties. This was after a long career as a warranted officer with significant experience in the covert aspects of policing. Geoff Sutton was never a high flyer through the ranks but, with a great deal of hard graft and reliability, coupled with integrity, he had become highly respected by his supervisors and peers. He had attained a rank that reflected his ability. Nothing more, nothing less.

Roger, Pete and Stew had followed their mate's life and career for nigh on forty years, including the dreadful time of the death of Sutton's late wife, Maria, following her brave and prolonged fight against cancer. Those life experiences gave his friends both the knowledge and the level of respect that allowed them to make fun of each other.

'Still investigating the missing staples at work?' Pete asked Sutton as he started on his third pint.

'Nope, he's moved on to the paper clips. They think it's the same person who's responsible. Isn't that right, Geoff?' said Stew.

'Bugger off,' said Sutton, his normal reply. His mind wandered back to the old days and the critical dealings he'd had with informants and covert authorities, which often ended in high-profile murder trials.

'Who's at home tonight?' Sutton turned to Stew Grant. It was always a good question as Stew and his wife, Tina, had been foster parents for problem adolescents for a number of years. Numerous children had passed through the Grant household, some more successfully than others. They had decided to become foster parents after several extremely emotional failed courses of IVF treatment.

'Possibly Simon, Sally and William, possibly not. Who bloody knows?' Stew said with the voice of experience.

'Who's William?' asked McIntyre. Simon and Sally were well known to them all.

'Well, believe it or not – and just between the four of us – William used to be Julie. It's a long story,' sighed Stew.

Stew took time out to address a small mark that had appeared on the right shoulder of his club waistcoat, making sure his appearance was as immaculate as ever. It was also a signal to change conversation; the foster caring had really taken its toll on them both. If Stew had his own way there would be no more but Tina disagreed.

Joe Benson, a parent of a player, approached Grant. 'How did you think our Bobby played today?' The underlying question was if 'our Bobby' would get a mention in the published match report. Could he even make it as Stew Grant's man of the match, a sought-after accolade for Bobby's peers?

'Okay, Joe,' said a non-committal Stew.

'You should be a politician, Granty,' shouted Sutton, overhearing the proceedings as he took a larger than usual mouthful of his pint.

Joe Benson soon realised he was wasting his and Bobby's time by continuing the conversation with Stew.

The level of common sense descended as they downed their fifth pint. It always seemed strange to Sutton that, in his own mind and those of his mates, the more he drank the better player he had been. He believed that the advice he gave was the best any young player could possibly receive. This, and the fact that as they got older the four of them spent more and more time discussing the weather, was yet another indisputable sign of advancing years.

'Time for off.' Sutton drained the last drops of his fifth

and final pint. He reached for his ancient, knee-length, dark-green Barbour coat with the fur-lined collar. Stew, Pete and Roger also finished their drinks. It was very rare that they did not all leave at the same time; their four-man team was bonded at the hip.

Although they left together, they had very different trips home. For Sutton, it was a walk up the bank after crossing the rugby field and a minor road. Tina had come to pick up Stew, and Pete was eager to cadge a lift to the other side of Parton where both families lived within half a mile of each other. Pete appeared to live the original happily married life, with two adult children and one infant grandchild; Benjamin was the apple of his grandpa Pete's eye. Each week there was yet another photograph followed by yet another story about Benjamin McIntyre. Sutton, Strong and Grant knew the lad inside and out.

Roger Strong walked down the clubhouse drive and across the road to the three-bedroomed bungalow immediately opposite the entrance to Upper Parton RFC. He was the only one of the four guaranteed not to stop for a toilet break on his way home. Strong had come through a turbulent divorce and, thanks to online dating, had met Cindy, a vivacious thirty year old. Two months later, after a whirlwind romance, Cindy had moved in with a rejuvenated Roger. She was a hit with all his friends and, much to their surprise, she seemed to adore him. The other three were extremely envious of him, more because he didn't have to stop for a call of nature than because of any sexual exploits that might be coming his way on a bitterly cold, sub-zero, February Saturday evening.

Geoff Sutton buttoned up his Barbour coat, feeling snug in his fur-lined hood, chin pointing down to avoid any cold air, and started his twenty-minute walk home. His new, low-level walking boots crunched on the now frost-bound ground, which was churned up and rutted from this afternoon's match. It was a beautiful clear night; stars and moon illuminated the way as Sutton skated home.

Crunch, crunch; boots on frozen ground as he desperately tried to stay upright, which was difficult on the slippery ground after five pints of bitter. He didn't bother with the warm leather gloves supplied by Maggie in celebration of his last birthday.

Crunch, crunch; he walked past the rugby posts where he and his mates had been standing earlier that afternoon.

Crunch, crunch; he turned left and started to cross the road by the bridge. Once over the bridge, it was through the stile, up the grassed field where there was a right of way, through another stile and he was at the end of the cul-de-sac at the bottom of his road.

As Sutton crossed the road onto the bridge, his attention was drawn to a white Bedford van, fully illuminated by the clear, bright sky. The van was parked in a small layby adjacent to a picnic area near the woodland walks. It wasn't unusual for a vehicle or two to park in these remote locations during the hours of darkness; it was a popular venue for some unbridled passion, although Sutton thought that the temperatures would deter anyone but the keenest – or the most desperate – of individuals tonight. What did catch Sutton's attention was the registration plate VE62 WFX.

He was some fifteen yards away from the van, with a clear and unobscured view of the rear of the vehicle. He continued across the bridge without stopping. Where was that registration number from? It rang a bell with Sutton as he tried to seek the answer through the foggy haze caused by the beer he had recently consumed.

What Sutton had failed to notice, nor would he have seen from his view of the van, was a small smear of blood above the rear nearside wheel arch. Furthermore, he would have no knowledge whatsoever of the carnage contained within the vehicle.

Crunch, crunch went Sutton's boots. He had crossed the first stile and was halfway up the steep, grassy bank that was making conditions underfoot even more precarious. His mind wandered between the registration number of the vehicle and what he was going to eat when he got home. The remains of his partially eaten chicken shashlik curry and a sag aloo, washed down with a glass of that particularly pleasant South Western Australian Shiraz was on the menu. The Shiraz always tasted that little bit better to the unrefined palate after a few pints. Sutton thought there was so much rubbish talked about wine nowadays; he was purely a 'drink what you like' consumer.

Crunch, crunch on the frosty surface. Sutton made it across the second stile then, with a Torville and Dean skating move, he just about made the tarmac surface of the cul-de-sac without falling. His arms were flailing around like an uncontrolled helicopter but he had made it home.

He entered his two-bedroomed bungalow and threw his Barbour over a kitchen chair. VE62 – why on earth was that registration number of significance to him? He had already forgotten the final letters despite racking his brain again and again.

His memory worsened by the minute as he took another large mouthful of his wine. He took the notepad from the kitchen bench, which was located next to the toaster and his all-important top-of-the-range microwave oven. Since Maria's death, this was Sutton's main cooking utensil both in terms of choice and necessity. He jotted down the letters and number he could recall, VE62.

Ten minutes later Sutton was tucking into last night's reheated offerings thanks to his beloved microwave. He recharged his glass and, with the gas fire blasting out its expensive heat in harmony with his central heating, he was in heaven. He played with the TV remote controls and searched for some appropriate Saturday-night sport. He finally settled for boxing on Channel 5, an obscure world-title fight involving a little-known British boxer shown live from Cologne.

The bell started the contest as Sutton finished the last of

his curry. Approximately two hours later he woke up, still in his chair. Channel 5 was now showing some equally obscure programme, a documentary on conservation in the Kruger Wildlife Park in South Africa.

Sutton wondered who had won the fight he had started watching. It was a complete mystery; the past two hours of his life had disappeared without trace.

He walked to the bathroom, undertook another very long call of nature, cleaned his teeth, took two Anadin Extra, then went to bed, rapidly sobering and becoming increasingly lonely.

He was totally unaware that the stabbed, brutally murdered bodies of DCs Linda Wrightson and Mike Chilter lay in the back of that freezing white Bedford Van bearing the registration number VE62 WFX. The vehicle he had observed on his walk back from the rugby club.

4

Billy Smith

The following morning at 9.30am exactly, Sutton became fully awake after a disturbed night's sleep punctuated by bathroom visits. He felt like a fully loaded washing machine in mid-cycle as last night's curry and booze tumbled around inside him.

He knew it was exactly that time because his mobile played its immediately recognisable musical rhythm of Dire Straits 'Local Hero', which indicated an incoming call. He kept his phone on the bedside cabinet, a habit of his for three main reasons: when Maggie was still living at home and painting the town red; his on-call duties, and when his now-deceased parents were both hospitalised. This time it was Maggie. He let it ring as he went again to the bathroom. He wanted to ensure he was on top form for his daughter's chat.

He climbed back into bed, fully awake now, and called Maggie back. It was always important to ring back immediately as it might be a one of the few opportunities to have a reasonable conversation with his daughter. Too often she would ring as she was walking to get a bus or a train and the conversation would inevitably end with the phrase, 'Got to dash, Dad, I'm just about to get on the bus/train.' It never ceased to amaze him that, if he didn't answer his phone immediately when she rang, she accused him of being selfish!

Ten minutes later, after a one-way chat about her new boyfriend Chris, Maggie said the immortal words: 'Got to dash, Dad. Meeting Chris and my bus has just pulled up. I'll speak during the week.'

Sutton hoped this was the truth and blanked from his mind the possibility that she was at home and Chris might have returned from the kitchen into the bedroom of Maggie's small rented flat in Watford with two cups of tea.

He decided that it was a day for household chores, interspersed with some TV sport and a trip to the leisure-centre swimming pool. He hated domestic duties with a vengeance, not the gardening, but the cleaning, washing and ironing. He honestly believed it depressed him. The more he thought of his day ahead, the more tempted he was to snuggle under the duvet in an effort to get back to sleep.

Another ten minutes of failed dozing passed before Sutton finally got out of bed. He dived into his scruffiest clothes before levering the hoover out of the packed storage cupboard and plugging into a depressing thirty minutes of pulling and pushing. One dust bag change was accompanied by a fit of obscenities then he kicked the hoover when it failed to work properly, like a spoilt child not getting his own way. It restarted for no apparent reason, despite his physical intervention. The damn thing had a mind of its own. An hour later, Sutton was feeling relief bordering on ecstasy. It's over for another week, he thought.

He was wiping the kitchen bench when he came across his scrawled note. He deciphered the letters and numbers, VE62, which he'd scrawled the previous night at the height of his alcohol consumption. It brought back the memory of walking home from the club and the white van.

'Why the bloody hell did I recognise the reg number?' he said out loud.

He shoved the note into his pocket and went into a

deeper depression as he attacked the toilet and bathroom. A further thirty minutes of gloom was followed by some unintentional light relief from the messages being read out on Steve Wright's *Love Song Show*. He couldn't believe people could be so emotionally dramatic as to have their innermost thoughts broadcast before the nation.

Steve Wright had finished on Radio 2, making way for the 11am slot of Michael Ball or whoever replaced him. Sutton enjoyed listening to music and had eclectic tastes; his age put him mostly in tune with Radio 2. He wondered if the replacement DJ scenario on Radio 2 was similar to circumstances when the Duty Senior Detective went sick or the force changed Sutton's duties because of holidays. You never knew who would fulfil the role; young and inexperienced individuals were thrown in at the very deep end, often at the last minute.

Brunch was in order as a reward and to bring him out of the depression caused by the cleaning. He decided to walk to his local cafe for something suitably unhealthy that would set him up for the day. The Parlour was rough and ready and he certainly didn't need to change clothes to go there. He could buy a paper, chat up beautiful Debbie, the cafe owner, and rack his brains over this bloody registration number.

He picked up his Barbour from where it had been unceremoniously dumped the night before and headed out. Late morning and the frost was still on the ground. He slid down the driveway, taking a direct route through his housing estate to a line of shops where the cafe was located. Hands in his pockets, he sought out Maggie's birthday present gloves only to find one was missing. He must have dropped it last night on his way back from the club.

Springfield Green housing estate was diverse with some social housing, council properties and what could be described as upmarket suburban dwellings. There were two care homes, a recently built nursery and a typical housing estate pub named The Falcon. This was the natural home for a weekly quiz in a very dark and not-so-cheerful bar, with cheap food served in the lounge.

Sutton slid his way across The Falcon car park on his way to The Parlour. It was situated in a line of shops that included a newsagent, hairdressing salon, Chinese takeaway and launderette, all of which serviced the estate. He caught a hint of Debbie's delights that would be coming his way as he passed the cafe door and entered Dillon's newsagents next door.

'Bit cold today, Geoff,' murmured Billy Dillon Smith, the owner and only member of staff. He had immediately recognised Sutton's distinctive coat.

'Just *The Sunday Times*, Smithy,' Sutton grunted, putting the correct money together with the previous night's lottery ticket on the counter.

Smithy scanned the ticket into the ugly black Camelot machine that apparently, in certain circumstances, changed people's lives. So far this hadn't been the case in Sutton's life and today proved no exception.

Smithy, as he did every Sunday, sighed. 'Bin it?' He asked the question in what Sutton thought was a pathetic voice of sympathy coming from the six-foot-four, twenty-stone shop owner. It was a question that needed no answer; Smithy had already thrown the ticket into the bin. Sutton thought that Smithy must repeat this scenario a hundred times each day.

Armed with his newspaper, and his scribbled note with the unknown reg number hidden deep in his trouser pocket, Sutton left Dillon's and pushed open The Parlour door, swapping Smithy's large physical frame for Debbie's attractive curves. The only slight similarity between Smithy and sister Debbie was their hair colour.

She swayed between the tables and sofas that she'd recently purchased to attract young parents. After ensuring that the apples of their eyes were safely deposited at the local nursery, many of them made their way to The Parlour for a catch-up over an Americano or latte or some other style of coffee from the new, shiny machine Debbie had bought to please this new and burgeoning clientele. Sutton couldn't believe how long it took to put the kettle on nowadays. His worst nightmare was being caught in a queue of parents, each ordering a posh brew out of a gleaming silver space machine that made noises similar to an overheated old Vauxhall Corsa.

'Geoff, how you doing, pet?' Debbie asked, making her way to his table. She was dressed plainly in black slacks, a blouse and her deep-purple pinafore with *The Parlour* printed above the left breast.

Sutton took on board her appearance as she walked towards him. 'Scrambled egg, sausage and mushrooms on toast,' he said, thinking irrationally that this was not a full English breakfast and therefore it was better for him.

Debbie turned and walked back to the counter that did its best to hide the kitchen. Sutton looked around the cafe, which was due to close at 1pm. It was almost empty apart from a young couple sitting on one of the sofas, each of them slurping some frothy little number.

'Pot of tea, please, Debs,' he shouted to the counter.

'Not a problem,' came the reply.

Sutton reckoned Debbie was in her late forties. She was slim, with the most engaging deep-brown eyes. His reliable source, namely Debbie's younger and much bigger brother, Billy Dillon Smith, had informed Sutton that his sister had divorced some two years ago after surviving a long abusive relationship.

As he went to unfold his newspaper, Sutton had a change of mind. He dug into his trouser pocket and pulled out his note. 'VE62, where the hell does that come from?' he asked himself. Despite racking his brain he was no further forward so he returned to the newspaper, pretending to read whilst really taking the time to observe Debbie.

It was some ten minutes later when his hybrid full-English breakfast arrived. 'Brown sauce,' she said in more of a statement than an enquiry.

'Naturally,' Sutton said, without looking up. He reached for a knife and fork; for a moment his meal looked even more appetising than Debbie.

He tucked in, not even noticing when Debbie placed a pot of tea, small jug of milk and large mug on the table. It took little time to demolish his meal.

Sutton looked up, again reflecting upon Debbie. He had been a regular at the cafe for nearly a year, had got to know her to an extent that, knowing his police background, she had supplied him with some intelligence overheard from cafe gossip. He had recorded it according to procedure as a confidential contact, protecting her identity should any criminal proceedings ensue.

Sutton took a last gulp of tea coupled with a last look at Debbie. 'Bye then, Deb,' he said almost sadly.

'See you, Geoff. Are you in during the week?' she enquired.

'Possibly tomorrow or Friday. Part-time working is highly recommended,' he replied.

'Look forward to seeing you then,' she said with a wink of those gorgeous brown eyes.

Sutton left The Parlour. Yet again, as he had done for at least the last six months, he asked himself why he hadn't asked her to go for a drink, or at least asked to exchange mobile numbers. The very few occasions he had managed to talk with Maggie on a subject that didn't involve herself, she always asked what was happening with him and Debbie from The Parlour. It had almost got to the stage when Maggie had given up on her father's potential love life.

The sun had started eating into last night's frost as Sutton made his way home, replenished from his brunch and feeling good to be alive. It was another beautiful clear and dry February day; his return walk home was noticeably warmer and considerably easier than his outbound journey.

Walking through the front door, he dumped his coat in its usual spot and pulled the scrap of notepaper, with the reg number VE62, from his trouser pocket. For some unknown reason it troubled him and he knew that the longer this continued, the greater would be his anxiety. He told himself he was no longer a DCI and didn't have the associated accountability; he was a three-day-a-week civilian support officer, enjoying the social interest that the role gave him. Yet it was always the same for Geoff Sutton. You cannot spend thirty years learning a trade and leave it locked away in some Davy-Jones-type locker, secure and untouched.

'Stuff it,' he tried to tell himself unsuccessfully.

Desperate to think of something else, he sat down in the living room and searched for the TV sport listings hidden deeply within *The Sunday Times*. As it was a non-European weekend as far as the Sky rugby coverage was concerned, he turned his attention to yet another 'Sky Super Sunday' and the latest coverage of the European Golf Tour.

An instant Sutton decision was made: Sky Super Sunday, Man Utd versus Chelsea. The top of the table 4pm clash would allow him to go for a swim at the leisure centre. There was an allocated-lane adult-only swim every Sunday between 2pm and 3pm. He'd have time to recover – a process that was becoming increasingly protracted and necessary. He loved exercise and the buzz that it gave him but his age was beginning to tell.

Collecting his damp towel from Friday's gym session and his chlorine-starched swimming trunks, he set off with his mind focused on his swim. Climbing into his racing-green Vauxhall Insignia, Sutton drove on automatic pilot to the recently refurbished leisure centre. He didn't turn on the radio; he hated Elaine Page's Radio 2 slot in the early afternoon. He was no lover of the musicals.

Parked up, trunks wrapped in his towel, Sutton walked through the car park. He passed a few posers who, in his opinion, looked more like they had attended a fashion show rather than spending time at the gym. In complete contrast, Sutton knew that in about forty-five minutes time he would be making his return journey with his shirt tail flapping, looking totally bedraggled and sweating profusely.

Sutton's swim was the same each time: a thirty-two length session, about half a mile, alternating breast stroke, back stroke and front crawl. The banality of swimming up and down lanes cleared his mind completely and allowed him time to refresh his thoughts, depending on how much he was punishing himself.

Twenty-three lengths into his session, Sutton pulled up suddenly. Fortunately, he was finishing a breast-stroke length in the shallow end; he'd already suffered the ignominy of being asked by the lifeguard to move from the fast lane to the slow lane. On his twenty-third length he finally cracked it.

VE62 WFX was a Confidential Unit vehicle; it had been done for speeding last month and got a ticket. He restarted his session. What was it doing there? An informant's meeting? The remainder of Sutton's swim was taken up with thinking about the pros and cons of having a meet at that location.

Some fifteen minutes later Sutton, sweating profusely, shirt tail flapping, with his untidy baggage of trunks, goggles and stolen hotel toiletry under one arm, left the leisure centre. On the way out he bought a can of Diet Fanta Orange. He walked across the car park, taking a couple of swigs from the can, and opened the Insignia car door before collapsing into the driver's seat. The radio activated with the ignition key: Jonny Walker, *Sounds of the Seventies*, one of the best programmes of the week.

Where to next, he asked himself, as he reversed out of the parking bay. His life would not be worth living if he had lost his leather glove so he headed back to the rugby club. It wasn't really out of his way and it was still daylight; at least if he had lost the glove, he could truthfully tell Maggie he'd tried his best to retrieve it.

He parked in the club car park, empty now after the mini

and junior morning matches. Sutton retraced his steps back across the first team pitch. Just as he was about to cross the road, he looked downward and saw a frost-covered, hand-like shape. His missing glove.

'Thank the Lord,' said Sutton out loud, picking it up then looking around to see if anyone had heard him.

What shocked him was not that he had an audience and could be overheard but the sight of the white Bedford van still in situ. Another informant's meeting? Surely not in broad daylight.

Without going any further, Sutton turned on his heel and returned to his Insignia. There was a lot going through his mind as he made the one and a half mile trip back home. With his thoughts racing, he narrowly avoided a cyclist on the back hill. As he pulled into the driveway, his decision had been made.

He entered through the front door, dumped his Barbour in the usual place and threw his trunks and wet towel in the washing machine. Donning his rarely used black quilted jacket, Sutton was out of the house again in less than five minutes,

He needed to make a call. The van should not be there now; it was as simple as that. How to call it in without getting anyone into trouble was more problematic. An anonymous call from one of the few pay phones would probably be the best option.

Sutton walked back towards the row of shops where Dillon's and The Parlour were situated; there was a public pay phone opposite. He knew that at this time on a Sunday both the newsagents and the cafe would be locked up for the day. As far as Sutton was aware, CCTV coverage was non-existent, other than a camera at The Falcon car park for monitoring disorderly youths at the weekend.

He walked around the front of the pub, avoiding the car park.

Sutton made the call, knowing full well what he was going

to say. He dialled the main police non-emergency number and, after going through the relevant options, he eventually spoke to a human voice.

'Partonshire Constabulary. You would like to report an incident?'

'It's the bairns, the kids, playing around the motor. It's near the river, they could be trying to nick it. It's a big white van VE62 or summat. It's in a layby at the picnic area next to Upper Parton Rugby club.'

Sutton couldn't do an accent even if he tried, so he didn't allow the call-taker to ask awkward questions. He just kept on talking. He also included some trigger points that would require a more urgent response than just routine observation: children; river; danger; possible crime in action.

'Can I have your name please?' Sutton heard the call-taker asking as he replaced the receiver.

He returned home, replaced the black quilted jacket with his Barbour and sat in a chair in his living room for a few minutes. He knew a check for the owner of the car via the Police National Computer would show a false legend, probably some fictitious business address down south. He needed, therefore, to return to the scene. Hopefully he would be able to identify a colleague or their supervisor who would make the right call about the vehicle. Why was the vehicle there? And who had put it in that location? Sutton knew full well the risk of compromising the vehicle but to his mind the priorities had changed.

***

Police Constable 8558 Steve Barker had just passed his driving course as he neared the end of his two-year probation. Keen as mustard, he was the first to answer the request that came via the despatcher after an anonymous call.

'Can anyone attend an incident sent in anonymously? Possibly children in danger, possibly crime in action, possibly an abandoned vehicle.

'P.C. 8558 responding,' came Barker's immediate reply. That was Geoff Sutton's nightmare scenario, a young inexperienced cop first on the scene.

***

Sergeant 1296 Ged Graham was stuck in the office dealing with a messy complaint, as he had been since his 2pm–12 midnight weekend shift had begun. He shouted in. As Barker's supervisor, he had the bureaucratic headache of confirming Barker's end of probation; a trip out to see him dealing with an incident, whilst not absolutely necessary, would provide good evidence for his report. Graham, dedicated to the force and with twenty years' service, was as conscientious as he was reliable.

***

Sutton drove the Insignia back down the hill to the rugby club, where he parked in exactly the same spot that he'd been in less than an hour ago. He left the car and walked across the first team pitch, thinking he'd now covered more of the field than some of the players yesterday.

He saw two police cars parked near the white Bedford van. To his immense relief he saw Ged Graham, a cop he knew and respected, having supervised him as a young detective constable.

Barker was on his radio asking for a vehicle check, quoting the number plate VE62 WFX.

Sergeant Graham looked up. 'Now who else would be wearing a green Barbour, boss, how you doing?' he enquired as Sutton approached.

'Well, I'm not your boss, Ged, as you'll be more than pleased to know!' Sutton replied as they shook hands. 'Can I have a quick word?' He knew that Graham would realise that the quick word needed to be out of Barker's earshot.

'Steve, just do a search of the area. Make sure there are no kids in the river,' Graham instructed the young PC.

'OK, Sarge,' came the immediate and unquestioning reply.

'Ged, I called it in,' Sutton said. 'The vehicle belongs to the Confy Unit. It will probably come back registered to some business address down south. On my drunken walk back from the rugby club last night, it was here about sevenish. I thought the reg number looked familiar but it took me until now to work it out. I had a speeder written off with this reg. I thought it might have been an informant's meeting going on, but when I saw the van again today I made the call. It just shouldn't be here.'

'No keys in the ignition,' said Graham thoughtfully.

Barker had finished his brief search of the area and returned dutifully to his Sergeant. 'Nothing immediate, but could you have a look at this?'

Graham and Sutton followed him around to the rear nearside wheel arch, where the eagle-eyed constable had spotted a blood smear.

'I think this could be blood,' Barker said, requiring confirmation.

Sutton and Graham looked at each other. 'Geoff, have you got some numbers on your phone?' asked Ged Graham, all formalities gone.

Sutton knew exactly what he wanted and immediately scrolled down his contacts' list for Sue Dalton's details. She was Detective Inspector of the Confidential Unit. He dialled her number.

One of the benefits of his long service, which continued in semi-retirement, was the number of contacts he still had within the force. He may not have been the most talented officer but his reliable, conscientious approach had earned him respect. His colleagues were happy to stay in touch.

'Sue, it's Geoff Sutton.'

'Geoff! To what do I owe this out-of-the-blue call on a Sunday?'

Straight to the point, Sutton carried on. 'Is the vehicle VE62 WFX one of yours?'

Dalton immediately replied, 'Why?' A shudder ran up her spine.

'It's parked up in the picnic area near Upper Parton Rugby Club.'

'Shouldn't be there, unless it's broken down and hasn't been removed. I don't know – but it needs sorting. I'll make a couple of calls and if that doesn't work I'll pop to the office and bring the spare keys. Whatever, I'll either be with you or will contact you in about twenty minutes.' Her voice was controlled but tense.

'Cheers.' Sutton finished the call then informed Ged of Dalton's response.

***

Shit, thought Dalton, as she contacted Mike Chilter's mobile. It rang, then went to voicemail.

'Mike, it's the D.I. When you pick this up, give me a ring.'

Shit, shit, she thought, after she called Wrightson and got a similar response.

Quickly believing that she could be in deep trouble, Dalton drove to get the spare keys via the Confidential Unit garage. Normally she would have insisted on a phone call from one of the informant handlers immediately after the meeting she had authorised had been successfully completed; that was the protocol when they were deployed on a job. But the informant's meeting had clashed with yet another date with her boyfriend who had become so very important to her over the last twelve months or so. Romance was a highly unusual occurrence in the life of Sue Dalton. She didn't want to be disturbed so she didn't insist that either Chilter or Wrightson call, just that they update her some time over the weekend.

The romance had been such a success after so many false

dawns that Dalton was only awakened from her dream world when she received Sutton's call. Work had been the last thing on her mind.

Almost twenty-five minutes passed before Dalton pulled up behind the two police vehicles. She immediately recognised Sutton and Sergeant Ged Graham from past incidents. She spoke briefly to them because they needed to know, but not to Barker who didn't.

Barker was asked politely by his Sergeant to return to his vehicle and ensure his pocket book contained his current shift duties. 'It needs to be available for inspection at all times,' Graham said.

After Barker had moved away, Ged said to the other two, 'We may need someone to help with a search and I would like Barker to be involved. It's good experience and I can fully debrief him a later date.'

'No problem,' Dalton said, as she walked towards the sliding door that was built into the side panel of the vehicle. The keys were in her hand.

Graham called over to Barker and summoned him back.

'Seen this, Sue?' Sutton asked, pointing out what appeared to be the blood smear.

Another shiver ran up Dalton's spine causing her to hesitate momentarily as she moved closer to the van. Quickly recovering her composure, she unlocked the sliding door and pulled it back.

Nothing could have prepared Dalton, Sutton, Graham or the young Barker for the sight in front of them. Carnage, as the wide and staring eyes of Chilter and Wrightson seemed to fix upon the eyes of their new audience.

Both officers had been brutally cut up. There was no other way to describe their injuries. The fact that they had both fought for their lives was blindingly obvious.

Barker gagged, seeking to control himself from being sick. Ged Graham was immediately in response mode and started listing instructions to the young constable, who couldn't react no matter how hard he tried.

Taking in the scene, Sutton sighed. He'd been to many murder scenes in his time, some with multiple fatalities, but never to attend a murdered colleague. He dug his chin even deeper into the collar of his Barbour. Not surprisingly, Sutton knew both Chilter and Linda Wrightson from his time as the Detective Inspector of the Confidential Unit.

Sue Dalton, an experienced officer of twenty-four years service, collapsed to her knees in tears, totally distraught. It seemed to Sutton that the staring eyes of the murdered detectives were trained on their former Inspector as her crying became hysterical.

Sutton was mesmerised, unable to move as he took in the tragic scene. It was as if total paralysis had taken over his body.

Graham called it in, as if going through a prepared speech that he had learnt word for word. 'We need further resources asap for scene management. Contact the Duty Inspector and Senior On-call Detective. I also need the Control-Room Supervisor to give me a ring on my mobile.'

When he finished, he turned to Barker who was trying hard to recover his composure. His eyes never leaving his Sergeant, the lad was like an obedient dog waiting for his next instruction. He had just witnessed a scene that he would never see again during his next thirty years of service. It was a scene he would always remember as if it were yesterday.

It was Ged Graham's instructions to his young probationer Constable that ended Sutton's temporary paralysis. 'Steve, let's make this scene as secure as possible before my phone goes crackers,' he said to the stunned officer, who was now aware he was at the scene of a double murder of two of his colleagues.

Sutton helped Sue Dalton away from the scene and placed her in the Insignia. Between her sobs, he just about made out the name she was muttering. 'Billy, Billy Spitz,' she repeated.

Sutton was not medically qualified in anyway, but he knew enough to recognise that Dalton had totally lost it, not unsurprisingly at the sight of her murdered officers. She was their supervisor.

Sue Dalton knew she would have some serious questions to answer when the circus came to town.

Sutton, more than anyone, knew her problems were just beginning.

5

Stew and Tina Grant

Sunday evening in the Grant household was proving more disappointing than usual. It was their custom to have dinner served at about 7pm. It was always a roast with all the trimmings, presented and served in the newly decorated dining room by the hosts who, as ever, would be equally well presented. Tina looked exceptionally smart in her recently purchased Monsoon dress; with her Pandora bracelet on her right wrist and River Island shoes, it looked as if she had walked out from the pages of a Vogue catalogue. Stew had a plain white Charles Tyrwhitt shirt beneath his navy waistcoat. Yes, it was over the top but the Grants were like this; however, you couldn't fault their efforts and intentions.

They logically thought that the efforts they made both in dinner and dress would not only provide a good example for whoever they were currently fostering but also give them an opportunity to chat about the past week and what was happening in the immediate future.

There were few rules in their house but the 7pm weekly Sunday dinner was what Tina particularly anticipated and looked forward to as their 'family time'. The event was recommended by Social Services for a weekly catch-up on what had happened over the past seven days, what was to come and how they, as foster carers, could help their protégés.

The Grants had embarked on fostering some twenty years earlier, having long given up on the expensive and emotionally draining process of IVF. Over the years they had had concentrated on children coming to the end of the care process, who were moving towards their later teens. Often they would subsidise the youngsters in their care long after the legal obligation of fostering had ended.

With their vast fostering experience, the Grants might have thought nothing of the continual disappointments caused by dealing with the some of the most vulnerable in society but this was far from the case.

Tina and Stew sat at opposite ends of the dining-room table, the aroma of a roast wafting from their elegant, newly-fitted Cavendish kitchen. The only thing missing was their foster children; not one of them was present.

Tina was in tears, floods of them. Stew was absolutely incapable of controlling her emotions when it came to 'her children'. This was yet another significant indicator, in Stew's opinion that as they rapidly approached their sixties their foster caring years were coming to an end, no matter what Social Services said. He and Tina had agreed to discuss the matter later when emotions were not so raw.

Yes, there had been numerous successes, a fact evidenced when you looked around the Grant's house. Numerous photographs of weddings, graduations and sporting achievements littered the rooms, providing warmth and comfort to them both, as well as giving the feeling of a true home. Significantly – and not surprisingly – the photographs always included either Stew, Tina, or both of them, a proud reflection of their significant contribution.

With the assistance of Parton Social Services most, but not all, of the children they had fostered had come from Holston House, a residential care institution for youngsters on the outskirts of a town called Firston, approximately thirty miles from the Grants' home in Parton. Firston was one of three county market towns, which, in addition to the city of Parton, were the main residential areas of the county.

The Grants were generous and regular benefactors for Holston House, as their bank statements testified. Such was the esteem in which the Grants were held by the authorities that they often attended foster caring focus groups and mentored other foster carers. In addition, Stew was an honorary member of the Holston House Board of Directors, and brought his vast practical experience to assist in the running of the home.

Stew thought the best way out of this current crisis would be to settle his wife down in the living room with a large Hendricks gin and Fever-Tree tonic, ice and lemon. Then he would switch on the TV with the surround-sound speaker system in the hope that Matt Baker, Julie Bradbury and the *Countryfile* team would ease her anxiety. If Tina had half an hour viewing Matt Baker, whom she always thought was pleasing to the eye; it could distract her from the emotions of foster caring. It would also give him the opportunity to complete his match report from yesterday's game and have a glass of Glenfiddich malt whisky, as he did so.

He prepared his wife's dinner on a tray. Whilst Stew was typing away on his iPad between mouthfuls of pork and apple sauce, reliving the nightmare of yesterday's Upper Parton RFC defeat, Tina was drooling – not over her delicious dinner but at Matt Baker high up in the Cheviot Hills. Yet another nightmare was momentarily forgotten but, as many times before, there would be another one heading over the horizon soon.

Stew loved writing the match reports and when he finished he chose his man of the match. He crunched his last piece of pork crackling and took a long gulp of his chosen malt. This was the most difficult aspect of his task. He thought back to the previous night's brief conversation with Joe Benson in the clubhouse. There was no chance of his lad Bobby getting it; his dad hadn't even bought Grant a pint.

The name of Pete Storey resonated, the tight head prop,

who in Stew's view was one of the team's unsung heroes. Pete was a consistent performer week in, week out; there wasn't a prop in the league that he couldn't take to the cleaners and yesterday had been no exception. Stew pressed the send button and in an instant his report appeared on the website and was also forwarded to the sports editor of the local newspaper, the *Parton Weekly*.

Stew had finished his whisky and took the opportunity to recharge his glass, in the hope that Tina would believe it was his first drink. He thought for a moment about the youngsters currently in their charge. Simon, Sally and William had all been former residents of Holston House. To be fair, Simon and Sally had proved to be as reliable as any foster children. It was highly unusual for them to miss out on their Sunday dinner. They were sixteen-year-old twins who really enjoyed their food and had never missed a Sunday dinner before, although both had become increasingly unreliable as new romances seemed to be occupying a great deal of both their time and energy.

Just as he returned to the living room, the front door crashed open. Simon and Sally stormed into the house and went straight through to join Tina, totally ignoring Stew as if he didn't exist.

'*Antiques Roadshow*, Tina. Don't you just love it,' said Simon in his most ingratiating voice.

'Can we watch it in here together with you, Tina, and eat our dinner without getting ponced up?' continued Sally.

They didn't miss a bloody trick, smiled Stew to himself, surveying the state of the recently purchased cream carpet in the living room, now splattered by the Terrible Twins' footwear. They both knew that there was no way Tina would turn down a request that included the words 'together' and '*Antiques Roadshow*'. Stew was already on his way to the kitchen to plate up two dinners on trays, as well as helping himself to his third Glenfiddich whisky.

'Take your bloody shoes off,' he said.

Ten minutes later, they were enjoying the kind of evening that made fostering the most rewarding job in the world. The two children from difficult backgrounds were totally immersed in conversation with their carers. Stew and Tina even got to know the names of their new partners. Tina naturally offered an open invitation to Sunday dinner for them and their new partners – without any dressing up.

Sadly, the same openness could not be attributed to their other current foster child, William, whom the Grants had looked after off and on for the last three months.

Despite their vast experience of fostering, William was causing the Grants some distress. As a seventeen year old, he was rapidly approaching the age when the statutory obligation for care would end. Stew's view was that this time could not come quickly enough. He had a genuine dislike for William and he didn't trust him one inch; he never knew where he was or what he was doing. Basically – and absolutely wrongly in his role as a foster carer – such was Stew's despair that he did not want to know, nor did he care, what William was doing. The relationship was completely failing despite Tina's heroic efforts, and Stew knew it.

William had arrived as Julie but he had stated that he had never felt comfortable in a girl's body and would seek a sex change at the earliest opportunity. From that point on, Julie wanted to be known as William, so William it was. He would go missing for days on end, come back to start another argument and leave again.

Both Tina and Stew, together with William's social worker, had genuine concerns about his safety and welfare. There were many instances when Stew was just about to contact the police because of another mystery disappearance, only for William to crash through the door and head for the fridge in a frenzy of hunger. He was probably on a downer from some illegal high. No sooner had he been in the fridge than he was off out again with the minimum of conversation.

The last time they had seen him was the previous Thursday

night. Stew and Tina were yet again anxiously deliberating whether to make his disappearance a police matter. They were fully aware this was an extreme course of action that they had taken only twice before during their long career of fostering.

Balancing a child's vulnerabilities and his or her welfare was easier said than done. Perhaps it wasn't surprising that there was no written policy and procedure on common sense. Stew and Tina knew that any police involvement would more than likely be the end of their already poor relationship with William.

The Grants had often wondered about moving away from the city of Parton to the uncommercialised rugged coastline of the county when their fostering days were over. Stew was against this proposal as it meant travelling further for his golf and to see his lifelong rugby mates. Nevertheless the coast had a great deal to offer in terms of scenery and had the added bonus of being guarded against tourism by the harsh weather conditions that often prevailed.

What they didn't know was that, sadly, there wasn't a hope of William returning to their sumptuous, four-bedroomed detached house in a very sought-after suburb of Parton.

***

Drip, drip, drip. He could hear the rain water making its way slowly down from the leaking roof. The stench of decaying wood permeated the atmosphere, creeping through to his very core. The seventeen year old was gagged but breathing relatively freely through a loosely fitted cloth hood. He was shivering in the freezing loft, bound hand and foot. He had absolutely no idea of the time or date and dreamt longingly of the sumptuous comfort of his foster parents' home and the Sunday dinners he rarely bothered attending.

Life had dealt William a poor pack of cards. He'd had a troubled upbringing and been in and out of care and foster placings. He was bright and could be a likeable individual, yet he had squandered opportunity after opportunity, whether as Julie or latterly as William. Various people and agencies, who had all gone the extra mile to try and support him, had finally given up after he continually let them down.

That said, the most recent emotional turmoil and the real reason for his wish to change sex were unknown to anyone except himself. It would remain that way, should he ever remove himself from his present predicament.

The Grants were now directly at the centre of William's most recent and serious problems. They were like two people facing a firing squad, with William pulling the trigger of some automatic weapon and spraying bullets in their direction. If only they had known the problems he was encountering; if only William could have told them.

In a life full of crises, this was the worst.

William was in significant danger. He knew it and shook even more, squirming around, desperately trying to make himself more comfortable. As he contemplated his dire predicament, he wondered what those people who had tried to help him throughout his life were thinking.

He had a very good idea why he now found himself being held hostage. He also believed that survival was extremely unlikely. He wondered why his kidnappers hadn't killed him immediately.

His head dropped inside the hood. With his chin resting on the upper part of his chest, he sobbed uncontrollably. Tears streamed down his cheeks and rolled onto the cloth until it was totally soaked.

***

Sutton turned right at the junction and into the new development where the recently deceased DC Mike Chilter had purchased a neat, three-bedroom semi-detached property.

Mike had been married for more than five years to his childhood sweetheart, Yvonne. The Chilters were known for their sensible, forward-looking approach to life, which attracted a lot of good-natured banter from Mike's colleagues. Their home was within the catchment area of the best high school in the Parton area, even though their recently born offspring Olivia had not yet reached her first birthday. A few enquiries with his former colleagues had established that, with Mike working at least some of the weekend, Yvonne and Olivia had gone away to see her mother and were due to return some time on Sunday evening.

That would explain the fact that no one from the family had raised the alarm about him being missing. Linda Wrightson was single through and through, and kept herself to herself. If she had a life outside her work no one knew about it and she'd always been determined that it would remain that way. Consequently there had been no enquiries about her absence either.

Whilst the initial scene was being preserved and the relevant supervisors were attending, Ron Turner, the head of CID, had rung Sutton directly. 'How well did you know Mike Chilter, Geoff?' he asked.

'I was his DCI before I retired and I've met his wife at a couple of social dos,' stated Sutton.

'Can you do me a big favour,' Turner said. It was not a question. 'Could you go and inform his wife? I don't want her to hear or see something on the news. I'm briefing the Chief, who will also want to see the next of kin sooner rather than later. But in the meantime—'

'No problem,' sighed Sutton, politely interrupting, knowing what Ron wanted. It made a fair amount of sense, particularly as Sue Dalton was incapable of doing anything at the moment. He also knew that the family liaison officers assigned to the Chilters and Wrightsons would not be appointed until the morning.

Sutton parked the Insignia outside the Chilters' house.

A young female constable, PC Wardle, accompanied him. There wasn't a manual or procedure for delivering death messages. Sutton always remembered the advice given to him some thirty years previously when he was a probationer. 'Get in, tell them, get out,' instructed his tutor Constable. 'You can't bring back the dead,' was his considered reasoning, without offering any crumb of comfort.

Because it was so late, Sutton couldn't start knocking on neighbours' doors to ask for their assistance, which might have been a comfort to the new widow.

Here we go, he thought to himself as he knocked on the door firmly enough to get attention but not loud enough to wake a slumbering baby.

Yvonne answered the door. 'Mr Sutton,' she started but never finished. Realisation dawned in her eyes. 'Mike!' she screamed.

Sutton heard the sound of Olivia waking inside the house. 'Can we come in, please, Yvonne?'

Yvonne couldn't speak. She just stepped aside, eyes wide open, hands over her mouth, oblivious to Olivia's crying.

Sutton walked through to the kitchen-diner and sat down on a stool at the breakfast bar without being asked. Yvonne followed him; PC Wardle was half-supporting her and helped her to a chair at the dining table.

Sutton continued. 'I'm sorry, Yvonne. I can't say anything that will make this any easier. Mike's been found in a work's car at the picnic area near the rugby club. It would appear he's been murdered, along with Linda, although how they died needs to be formally confirmed. Ron Turner, the head of CID, asked me to come and tell you. I'm so sorry.' Sutton immediately regretted those last three words. They were platitudes, they couldn't express what he was feeling – but what else was there to say?

It was blatantly obvious that Yvonne was in shock. Olivia was now howling. Sutton caught PC Wardle's eye and nodded at her to go and check on the baby. Yvonne couldn't even hear her own baby crying; she was oblivious to everything that was going on around her.

Again without asking permission, Sutton walked over to the gleaming silver kettle and flicked the switch. 'How do you take your tea?' he asked firmly, almost as if he were giving an instruction.

'Milk, no sugar,' Yvonne replied automatically between sobs.

The next five minutes were filled with questions from Yvonne. She scarcely drew breath except for intermittent moments when she drew in great mouthfuls of air. She didn't give Sutton any time to answer before the next enquiry was on its way. Sutton politely deflected them all with the standard response that he would arrange a further visit in the morning and send over the Family Liaison Officers.

No doubt morning seemed an eternity away for poor Yvonne – and for baby Olivia, who was now to have a life without her doting, dedicated father.

It was some twenty minutes later, after Sutton had managed to contact Olivia's godmother who lived nearby to come over and comfort the grieving Yvonne, that he was able to extricate himself from the Chilter household. He cursed Ron Turner as he did so. Informing the bereaved was a crap job. He hadn't needed to accept Ron's request – but both Ron Turner and Geoff himself knew that there was no question of him refusing. When Sutton was asked to do a job, there was never a chance that he would refuse.

He drove back down to the crime scene. Ironically, it now looked like a fairground with lights and torches reflecting back in the starry sky on this freezing February night. But, unlike a fairground, there was little noise and no fun and laughter as the police investigation began in earnest.

After thanking her, Sutton dropped PC Wardle back with her harassed and stressed Sergeant, who was responsible for the crime scene management. He was about to ring Ron Turner when his car pulled alongside Sutton's Insignia.

Turner, who was more than stocky, always wore a tie and expensive dark suit whatever the occasion; he looked as if he were about to attend a meeting. He also looked as though he were trapped in the driver's seat.

Turner activated his offside electric window and beckoned Sutton to join him.

Sutton lip read, 'In you get, Geoff.' He joined the head of CID in his flashy, powder-blue Jaguar with its cream leather seats.

Turner didn't bother asking about Yvonne Chilter's welfare; it was a pointless question. He knew Sutton would have delivered the message and that Yvonne would be distraught. She would be looked after as much as was possible, given the circumstances.

Neither did Turner bother to thank Sutton. 'Geoff, have you got any plans coming up?' he asked. It wasn't an enquiry, it was more to indicate that whatever Sutton might have had planned was not going to happen.

'Nope, I'm fine, sir.' Sutton could never call Turner by his first name, even though he was no longer required to respect his rank. After so many years of addressing him as 'sir', which Sutton always preferred to 'boss', a term that his colleagues often used when they were addressing their superiors, he couldn't break the habit.

'Geoff, we need you in on this. It's informant-related. It's going to involve the authorities and there's a need for absolute confidentiality. Sue Dalton is absolutely knackered, both physically and mentally. I'll need to OK it with the Chief because of your current job role and status. He's meeting with the Police and Crime Commissioner as we speak. Go home. The scene is secure and work has been actioned for tonight. We're still trying to find Linda Wrightson's next of kin. There'll be a full briefing tomorrow at 9am at Parton City Centre Police Station.'

Sutton didn't speak but merely nodded his agreement. He got out of the Jag, noticing the mess he'd made with his muddy shoes on Turner's previously immaculate dust mats.

***

Sutton pulled the Insignia onto his driveway. It had just gone midnight. He needed a drink.

As he entered the bungalow, the heat billowed through the front door. Sutton's technical ability was such that the heating was either off or on; he couldn't be bothered to read the timer's operating instructions. He dumped his Barbour in the usual spot, carefully wiped his muddy shoes that had made such a mess of Turner's car and deposited them in the small porch by the front door.

Within five minutes he had a glass of Australian red in his hand and was sitting in the living room, safe and warm. His mind was racing, taking in the last thirty-six hours or so. He took a large gulp from the large wine glass.

He'd enjoyed the golf but the rugby was crap, and so was the result. Then seeing the van on his drunken walk back up the hill. Why didn't he call it in there and then? Were Chilter and Wrightson already dead by then? Tomorrow's post-mortem would provide that information.

As he took another gulp of wine, larger than the last one, a teardrop ran down his right cheek. The last time he'd cried was when Maria had passed away. Another tear, this time on his left cheek, running down as if in a race, both drops making their way to his upper lip.

Sutton closed his eyes. The sight of Chilter and Wrightson staring at the officers as Dalton pulled back the van door haunted him. It probably always would. He knew that.

Sutton drained his glass and went to bed. He wouldn't sleep properly; he had no right to do so, and the wine would be of little benefit. Despite the tragic events, he had a big day tomorrow and the adrenaline arising out of yet another tragedy was already coursing through his veins.

6

Briefing

It was absolutely the worst possible scenario for the Temporary Chief Constable, Alan Conting. He had been the force's deputy until, due to the illness and recent forced retirement of the current Chief, Conting had been left with an opportunity to become the new force commander pending confirmation by the Police and Crime Commissioner. After twenty-eight years' service in various parts of the country, he now had the opportunity to become a Chief Constable, the height of his ambition and something that he thought had passed him by.

As far as the police force was concerned, Parton Constabulary was a medium-sized organisation in relation to the forty-three forces currently in existence in England and Wales. After recent restructuring by the former Chief, due primarily to cost-cutting and austerity measures, the Parton Constabulary now consisted of three area commands in place of the previous five. The new force areas were County North, County South and Parton Central, which included the main City Centre Police Station with Parton Constabulary Headquarters in the adjacent buildings.

Conting just needed a quiet three months. Crime figures were good and there were no scandals. Hopefully he could convince the Commissioner to ratify, via the Home Office, his position as the new Chief without going through the rigours of advertising and interviewing. A new five-year contract would see Conting into retirement, with a Queen's Police Medal to fulfil his ego, not to mention the enhanced pension and potentially lucrative consultancy work. That would certainly go a long way to satisfy his wife's lavish lifestyle.

Permanent Chief Constable seemed a long way off as Conting sat in his office, head in hands, awaiting a call from the Police and Crime Commissioner Peter Roberson. What a bloody nightmare. What a shitting nightmare. Not one thought passed through Conting's mind for his murdered colleagues or their distraught families; for him it was about his own survival.

Conting had received his own briefing an hour earlier from the head of CID, Ron Turner, whom he despised. He thought that the Commissioner would think better of him if he was at his office as opposed to being at home.

It didn't surprise Turner at all that Conting asked no questions about the investigation or how the next of kin took the news. Turner, the operational animal that he was, much preferred the third degree when briefing senior officers: Have you considered this? Why have you done that? In his view Conting was not up to the mark, never had been, never would be. Turner had little respect for him and Conting knew it. Turner did not suffer fools and in his mind Conting fell clearly into that category.

Conting's mobile rang. It was Roberson. Conting answered and went through Turner's briefing. Roberson asked a lot of questions, which Conting struggled to answer. He kept repeating his stock phrase: 'Peter, the investigation is at an early stage. I will have an answer for you in the morning.' It wasn't his best performance.

Unknown to Temporary Chief Constable Conting or Ron Turner, as soon as Roberson finished the conversation he picked up another mobile phone secreted deep inside his jacket pocket. He scrolled through the contacts and brought up Sue Dalton's private number. Her phone rang repeatedly before going to voicemail and affording the caller an opportunity to leave a message. Roberson declined to do so and replaced the phone in his jacket pocket.

***

The following morning, Sutton awoke early, well before his alarm. His body told him immediately that he hadn't slept. That wasn't a surprise as he had spent a restless night mostly trying to remove the vision of the staring eyes of Chilter and Wrightson.

There were a lot of thoughts running through his mind. Did he really need to be involved in such major investigation? Surely those days were well behind him. The answer was short and sweet: definitely not. The main reason he continued in his civilian role was social as far as he was concerned; it certainly wasn't financial. He was well aware of how lucky he was financially. He had no idea how long he would continue working but at the moment it suited him just fine. He knew that when his contract ended it would create a void in his life, giving him a great deal of unwanted time to occupy, despite the golf and the rugby.

Yesterday had provided him with a huge adrenaline rush, which maybe he could do without. He got a few hours excitement every Saturday on the golf course. Any mistakes on the golf course could be dealt with by some classic piss-taking by his mates. He knew full well that mistakes in murder enquiries could be irretrievable, costly and potentially life-changing. And not just for the victims.

This case would be one continuous pressure cooker, particularly if it proved a 'runner'. Sutton knew the national press would be all over the murder of two British bobbies in little old Parton. Do I really need this, Sutton repeated to himself over and over again? He had called it in, thinking and acting as a police officer, involved himself, but he could quite easily walk away. He could see Turner first thing and politely decline his request. He wasn't a warranted officer and it didn't form part of his contract – yet Sutton, being Sutton, rarely refused a request.

He showered and changed, mind racing, making an effort to be smarter than usual but not going as far as wearing a tie. He always hated wearing ties.

By 7.30am Sutton had time on his hands. He decided that a trip to The Parlour and a hybrid full breakfast, served by Debbie, would just be the ticket. Wearing his Barbour and his Ted Baker sunglasses, another Maggie present because she thought they made him look trendy, he reversed the Insignia out of the driveway.

He stopped on the road immediately outside his house, realising that if he didn't make some attempt to clear last night's frost off the windows he would be the cause of the next unwelcome incident for the local police.

He drove to The Parlour, using the empty Falcon Pub car park as opposed to the few parking places on the road outside the group of shops where The Parlour was sited. He removed the Ted Bakers; he didn't have enough bottle to wear them anywhere but when he was driving alone in the car. Wearing them down at the rugby club would give too much ammunition to Roger, Pete and Stew.

'Shit the bed, Geoff?' said Smithy, as Sutton purchased *The Times*.

Sutton grunted a response and threw the change on the counter.

'Have a nice day now,' continued Smithy, counting out the various newspapers for the day's deliveries.

Sutton left the shop and made the short trip from Dillon's, turning immediately right and entering The Parlour. Within seconds, his mood change was complete. That vision of loveliness, Debbie, was serving a table of two contractors, whose bright yellow fluorescent jackets were draped over their chairs. They looked as though they were about to start work on one of the many extensions taking place on the Springfield Green estate. It would be a full English, with two piping hot mugs of builder's tea, for the real workers.

The sofas were vacant, awaiting the school-run parents. No doubt in an hour or so the place would be a buzzing with young parents, accompanied by toddlers of non-school age, having skinny lattes, cappuccinos and the like.

Debbie swayed over to Sutton's table near the window. 'Unusual, but still lovely to see you at this time, Mr Sutton. Americano with semi-skimmed milk and a croissant, sir?' she enquired, looking at him with those gorgeous brown eyes.

Sutton replied, almost in a trance, 'No, ta, Deb. Usual fry up, toast and a mug of tea, please.' He felt like a nervous schoolboy waiting to go and see the headmaster for another bollocking rather than a grown man speaking to a mature lady whom he fancied like hell.

'Can I just say you're looking really smart,' said Debbie admiringly. Sutton blushed embarrassingly, taking in the compliment but not knowing how to continue the conversation. Debbie turned away and floated off to prepare the order.

Yesterday's events had happened too late for all but very scant coverage in the morning's press and, whilst there were rumours abounding in social media, there didn't appear to be any great clamour for information at this stage. The explosion would happen later this morning no doubt, thought Sutton. He certainly had no wish to engage in local chat or rumour with anyone, even Debbie.

Ten minutes later Sutton was tucking into his food, delicious as always and, more importantly, served by Debbie. He had ignored his paper but now took the opportunity to study the sports pages as he took mouthfuls of piping hot tea.

He finished his breakfast then took the paper serviette that also doubled as a wrapper for his cutlery to wipe away the remnants of food from around his mouth. He sighed. It had been a while since he had attended a major incident briefing and he had very mixed thoughts about it.

Those thoughts were interrupted. 'Five pounds fifty, Geoff,' said Debbie as she came towards the table with a definite glint in her eyes.

In a quiet voice, from a place within that Sutton never really knew existed, he said to her, 'Debbie, would you like to go for dinner sometime soon?'

'What did you say, Geoff? You'll have to speak up,' Debbie said, arching her neck to hear what he had said as the cafe door opened.

Sadly the moment had gone and Sutton knew it. The courage he'd just shown retreated as quickly as it had arrived. 'Sorry, must dash, Deb. See you later in the week.' He caught the door before it closed fully and headed out into the cold like a scolded cat scampering away, tail between his legs, his coat hanging limp over his right arm.

Sutton began talking to himself. 'I'm bloody pathetic, like a schoolboy asking a girl on his very first date.' He repeated these thoughts as he collapsed in the driver's seat of the Insignia, breathing deeply.

He looked back at The Parlour, only to see the blinds open slightly and Deb peering out in his direction. What the hell must she think of him? He wasn't aware that, in the warmth of the cafe, Debbie was hoping that Sutton's next visit would be tomorrow rather than later in the week.

Sutton reached in the well of the driver's door and removed the designer Ted Baker sunglasses from their expensive case. After receiving them on his birthday, he'd decided to check how much they were worth. The price came as a shock to him that was lessened only slightly, when Maggie said he looked ten years younger when he wore them. At that price, Sutton wore them at every opportunity when he was driving, sometimes when there was absolutely no sun at all.

He decided Radio Five Live was the appropriate option;

there might be breaking news on the investigation and some light sporting relief. When you're making a familiar journey that you've done hundreds of times before, your mind can become numb and dangerously occupied by other thoughts rather than concentrating on the road ahead. That was exactly what happened to Sutton as he made the six-mile drive to Parton Central Police Station. Three separate motorists remonstrated with him during his journey, as well as a mother and toddler whom he nearly wiped out as they walked across a pedestrian crossing. It was both a relief and a minor miracle that he'd arrived unscathed.

Such was Sutton's lack of attention that he failed to notice the media trucks camped out in the car park immediately opposite the station entrance. He reached out to the keypad and activated the metal slide gates into the police station car park. His actions came to a halt as he noticed the half-mast Union Jack hanging limply around the flagpole on this windless morning, obviously in memory of their two stricken colleagues. The flagpole, sited above the Parton Police HQ, was an iconic landmark and could be seen for miles. It was a poignant reminder of what was occurring here and now, and not a living nightmare.

Sutton's mobile rang from deep in his pocket, the muffled sound of the *Local Hero* ringtone followed by the ping to denote a message. He ignored the call.

It was 8.30am on another bright, sunny, but bitterly cold February morning. Half an hour before the scheduled briefing and the car park was almost full. Sutton managed to find a parking bay farthest away from the staff entrance. He collected his coat, checked his phone and saw the missed call was from Stew Grant. There was no time to call him and he wondered momentarily what his mate wanted. He would ring back later. Grabbing his imitation black-leather A4 Parton Constabulary wallet, containing a writing pad and pens, he made his way to the staff entrance.

Ron Turner caught up with him as he crossed the car

park. 'Geoff, I've spoken with the Chief and Personnel. No problem with your contract. Basically you're on a 37.5 hour week. Any overtime, just put it through and it'll be paid at time and a third. You will be working specifically around the informant angle within the Intelligence Cell.'

Sutton was in, absolutely in, right up to his neck. It was inevitable, he thought to himself; he had known that right from the start and all his procrastinating was total bullshit.

Turner continued. 'I'm going to hold an intelligence meeting after the main briefing where there will be specific actions.' Typical Turner, do this, do that. He was in his element when there was no need for him to consult; this was currently a dictatorship and he would be asking the questions once he'd got the investigation truly underway.

Turner knew that he would have an abundance of resources; after all, it was two of their colleagues who had been brutally murdered. The team wanted to get stuck in without any delay; they needed some action and strong direction. In Sutton's view, Turner was the ideal person to provide that leadership.

Five minutes before 9am, Sutton entered the briefing room, which also doubled as the Murder Incident Room (MIR). The room was lined with whiteboards; the windows along one wall were blocked out by blinds. The floor space consisted of orderly lines of desks on which IT equipment was placed. The whiteboard on the back wall of the room had been updated with some key details: the names of the two detectives, the van details, make, model and registration number. It also listed the last positive sighting of the officers and the location where the vehicle was found.

The room was packed, yet quiet and subdued. Sutton acknowledged several familiar faces from a variety of different departments, as was the norm in major investigations. He made his way over to DI Bill Singer, another highly experienced officer whom Sutton had worked with and known for more than twenty years.

Singer was a detective through and through, with vast experience in the intelligence arena. He was rapidly approaching retirement and looked to be in a certain amount of shock at the thought of being involved in such a high-profile enquiry at this stage of his career. The double murder of their colleagues was unchartered territory for them both. They shook hands without speaking and Sutton sat down beside him in one of the few remaining vacant seats.

There was a tremendous sense of anticipation in the room. They were moving into uncharted territory. The trauma and tragedy of any murder is unique, yet out of the trauma comes a sense of excitement.

Ron Turner entered the room, followed by the Temporary Chief Constable and Police and Crime Commissioner. Turner looked resplendent in a grey pinstripe suit; Alan Conting was in full-dress uniform. The dapper Roberson wore a plain navy-blue suit and matching waistcoat, with a sky-blue tie and matching dress handkerchief just visible in his left breast pocket.

Everyone stood up immediately in respect of their rank.

Turner was in front, totally focused and not acknowledging any of the seventy-five or so personnel he was shortly to address. Sutton thought Turner's presence was far greater than his two VIP colleagues.

Temporary Chief Constable Alan Conting spoke to his staff. 'Please remain standing for a minute's silence for our two colleagues, Mike Chilter and Linda Wrightson, who lost their lives in the line of duty.'

You could have heard a pin drop. Sutton, head down, stared at his shoes. His mind wandered back to the staring eyes of the two officers, lying brutally murdered in the back of that van. That sight continued to haunt him. As ever, the minute's silence seemed to go on for an hour.

'Thank you. DCs Mike Chilter and Linda Wrightson were both serving officers with Parton Constabulary. They both had exemplary records and will be sorely missed. Some of you within this room will have known and worked with Mike and Linda. The investigation may well affect some of you more than others. If there is anyone who needs support, or who may wish to remove themselves from the investigation, then please speak to your line manager. It is only to be expected given the tragic circumstances.'

Sutton watched Turner as Conting gave his short, polite address. He knew what Turner thought of Conting; Turner's face portrayed both impatience and disdain. Turner wanted to get started and this was a distraction, despite the fact that Conting's words and thoughts were both sympathetic and appropriate. He just didn't rate the man, whatever he said.

'Please be seated,' said Turner, in an unusually polite tone. 'I want to keep this brief. We will meet again this evening at 7pm for a further update.' He paused then continued. 'On Saturday afternoon, Chilter and Wrightson left for an informant's meeting authorised by DI Sue Dalton. At the moment we don't know if that meeting took place or not. The informant's nom de plume was Billy Spitz.'

Turner looked up from the lectern and his carefully prepared briefing document. His eyes scoured the room, making contact with anyone who dared to look at him. 'That pseudonym does not leave this room. Do I make myself absolutely clear? For press purposes and anyone not on the enquiry, the two officers were in plain clothes and deployed on an operation. They left the police station in a Confidential Unit vehicle bearing the registration number VE62 WFX. That van was spotted at approximately 7pm on Saturday in the picnic area at the rear of Upper Parton Rugby Club. Currently we cannot say definitely whether Mike and Linda were in the vehicle at that time, or indeed if they had already been murdered. On Sunday afternoon the vehicle was still in the same location and a concerned member of the public rang the police.'

Turner again scanned the room, making sure he caught Sutton's eye. 'The police were called and the bodies of the two officers were discovered in the rear of the vehicle, which is utilised for mobile informant meetings. The scene was secured last night. There were no van keys in the ignition. Both officers' next of kin have been informed. Fortunately we managed to trace Linda Wrightson's aunt first thing this morning. These duties will now be taken over by appointed Family Liaison Officers.'

Despite the length of Turner's speech, he had the absolute attention of everyone in the room.

'As head of CID, I am senior investigating officer. The Temporary Chief Constable and Police and Crime Commissioner will hold a press conference at 10am this morning and another one is scheduled at 6pm.'

Turner hardly gave the Temporary CC and the PCC a glance.

'As a matter of urgency I need the following priorities addressed. One: the crime scene. There needs to be a full search of the van and also the bodies of the officers. Was the informant's money with them? Did they have the informant paper receipt signed? Two: a search of the surrounding area for the murder weapon and other potential evidence. Three: samples – blood, DNA, etc. Get them run through the various systems. Four: the van was not fitted with a tracker, so we don't know where it went after leaving the police station. Check out any potential CCTV and number-recognition cameras. I believe from the logbook back at the unit that the petrol card was taken out, so nearby garages need to be visited.'

Turner's voice deepened, reflecting the gravity of what he said next. 'Billy Spitz needs to be identified, traced and eliminated. He is our number one starting-point in this enquiry. He may or may not have been the last person to see DCs Chilter and Wrightson. When he is traced, contact me immediately whatever time of day or night it is. I will make the decision, based on the evidence we have at the time, to arrest him or not. The intelligence unit will have a separate briefing, which will allow for the degree of confidentiality necessary in this operation.

'Finally, I have mentioned before about certain matters that need to remain inside this room. Whilst inevitably there will be an issue of informant compromise when we identify Billy Spitz, I want to minimise the potential fall-out. And remember that, for all we know, Billy himself could be in significant danger and we have a duty of care.'

Turner's eyes were hard and staring as they swept the room. 'If I hear of anyone breaching this confidentiality, they will be removed from this enquiry immediately and they will not, as long as I'm Head of CID, be involved in any other murder investigation.' Anyone who knew Ron Turner was well aware it was not an idle threat but a promise.

'This investigation will carry the name of Operation Trust. Geoff Sutton and DI Bill Singer, in my office please for an intelligence brief,' Turner said as he finished.

Two minutes later, each armed with a cup of coffee, the three men were sitting in Turner's immaculate office. Turner was sitting behind his desk with his subordinates facing him. The walls of the office were adorned with his many service awards, commendations and landscapes of the Lake District, where he spent all his leisure time. He loved the scenery and the relaxed atmosphere of the Lakes. Despite his big frame, Turner was a keen hill walker.

On his desk, apart from his laptop, were just three family photographs. There was no sign of any paper, notes, lists – nothing apart from the jet-black fountain pen, inscribed with his initials in gold, in a black stationery holder. Turner's desk was so tidy that Sutton was convinced he must be suffering from some disorder and be a real nightmare to live with.

Turner was typically direct. 'As a matter of urgency, I need to know Billy Spitz's real name and what he was reporting on. Who authorised the meetings and how much was he paid? I want his mobile details. We might be able to trace him from this information. I need to know his antecedents so I can feed it into the Incident Room. We've got to get a hold of him – he could well be our murderer but alternatively he could be in grave danger if he's been compromised as a police informant.'

He took a sip of his coffee before continuing. 'Your passwords have been updated and you're cleared to access the confidential files. Sue Dalton is knackered. It's a non-medical term – she's currently bedridden and sedated. When she's up to it, she will have questions to answer over her supervision of this affair. She has to explain why, after authorising the informant meeting, she did not request an update from the officers within a certain timescale. It's fairly bloody basic supervision in my view. But those questions are some way down the line.'

Sutton left Turner's office with Bill Singer, both of them heading straight to the Confidential Unit to log into the nearest computer screens.

Sutton was pleased to be working with Bill again; they knew exactly how each other operated. Respect had been born from a number of operations but neither of them, even in their worst nightmares, would ever have thought they would be back working together on a double police murder.

Singer needed to sort out the staffing for the Intelligence Unit and a tasking for active informants to see if any information was forthcoming about the murdered officers. Additionally he would be assisting Sutton.

Geoff checked his mobile. There was another missed call from Stew Grant. What on earth did the miserable bugger want? Well, whatever it is, it would have to wait. Head down, he logged on to his computer.

***

The press conference given by Alan Conting was primarily about the lives of the two officers, how sorely they would be missed, and their exemplary service to the community.

'At this stage, we can tell you that the officers were deployed on a plain-clothes operation when they were brutally murdered.'

Conting appealed to the general public for assistance in determining if anyone had seen a white Bedford van VE62 WFX between 3pm and 7pm on Saturday in the picnic area adjacent to Upper Parton Rugby Club. He also asked for any sightings of the vehicle over the weekend in the Parton area. He concluded by saying, 'I will be attending the scene later today to lay a wreath for Detectives Mike Chilter and Linda Wrightson.'

Murdered unarmed police officers always struck a chord with the British public. There was massive interest on a national scale and the press could well stick around for some time, depending on developments in the investigation and other news stories that arose to claim their attention.

PCC Roberson was at Conting's side throughout, as if in support of his Temporary Chief Officer. He kept his head bowed in respect for the fallen officers. Prior to the press conference, Roberson had discreetly asked Conting about the welfare of DI Sue Dalton, who had been present when the murdered officers were discovered. Conting was unusually sympathetic in his reply, saying she was bedridden and under sedation due to the shock of seeing her officers' murdered bodies.

So that's why Dalton hasn't answered my calls, Roberson thought. He certainly didn't think she was ignoring him – Roberson was someone who was rarely ignored.

The final speaker at the press conference was the force's recently appointed Head of Media, Roz Nolan. Having been promoted from within the force she had a wealth of experience, but she had never imagined when she took on the role that she would face a situation like this. Nothing could have prepared her for this particular scenario. She looked like the proverbial rabbit caught in the headlights.

Operation Trust was in full swing and the expectations

were immense. The press would ensure that there would be no let-up in the investigation.

7

William

Drip, drip. More bloody drips. William thought it must have been raining as the drops increased in their intensity, as did the smell. How long had he been here? How long was he likely to be here?

He worked out that during his captivity he'd been fed and watered four times. His current circumstances were in some ways similar to the many occasions he had been arrested in his short life and placed in a cell, awaiting his approved social worker and the duty solicitor.

The police cells had four bare walls, concrete floors and blue plastic-covered mattresses placed on a slightly raised area that served as a bed. The only other piece of furniture was the built-in chrome toilet. William's favourite food when he was arrested was the all-day breakfast, served in a carton with white plastic cutlery, washed down with lukewarm milky tea.

His current captors had supplied him with a heavily stained and grubby mattress, which smelled of stale milk. Thankfully, they had brought him a blanket at the last meal time. Although it carried the same smell of stale milk, at least it enabled him to find some warmth.

The police cell seemed like a hotel room, given his current conditions. How he now wished for the luxury – and more importantly the opportunities in life – offered by people like the Grants.

The system for bringing his meal seemed to have been well rehearsed by those responsible for looking after him. It began with knocking on what William thought must be the trap door that gave access to the attic, then the noise of the hatch area opening, followed by the pulling down of a set of extended ladders.

William could hear the tell-tale steps of two people ascending into the loft space as his captors climbed into his upstairs room. His hood and the binding securing his hands behind his back were removed. William was faced with two of his captors disguised in clown masks. The masks reminded him of some ancient Netflix films of bank robberies. No words were spoken. He was supplied with a clear Tupperware box half full of cold chilli, accompanied by equally cold and rubbery toast and washed down with water from a bright red plastic sports-drink bottle.

He ate his meal quickly in order both to satisfy his hunger and keep his captors happy. No sooner had he finished than his hands were rebound and the hood replaced loosely over his head.

He wondered constantly about escape, particularly when his hands were momentarily free, but it seemed a pretty pointless thought considering the odds of having to take on two people with his feet bound. There was also the distinct probability that they were armed in some way. He thought of shouting, attracting attention, but what was the point? Then again, although his predicament looked grim, if they wanted to kill him why hadn't they already done so? There must be a reason why he was being kept alive and being looked after.

When he'd been taken, kidnapped, and bundled into a white van, he felt the familiar sharp pain of a syringe entering his skin. On this occasion, it was in his right thigh. Within seconds, he lost consciousness. He had awoken to find himself in this room, fighting both against the drowsiness of his intoxication and what seemed like concussion. He was here but not here. He had shaken his head violently around the inside his cloth hood to try and locate his senses.

He heard his two captors retrace their steps back across the attic floor to begin their descent down the extended ladders. Suddenly a mobile phone rang; the ringtone was the distinctive sound of Robbie Williams's ballad 'Angel'. One of the men must have reacted quickly to silence it; the tune didn't even get as far as the first lyrics.

The ballad was well known to William; it was the first dance at his mother's third wedding at the local leisure centre. William was still Julie then, and incredibly surprised that his mother had wanted him to attend. She had sent an invite to William's address at Holston House. He didn't have to accept the invitation but wrongfully, yet maturely, thought of it as a potential opportunity to build bridges. He loved his mum, despite having only sporadic contact with her throughout his short life.

Ironically the wedding took place on William's seventeenth birthday, though this was not noticed or recognised by his mother. His birthdays never were. What really attracted William to the wedding was the possibility of seeing his eldest sister.

His sister was some ten years older than William and, although their paths had separated some years previously, there was nobody closer to him. They had lost contact completely but, despite this, William loved his sister far more than anyone else in this world. He wondered every day where she was living and what she was doing.

At the wedding, as William should have expected, most guests were drunk even before the ceremony began. The wedding breakfast broke into a mass brawl before the speeches. When William met his sister, her appearance was a shock. She was obviously heavily dependent on drugs and unable to have anything approaching a coherent conversation. Yet William came away from the occasion clutching a birthday gift; whatever her problems, his sister had remembered the date.

Despite the years apart, despite her obvious problems, she had remembered William's birthday. The gift was a photo frame. William took a selfie on his phone that included his sister and mother. Sadly, the wedding invitees also included a close relative, an uncle who had abused William when he was four years of age. It was one of the many events in William's short life that he had never forgotten nor recovered from. He could no more tell his mother about the abuse now as he could have done at the time it occurred.

It was a real and utter living nightmare.

William broke down in tears again, soaking the loosely fitted cloth hood. It was yet another traumatic memory of abuse which continued to haunt him.

***

Police and Crime Commissioner Peter Roberson had dutifully attended the press conference. Conting had surprised him by doing an excellent job, pitched at the right level. Afterwards Roberson also attended the murder scene with Conting and laid a bouquet.

His thoughts were about himself, about being in the media spotlight and what the public thought of him. Any thoughts of the two murdered officers were purely secondary; one thing mattered to Peter Roberson and that was himself.

Roberson had already made up his mind that if Conting applied for the job as Chief Constable then there was every chance he could be successful. Roberson reasoned that Conting was weak and could easily be manipulated, so Roberson himself would have more control and as high a profile as possible as Crime Commissioner. That was an integral part of his plan to fulfil a lifetime ambition and become an MP.

There were obvious issues. As with many cities, Parton

had become increasingly diverse, particularly in the last forty years. In Parton's case there had been an influx of Eastern European migrants, which had provided some of the establishments on the popular and emerging East Parton Marina with cheap labour as well as enriching the local community with new and different cultures.

The influx of migrants had sadly also involved associated racial-hate crime. Conting, in his former role as Deputy Chief Constable, had established some good working relationships and was well respected by local councillors. Roberson recognised this achievement; Ron Turner did not.

The only major factor that could affect Pete Roberson's ambition and push his plans off course was Dunc Travis. If only Roberson had made his way straight home on that foggy evening, a year or so earlier, his path to achieving his ambition would be clear and unhindered.

Roberson made an excuse to leave Conting. He confirmed he would ring him in a couple of hours and then left the police station in his silver top-of-the-range Lexus, a car with enough bells and whistles to satisfy his status. Roberson was not only big on ego, he was also substantial in size. At well over six feet in height and weighing more than eighteen stone, it was a struggle for him to get into the driver's seat. He could never make a quick getaway. There was no doubt that ego had been the dominant factor in that purchase.

He had carefully planned his new Lexus purchase, allowing sufficient time to pass following his 'accident'.

Some years earlier, he had bought a penthouse in the new quayside developments overlooking the small marina in the rapidly developing East Parton Marina. It was the time when most cities were completing waterside developments, using the old bonded warehouse sites and converting them into accommodation that in the 1980s would have been called 'yuppie apartments'. This appealed to Roberson, a single man, as he drove the Lexus up to the gates of the block where his apartment was located. Due to the use of a number-plate recognition system, the gates opened without prompting so he could access the underground car park.

Waterside was the name of Roberson's block of apartments. It had its own gym, not that Roberson ever darkened its doors, concierge and extensive CCTV system. It was just the ticket for a man of his stature.

He made his way to his allocated parking bay, identified by the gold-plated apartment name pinned on the car park wall. His apartment was named Grebe and was on the top floor with the best views of the marina.

Roberson walked towards the lift, pressing the Lexus key fob to ensure the car was secure. Entering the lift, he activated the pad to allow him to exit on the eighth floor. After he used the scan system on his mobile phone, the door to his apartment seemed to open as if by magic. The kitchen-diner and living room gave access to the two bedrooms, one ensuite, with another having a bathroom next door.

What took your breath away when you entered Grebe apartment was the panoramic view of the East Marina. It was undoubtedly the best in Parton. It did not matter which room you were in, you always had the view. The East Marina side was the money side and with it came status and prosperity.

From here, Roberson could look out at his boat, aptly named *ROBES*. Not that he was particularly keen on sailing; he had purchased the vessel at the same time as the apartment because that was what was expected when you owned property on the Waterside.

The apartment was open plan, with minimalist designer furniture, almost all black and white. Everything was of the latest style and the highest quality. Roberson was a man who had to have the trappings. It was a sought-after residence in a sought-after area.

Through voice activation, Roberson started his music playlist. He sat down at the lacquered black surface of the dining-room table that often doubled up as his home office.

He pulled out his two mobile phones from the inside pocket of his Hugo Boss suit . He used one mobile phone under a Vodafone contract for work; the other was a pay-as-you-go for his 'social activities'. Dunc Travis had ordered him to get it. A pay-as-you-go phone allowed them the freedom of non-attributable communication.

Roberson's work phone rang. It was Simon Keys, head teacher of Holston House. He was due to attend a meeting tonight at which Roberson, who was chair of the management board and a trustee, would be in attendance. Holston House was yet another organisation that Roberson thought provided evidence to the general public of his commitment to the community. It was another role that would attract positive publicity for his parliamentary ambitions.

For Dunc Travis, Roberson was an ideal target for blackmail because he moved in the best circles. Not only that, as Roberson was the local Police and Crime Commissioner Travis really had hit the proverbial jackpot. Should anyone question any aspect of Travis's business empire, he had Roberson on the payroll. Roberson had all the contacts that would allow Travis to expand his business activities. The contacts and position that Roberson had sought over the past years in his successful efforts to be the apple of the public eye had returned to haunt him with a vengeance.

Roberson was rapidly becoming a puppet, with only one person pulling his strings. It was a situation alien to him and one that he found far from comfortable.

Since the night in question when Nina died, Travis had purchased his late uncle's garage where his hand car wash was located and placed Stan in charge. Stan was highly trained and an excellent mechanic. His brother, Seb, promoted because he also never asked questions and was totally loyal, became the new person in charge at the car wash. The garage and car wash were reasonably successful but, more importantly, provided a smokescreen for Travis's other businesses. Blackmailing Roberson was not only proving highly profitable but it also catered for the perverse and controlling side of Travis's character.

Roberson decided not to answer Keys call. The headmaster was always on the phone updating him on this, updating him on that, and telling him how well the school was doing. The only aspect that interested Roberson was the next positive media opportunity. You could bet your mortgage on the fact that whenever there was press coverage of Holston House Roberson would be in the photograph. He appeared at the home's annual outward bound visit to North Wales, as well as the outings to local attractions. Not only did these events enhance Roberson's popularity in the eyes of the general public, they were also the ideal opportunity for Roberson to make young friends and exploit their vulnerability.

Roberson found that, without trying, he had become popular with the vulnerable youngsters at Holston House. Dunc Travis hoped that Roberson's ability to influence and have youngsters depend on him would continue. Roberson's role at Holston House would become Travis's main asset, as far as blackmail was concerned.

Roberson was not short of money; as an only child, he had inherited a small fortune from his parents scrap-metal business when they were tragically killed in a car crash some five years previously. Despite the price of metal going through the roof, he had sold the business in which he had never taken any interest. That was another aspect that Travis exploited to the full.

Roberson's personal campaign had been plain sailing over the last ten years as his ego and portfolio expanded at a similar rate. The tragic and avoidable events of that fateful night twelve months earlier had dented but not broken his arrogance. Nevertheless, the accident at the trading estate haunted him. The nightmares never left him. He woke up at night, thinking the police were at his door. Why was his timing so wrong? Wrong place at the wrong time, was a phrase he continually repeated to himself. That said, those nightmares were nothing compared with having to endure Dunc Travis's blackmailing.

Roberson reflected that he would have been in a far better situation had he reported the accident at the time. The publicity would have been brutal, as would have been the public humiliation. There would probably have been a jail term and the abrupt end to his lifetime ambitions. However, the continual mental anguish and torture might well have lessened.

Roberson was approaching his fiftieth birthday and needed to achieve his goals soon, but the demands placed on him by Travis had grown. Roberson's life was now fully in the hands of Dunc Travis and his emerging illegal business empire.

Travis had hit on Roberson at exactly the right time for himself and the worst possible time for Roberson.

For the first month after Nina's death, Travis sent the video through to Roberson each week, always at the same time. There were no comments attached; there was no need because the video itself was a graphic reminder of that horrendous experience.

Travis's timing was always immaculate. He usually made contact late at night. As he sat with a glass of gin and tonic in his hand, Roberson's phone would ping. For Roberson, it usually resulted in yet another broken glass followed by the obligatory sleepless night.

Roberson had scoured all possible avenues to enquire whether or not there was a missing-person enquiry or a hit-and-run accident investigation. There was absolutely nothing. Travis and Roberson had made the same decision independently that no one, other than themselves, had witnessed the tragic events. Both men were also correct in their assumption that nobody was bothered about Nina's disappearance.

After the first month, Travis began to turn the screws on Roberson. Slowly, the messages started to accompany the video. He told Roberson to get the non-attributable mobile for 'our business'. The first demand was for a small amount of cash to be placed in a bin at a location at a certain time. Perversely, the location was the very same trading estate, where Roberson had had the accident.

During that first drop, Roberson was a quivering wreck as he pulled up in a different Lexus to the one that had run over Nina. Hands shaking, he carried a paper bag containing the required amount of money. He placed it in the bin as directed and scanned the surrounding area.

As ever, Travis was one step ahead of him. He had used one of his well-researched pimping observation points to watch the drop. He was relaxed in the knowledge that he couldn't be seen but had a clear view of Roberson's actions.

Travis laughed as the petrified figure of Pete Roberson walked nervously back to his vehicle before driving off. After recovering the package, he counted the £1000 cash. He could not believe his luck.

Roberson had made his way not home but to the nearest police station. He was no fool and he knew full well this would be merely the start of a number of demands from Travis. He had made up his mind there and then that it had to stop. Bugger his ambitions; there was only one way this was going – downhill rapidly, like an unstoppable avalanche. Life was not worth it.

Roberson had pulled up in the parking bay for the general public at the small outlying police station named Parton East. A blue-and-white checked police sign illuminated the building. He got out of the car and walked into the foyer. He was shaking and panicking. The confidence and arrogance shown in his many and varied public appearances was totally gone.

He looked around the foyer. It was well illuminated, and the walls covered with posters and appeals. There were helplines for domestic abuse, homophobic crime and an advertisement for scrap-metal anti-theft markings. It seemed to have a unique and awkward smell of its own, both musty and dirty. Roberson made a mental note to speak to Conting about how unwelcoming the foyer would appear to a member of the public.

He was about to ring the bell to attract a member of staff when he saw a pair of eyes looking straight at him. It was a large poster of himself, prominently displayed, the Parton PCC Peter Roberson. He was looking straight ahead, relaxed and smiling; his full contact details, mobile phone number and email address were shown in large print.

Roberson's index finger hovered above the bell on the front desk as he looked at the poster. Not bad, he thought in a moment of supreme arrogance, a moment where he completely forgot his current predicament. Still looking at the poster directly above the public counter, he rang the bell. Some thirty seconds later, after no one arrived, he pressed the button again this time for longer. He was not accustomed to being ignored.

'Coming,' said the welcoming voice of Civilian Support Officer 812 Jessica Davies, who was working the 2pm to 12 midnight shift as the Duty Front-Desk Officer. For once she opened the sliding frosted glass doors without first checking the CCTV camera where she could view her customers from the relative safety of the front office. When the sliding doors were fully opened Jessica Davies was faced with the large frame of the Crime Commissioner, standing directly in front of her.

Davies was dressed in a black polo shirt and plain black trousers, with navy-blue epaulettes bearing her force number perched neatly on either shoulder. She immediately recognised Roberson.

'Yes, sir. How can I help?' she enquired in an admirably composed voice, even though she could hear the thump of her heart rebounding against the black polo shirt.

'I'm the Police and Crime Commissioner, Peter Roberson. Can I see the Duty Sergeant please?' Roberson said, having recovered his own composure. He loved being called sir. He was now focused and ready.

'Please have a seat.' Davies politely directed Roberson to the metal bench fixed to the floor directly opposite the front desk and sliding doors. Surprisingly, Roberson did as he was asked.

Jessica removed her airwaves radio from the buckle on her belt to use the telephone facility. She rang Sergeant Ged Graham. Out of Roberson's earshot, Jess informed Ged that they had a visitor, the PCC.

Ged Graham had just finished drying his hands after a call of nature when he took the call. He was experienced enough to think immediately of some operational necessity that made him unavailable to meet with his unexpected guest, or even to attend the front office. Then he decided that it would be unfair to ignore Jessica's request and land somebody else with the problem. He would take any flack going.

Graham also had sufficient nous to think that Roberson's unannounced visit would probably be a spot check on resources and how he deployed his staff, or possibly a general look around the station. Anyway let's face the music, he thought to himself. 'I'll be there in a couple of minutes. Best not to keep Mr Roberson waiting,' he told Jessica.

Within a couple of minutes the door of the main station opened and Ged Graham was extending his right hand. 'Mr Roberson, I'm Sergeant Ged Graham. Very pleased to meet you. Would you like to come this way?' He ushered the Crime Commissioner through the opened door, surprised at the weak handshake Roberson had offered in return.

Roberson was about to walk through the door when his eyes caught yet another poster, immediately to the right of the main entrance. It was one of many posters that he'd initially missed when he was looking around the foyer and he had become engrossed with his own prominently displayed portrait. This particular poster was a helpline for sex workers and featured a black male and a white female. A heading before the relevant contact numbers and website bore the title 'Keep Safe'. The face on the white female could well have been Nina's.

Roberson pulled himself upright and walked through the main door after Ged Graham. 'Sergeant Graham, could you inform me what resources you have on your shift this evening?' he asked.

Shit, thought Ged. Another administrator, more concerned with statistics than catching criminals.

Roberson had bottled it totally.

That was the only occasion that he came close to confessing to his situation and reporting his accident. Consequently, the blackmail was ongoing.

8

Travis, Roberson and Dalton

Time had moved on since the first incidence of blackmail and Roberson's failed attempt at a confession. Travis's operation was both simple and straightforward. Using Roberson's influence, and with the promise of soft drugs, over the following months Holston House became a source of absconding youngsters, either on their own or more often in pairs. They attended locations and were met by one of Travis's more trusted sex workers, where drugs would be promised on the understanding that they would have to pay their way by some other means.

Drugs for sex was Travis's business model.

Sadly, the younger and more vulnerable were worth the better price. It couldn't fail, thought Travis, as the youngsters became more and more dependent on drugs.

He had more punters than ever and they were paying even more money. Roberson, who was in Travis's back pocket was the pivot to this enterprise because of his contacts and influence.

Travis was always ahead of the game, always looking ahead for more potential customers, for more providers. He was brought up on the streets and he knew where to look for those most vulnerable, those likely to want drugs and whose backgrounds made them easy to control.

The word had got around the streets. Many would make their way to the car wash, waiting for the next fix to meet their increasing needs. Travis stopped this practice almost immediately, telling Stan it was far to close to home and likely to attract unwanted attention. What these youngsters didn't realise was that everything came at a cost and would lead to scars that would last a lifetime.

William had come on his books during this recent business expansion when he was known as Julie. He was sixteen years of age. Travis recognised the face from somewhere, but couldn't quite place where. He saw the tell-tale signs – hanging around the streets, already worldly-wise in that respect. Julie, as she was known to him initially, certainly gave the impression that she had tried drugs, and the way she dressed left very little to the imagination.

He assigned Stan to do a bit of grooming. It didn't take long; it never did. A couple of freebie drugs set the ball rolling and, within a month, Julie was signed up and on board.

As was the norm, Travis took her out the first night she worked for him. The trading estate was always the place; he could keep an eye out and ensure her safety. Julie, despite her years, knew what was expected and needed little encouragement. She was off and running.

Roberson either knew exactly what was occurring in Travis's operation, or had a really good idea and chose to ignore it. Keeping Travis off his back was his main aim, thereby enabling him to continue with his ambitions. Roberson had, on more than one occasion, looked to pay Travis off with a lump sum but the offer fell on deaf ears. It just didn't make business sense to Travis. It became increasingly obvious to Roberson that not only was the blackmail more profitable in the long run but Travis actually enjoyed controlling him.

Since the accident there hadn't been a single moment of every hour of every day that Roberson didn't regret that extra drink at the leisure centre and being in the wrong place at the wrong time. Now he was racking his brain at the information he'd been given, both by Conting and also at the briefing given by Ron Turner, to glean anything that indicated a connection between his involvement with Dunc Travis, and the murder of the two police officers.

He gave a sigh of relief; even he, in his worst moments of despair, couldn't envisage that this tragic double murder was linked in any way to his own blackmail predicament.

The only positive aspect of that horrendous night was the fact that it was the evening he met Sue Dalton. She was an ideal ally for Roberson. He was a man who needed female company and had done so throughout his life; he preferred the company of women rather than men. This became very apparent when he attended his various public functions.

Dalton kept herself to herself; she was a lonely lady in middle age. She never dressed in a particularly trendy manner; for Sue Dalton, clothes were a convenience to cover her full and curvaceous figure. She was a forty-five-year-old single woman who had lived in and around Parton City all her life. Having attended local schools, she had decided to embark on her childhood ambition without delay by joining her local police force straight from school, despite the fact that her excellent A-level results would have guaranteed her the choice of some high-ranking universities. The fact she joined the force straight from school instead of going away to university, created a widening gap between her and her peers. Not for Sue the late-night parties over the Christmas university break – it was a continuous spell of night shift over the festive season.

She didn't mind; it was her choice and her chosen career. The additional bank holiday overtime was a welcome bonus, carefully put away towards when she could afford her own property and move out of the single-person's accommodation provided by the police when she first joined the job.

She had no children and, with both parents having died, her only living relative was her sister with whom she had fleeting contact, and who lived at the other end of the country. They rarely saw each other, even at Christmas time. Her sister Helen had her own life to live, with her doting husband and their three adult children, Sue's nephews and nieces.

Sue Dalton had her job and now she had Pete Roberson in her life. Maybe one day they would travel down to see Helen and her sister's family but that was a very long way off. She often wondered what Helen would think of her boyfriend.

It quickly became apparent to Roberson that Dalton was a very dedicated police officer, who had risen through the ranks to become a Detective Inspector in a very specialized and responsible role. She was a local girl, totally dedicated to Parton Constabulary, with an old-fashioned outlook in that she was proud to serve her community.

Roberson took his time with the relationship, never rushing it but quietly assuming control as it became apparent that she was infatuated with him. He knew that, as well as providing him with some solace in terms of female company, Dalton could also be very useful out of the bedroom.

His patience was rewarded as slowly, for the first time in her life, Dalton fell in love. She had had only one other serious boyfriend in her life and that was back in her early twenties but Pete Roberson was different. He was the local Police and Crime Commissioner, bound by the same rules of confidentiality as she was. For the first time in her successful career, performing a role she loved as the Confidential Unit Inspector, she could discuss her problems at work as opposed to coming home to her tidy, well-maintained flat and somewhat lonely existence.

Her place was located on the opposite side of the city to the bustling Marina, far quieter. The premises had once been a large old town house, one of many on a long street that would have been *the* place to live back in the early 1930s when it was built. Nearly all the houses now had been converted into separate flats, with one on each floor.

Dalton's flat was a first-floor gable-end home that she had purchased after her mother had died three years previously. It was simply decorated and furnished; Dalton had similar taste to Roberson in that she had modernised the flat and created the idea of space even though the property was fairly small in size.

Her bedroom was neatly decorated and gave the impression of a well-organised and tidy single person. Above her double bed there hung a very large poster of her hero, Bruce Springsteen, which also included details of venues from a recent worldwide concert tour. More recently, she had added a small photograph of herself and Roberson in the Lake District on the only occasion she had been able to persuade him to go for a weekend away when she was not on call and he had no civic or public commitments. This was housed in a plain silver picture frame and placed on the dressing room table opposite the bed.

The weekend away took place on the six month anniversary of that fateful night after the leisure centre reception. It was also the first time in their relationship that they had spent the full night together as a couple. It meant so much for Sue Dalton but very little to Pete Roberson.

It was not the outstanding success that Dalton had hoped for. Pete seemed to be on his phone a great deal, paying little attention to her except in the bedroom. When she reflected upon the location, she admitted to herself that it was probably not the best place to choose. It was a last-minute bargain that she had chosen despite the fact that neither of them were particularly athletic. She drove as she always did. Roberson didn't offer a single penny towards the petrol costs.

There was a disagreement as soon as they set off when Dalton picked up Roberson from outside the plush Waterside apartments. She was listening to Springsteen's CD, *High Hopes*; Roberson immediately changed over to Radio 4. She began to object but thought better of it and resigned herself to performing her normal submissive role.

Never mind; it was really good to get away and the countryside, which they both enjoyed, was stunningly beautiful even from the car. She had really become infatuated with Pete, having never felt this way about her only other serious boyfriend.

After that, not too successful weekend, the relationship continued its unbalanced path.

Roberson only stayed over at Dalton's flat on the occasions he needed female company and when it suited him. He never invited Dalton to his Waterside apartment. He could never now return to his old haunt, the trading estate; he already had too many nightmares of that awful night. On the occasions he stayed with Dalton, she cooked his meal, gave him a glass or two of wine, some small talk and some satisfying sex. Roberson was usually up and away the following morning before she woke.

She would always make the meal and chat about work, staffing matters at first, but as the relationship grew and Dalton became more confident in his company she began confiding about operational matters. Roberson found this far more interesting, not least if there was any mention at all of a missing person or a hit-and-run accident enquiry.

A month ago, Roberson realised why he placed any value on his relationship with Sue Dalton. It came about on one of his few sleepovers. Sue had started up a conversation that she hoped would create some interest with her new lover.

'We've got a job and half developing, Pete,' said Sue. She placed the fresh salmon in the pan whilst turning down the heat.

Roberson ignored her; he usually did, then she would inevitably continue.

'We have reports on some abuse. It's basically drugs for sex and involves some high-profile people. Seems the bastards are picking on very vulnerable youngsters.' Dalton took a large swig of some high-quality Sauvignon Blanc.

Roberson had been checking emails on his phone but her

words caught his attention. He took a large gulp of gin and tonic; it allowed him to gather his thoughts and gave him some time to consider his next comments. His heart was beating fast beneath his waistcoat.

'Sounds interesting stuff. A bit tragic though,' he replied, hoping his words sounded suitably outraged yet expressed some concern for the victims.

'Well, if this develops it could end up on your desk, darling, certainly from a media perspective,' said Dalton.

'It would be a major coup for the force,' Roberson replied confidently. Then, after a pause, he added, 'Where are we with the operation?' It was an open question; he was not keen to raise any suspicion but he wanted Dalton to expand upon her knowledge.

'We have someone, a really vulnerable person, who is currently on our books as an informant. She's a juvenile who used to be a resident at Holston House but is now in foster care. A bit unreliable as an individual because she has a few convictions for theft, but she seems to be as reliable as an informant can be – always makes meetings, always on time, etc. Time to make the salads,' Dalton said matter-of-factly, moving onto a completely different topic as supper became more of a priority. 'Could you set the table, love, or should we have it on trays watching something on the box?'

'I'll set the table, Sue. More wine?' Roberson wanted the previous conversation to continue. He needed to push her ever so slowly, like a dedicated mother persuading her infant to attend nursery on their very first day. He wanted to encourage her to give more information freely. He couldn't afford to raise any suspicion and make his own vested interest apparent.

Roberson's skilled prompting, coupled with Dalton's increasing infatuation with him and a wish to have some meaningful dialogue and interaction, enabled him to find out everything he needed to know about this high-profile operation.

Following that brief conversation with Dalton, in a bid to appease Travis but more importantly to safeguard himself, Roberson passed on the limited information he had obtained. When he did so, he thought Travis's reaction was extremely strange – Travis seemed neither surprised nor particularly worried.

The major enquiry that was now underway had caused Roberson to reflect upon his previous conversations with Dalton and the information he had subsequently supplied to Travis. Just to be on the safe side, when Sue Dalton had recovered and was contactable, Roberson would make some very discreet enquiries. Belt and braces, he thought, just to ensure that the informant reporting that Dalton had alluded to regarding drugs for sex involving some important local people had no connection whatsoever with the double murders of Chilter and Wrightson.

9

Intelligence

Geoff Sutton was almost complete in his update for Ron Turner regarding the informant Billy Spitz. He had been using Sue Dalton's vacated office. The unit detectives were at a briefing at the force's Occupational Health Unit, providing counselling for the staff because they were the immediate work colleagues of Mike Chilter and Linda Wrightson.

Sutton was joined from time to time by Bill Singer who, in between working with Sutton, also had to ensure staff within the intelligence unit of the investigation were progressing the various actions churned out from the Incident Room.

As Sutton was completing his report on Billy Spitz, he again checked his phone, which he had previously placed on silent. Stew Grant had made further unanswered calls. It must be important, Sutton thought. Knowing Stew, he must have split a nail, he chuckled inwardly.

He pressed the relevant buttons and the phone rang through to his mate. 'Thanks, Geoff. About time.'

'Been a bit busy, Stew.'

'Bollocks, you have a new batch of drawing pins to distribute,' Stew said, laughing down the phone, which was the first time he had laughed all day. 'It's William. He's been away for three days. No sign, no contact at all. As ever, we are reluctant to call the police in these matters.'

Sutton interrupted his mate. 'Call them straight away.' Sutton knew his friend well and if Stew was calling him and having this sort of conversation then he knew there was a concern that needed action without delay.

'I'm involved in the cop murders so will be busy for a few days,' Sutton said, explaining why he hadn't replied earlier. 'But if you don't get the right response give me a bell. Speak soon.'

'Thanks, Geoff.' Stew, knowing his mate was busy, ended the call without delay or any further small talk. He had seen the press conference and knew full well from past experience that if Sutton was busy, he was up to his neck.

Stew rang the non-emergency number and then told Tina.

Sutton had been head down and very focused for the last two-and-a-half hours, scrutinising the information the force held about the informant known as Billy Spitz. For almost the first time in that period, he looked around Dalton's office. Nothing much to it, no pictures, no flowers or plants. Absolutely nothing that would give you an idea of what sort of person worked here. Usually you would pick up on photographs, flowers and items of interest that gave you an indication of the occupant's personality but in this case you would find nothing at all about the life and personality of Sue Dalton.

She must be someone else who has one of these syndromes, thought Sutton.

Bill Singer returned to the room. 'Ready, Geoff?' he asked, looking at Sutton.

'Just need a paper clip,' Sutton said as he shuffled his A4 notes.

Sutton looked at the main desk, which was locked with no small, plastic stationery container on the top surface. He checked to see if the desk had one of those flat, sliding drawers immediately below the desktop. Standing behind the desk, he located one on the right-hand side. Sliding it back towards him, Sutton found what he was looking for underneath what appeared to be a face-down photograph.

He turned over the photograph and saw a picture of Dalton, arm in arm with Police and Crime Commissioner Peter Roberson. The landscape background of the photograph, which Sutton didn't recognise, suggested a holiday or weekend vacation,.

'Bill,' he said, showing the photo to Singer.

'Bloody hell! Never knew that, never heard any rumours, nothing. Don't suppose it's a crime. No wonder she kept herself to herself.'

Sutton put the photo back from where it came and left the office with Singer, en route to Turner's office to give him the briefing he had requested. It would be interesting to see his reaction.

Ron Turner was still immaculately smart – no loosening of the tie, standards had to be maintained. He was just updating his Senior Investigating Officer policy book when Sutton and Singer knocked on the open door.

'Geoff, Bill, come in,' he said, offering them a glance before going back to his policy log, a pivotal document and a bible for any Senior Investigating Officer in recording his key decisions and strategy for the investigation. If there was a subsequent hindsight enquiry Turner would stand or fail by his policy book.

Sutton glanced around at Turner's office. It was such a change from Dalton's, full of his career landmarks, photos of CID courses and his many awards. The difference between Dalton's stark office and Turner's museum of self-adornment could not have been greater.

Turner rang through to the outer office. 'Can I have a coffee, please, milk and no sugar. Gents?' He looked up at Sutton and Singer who were now sitting in front of the desk.'

Singer took the initiative. 'Same for us both, please.' It had been a manic start to the day, as it always was in any major investigation, and all three needed some sustenance.

Sutton thought that this was probably the first time in nearly ten years of his association with, and reporting to, Turner that he had been offered anything, let alone a cup of coffee. He couldn't ever recall Turner buying him a drink at any of the many social functions that they had both attended. Turner's reluctance to buy a round was infamous.

'The informant Billy Spitz,' said Turner, looking directly at Sutton.

Sutton looked at his notes. He knew that Turner would only interrupt if he didn't understand any of the terminology or some other aspect of his report.

Sutton was about to begin his narrative when the coffee arrived, via a very quiet knock on the door delivered by Jerry Cowley, a young lad who recently became part of the secretariat at Parton Central CID. He looked rightly nervous at having to transport Turner's coffee.

Sutton started. 'Billy Spitz is a seventeen-year-old juvenile registered informant, who has been on our books and receiving payments for the past six months. The motive for the informant is purely financial. He has a background of theft and low-level drug abuse, Class C. Presumably one fed the other. He was turned into an informant when he was arrested for shoplifting in the city centre. While he was in custody, he had either the knowledge or wherewithal to ask to see a detective. He was subsequently handed onto the Confidential Unit, where Mike Chilter spoke to him, and had him registered with Mike as handler and Linda Wrightson as co-handler. She was introduced to him soon after Mike had established the rapport.'

Sutton took a sip of his coffee then continued. 'Billy became a reliable informant, albeit a great risk not only because he was a juvenile but also as he had convictions for dishonesty. He was always on time for meetings, always met contact deadlines and was paid accordingly. This is where it becomes interesting. Billy was reporting on abuse that was occurring amongst his peers. It seems youngsters of a similar age, both male and female, were being supplied with drugs in return for sex. It seems that Mike and Linda were in the process of providing excellent intelligence into extremely widespread, well-organised abuse of vulnerable youngsters.

'There were multiple abusers and Billy seemed to think that there could be some important local people involved. Billy Spitz was one of many people being exploited. As far as he was concerned, it seemed to be a well-run operation. The reporting suggested youngsters were asked to be in a location at a certain time and date. They were picked up in a van and transported to a safe house. Drugs were then supplied in return for sex. They were given a lift back and dropped off at a different location. Billy's information suggests that this had been developing over the last nine months or so.'

Turner interrupted. 'What is the provenance for all this? And what are his antecedents.' His tone was sceptical. 'I've been down this road many times before,' he sighed.

As Head of CID, Turner had almost daily intelligence briefings, many claiming this and that, but when simple and very basic enquiries took place the intelligence had been proved to be personal motivation on behalf of some untrustworthy criminal – usually either sheer greed or satisfying a grudge. Consequently Turner sought immediate reassurance that Billy Spitz was the genuine article. The fact that he was a juvenile and a proven thief immediately raised concerns.

Sutton continued. 'Billy Spitz was previously a resident at Holston House in Firston. For the past three months he has been fostered but, as yet, we do not have the details of his current address. It's not been recorded. The meeting on Saturday was authorised by Sue Dalton and ACC Bob Harries. The amount he was to be paid was £2000.'

Turner stood up from behind his desk, pushing his chair with the back of his legs as he did so. He placed the flat of his hands firmly on his imposing desk. 'Two thousand pounds for a juvenile informant? You're bloody joking! Was he reporting on Bin Laden? I don't believe it. Shit, two grand authorised to a juvenile! I wonder if Chilter and Wrightson still have the money with them.' He paused then asked, 'Geoff, am I right in saying that if a payment is to be made, it would need a senior officer to be present as a witness, particularly for such a large amount?'

'Correct,' said Sutton. 'According to the records, the matter of the payments being witnessed was authorised by Sue Dalton and endorsed by Assistant Chief Constable Bob Harries. On this last occasion, both of them authorised the payment without a senior officer being present. This is contrary to force policy,' Sutton added reluctantly.

'Is there any recorded reason as to why these officers made that decision?' Turner asked, returning to his seat.

'No recorded reason,' said Sutton, again reluctantly, knowing full well that the two officers mentioned were in deep shit. In Dalton's case, the depth was increasing by the minute. For somebody as high ranking as Harries, his successful, high-flying career would likely return to earth with a resounding thud.

'How much has Billy Spitz been paid since his registration?' Turner enquired.

'Five grand,' Sutton said quickly, already guessing what Turner's amazed reaction would be.

'Well, there must be some extremely vulnerable youngsters and some very important people involved,' said Turner, trying to justify his colleagues' work.

Sutton continued. 'As far as we know, Dalton and Harries are the only two people within the force who knew the real identity of Billy Spitz,'

'And his name?' demanded Turner with a hint of impatience.

'William Carr,' Sutton replied. 'But what is interesting is that I have referred to the informant as "he" throughout. William was originally a "she" but wanted to change sex. William was previously reporting as Julie Carr. The intelligence suggests that Julie had a troubled upbringing with some horrible abuse. He thought that by changing sex from female to male and becoming William, his problems with abuse would come to an end. Odd logic, as it appears his reporting included abuse of both males and females.'

'Poor kid,' said Singer, who had been listening intently to both Sutton and Turner.

'That may be, in some small way, a reason why the high amounts of money were authorised,' Turner said. 'We don't know where William lives? What else do we know about him? Phone number, any bank details, something we can trace?'

'We have a contact number but it was one of our own pay-as-you-go mobiles, given to him by Chilter and Wrightson in case of emergency.'

***

Had Dunc Travis been listening into this conversation, he would have been smiling. Unbeknown to anyone within Parton Constabulary, Dunc Travis had noted a distinct change in William's recent behaviour. William had become unreliable to contact, unreliable at turning in for work. He'd also started dressing down in a fashion that would not please the punters.

That began to cause Travis some concern. His experience was that when one of his 'employees' started acting in this way, they were either getting their drugs from somewhere else, working for someone else, or had some sexually transmitted disease. Travis tried again to think back to where he thought he had seen William's face somewhere before, but he couldn't place it.

He was sure that the kid was not an undercover cop; he was far too young. After William didn't turn up for work as he'd promised, it was time for action.

Travis took the decision to have William followed and

called Stan. The cops always thought they were good at surveillance and covert work but Stanislav Zenden was more than a match for William Carr and his police informant handlers. Stan's previous work in the Agencja Wywiadu, the Polish Intelligence Agency, came in very useful.

It only took two weeks but Dunc Travis's suspicions were confirmed. Stan covered three meetings between William and his police handlers. He covertly observed William from the street and watched him make a phone call. Then William moved to another location not covered by any CCTV cameras and, within a couple of minutes, a white Bedford van arrived. Stan was convinced, due to the thickness of the number plates, that they were false and glued on. William slid open the side door before climbing into the rear of the vehicle. Stan could just about make out a shadow of someone else already seated in the vehicle.

William Carr was a police informant. Travis was one step ahead; his motto was 'Never trust the untrustworthy'.

***

Turner took a deep breath after listening to Sutton's comprehensive briefing. He assumed control and began spitting out instructions. 'Contact Holston House. We still need to locate William Carr. The foster carers' current address would be a good start. I also need to know if there is anything at all from the crime scene, blood, fingerprints, etc, that connects William to the bodies of Chilter and Wrightson. We don't even know for sure if the authorised meeting actually took place. Finally, did Chilter and Wrightson still have the informant's money in their possession?'

Singer tasked Sutton with the Holston House enquiry whilst he made off towards the Incident Room to action the forensic requests of the crime scene.

Turner needed to update the Chief about the actions of Assistant Chief Constable Bob Harries. A grin appeared across his face; he knew full well that Temporary Chief Constable Conting had a difficult job on his hands with this particular matter.

Unfortunately for Sutton he knew that in these days of data protection, a phone call to Holston House in order to obtain foster parent details for William Carr was out of the question. However, as a matter of courtesy he rang ahead and informed the home he needed to speak with the head as a matter of urgency.

Donning his Barbour and sunglasses, he went back to the Insignia, listening to Steve Wright in the afternoon on Radio 2 as he made his way across town and out to Firston.

'Nutbush City Limits' was blasting away as Sutton turned left, passing the large entrance sign, with its large gold lettering on a blue background. On the sign were the words 'Holston really cares', followed by an Ofsted rating of good and the name of the head teacher, Simon Keys BA.

Sutton had never had the pleasure of attending this location before but 'institution' seemed the appropriate word as he made his way up the quarter of a mile driveway towards a Victorian building that looked something like a picture from an old horror movie. Immediately to the left of what he assumed was the main building was a two-storey flat-roofed structure. As he got closer to the buildings there was signage indicating the main Victorian building as the teaching and administration centre. The flat-roof structure was a residential block.

The gathering dusk added to the totally unwelcoming atmosphere. Despite the dusk, Sutton could make out a sports area consisting of a five-a-side concrete football pitch, which obviously doubled up for netball and basketball. A wooded area to the immediate right of the main building had rope swings and a tree house, presumably some sort of assault course.

Throw them out there to play. Hopefully the young buggers will get knackered and then they'll cause you less hassle, thought Sutton.

He rang the doorbell. An adolescent voice shouted 'Fuck off' from within.

The door was opened by a slim male in his forties wearing denim jeans, black Nike trainers and a black-and-white gingham checked shirt. A tell-tale striped lanyard with the obligatory picture identification card doubling as a pass key, hung around the neck of its owner. Simon Keys, Head of Holston House stood in front of Sutton.

'Mr Keys, I'm Geoff Sutton, Parton Constabulary. Pleased to meet you.' Sutton was greeted with a very limp handshake as he produced his own identity card. 'Is there somewhere we can talk?' he enquired.

Keys showed him towards his own office. Sutton noticed the huge wide staircase that spiralled upwards from the entrance hall. He ignored the swearing coming from a nearby classroom.

Sutton followed Keys into his spartan and extremely untidy office, littered with staff rotas, timetables and an old-fashioned computer perched on his desk. On the office walls there were many pictures of the school activities from various events that took place outside the school premises.

Not for the first time today, Sutton noticed the larger-than-life figure of Peter Roberson, who appeared on more than a few of Keys' photographs.

'How can I help, Mr Sutton?' asked Keys agreeably.

'I'm trying to find out who is currently fostering William Carr. You might have known him as Julie. He was fostered a couple of months ago, after being a resident here for a few years, I believe.'

Sutton had to endure a lecture from Keys on data protection, until he decided to interrupt. 'Look, Mr Keys, I need to stop you there. Above all, this is a matter of urgency and there is a duty of care. We need to trace William immediately. At this moment in time I am unable to disclose the nature of our enquiry, except that he is being dealt with as a missing person. Any delay in finding William could put him at substantial risk. I hope I am making myself clear.'

Without replying, Keys started searching his strewn desk and eventually located the access code for a metal cabinet that was located behind another pile of paperwork. Despite his obvious disorganisation, Sutton got the impression that Keys was a genuine, hardworking and caring individual, who was probably very dedicated in dealing with difficult youngsters. Sutton had actually taken an immediate liking to him. It must be one hell of a job keeping a lid on an establishment like this and caring for some of the most vulnerable kids in society.

After what seemed to take ages, Keys took out a file. He cursed about people not putting things back in alphabetical order.

A couple of minutes later Sutton was back in his car. He had left the headteacher's office at speed, running out of the building. He turned off the car radio. Unusually, he needed the silence.

He was stunned. Stew and Tina Grant were William Carr's foster parents. The records at Holston House still had William recorded as Julie.

Sutton took stock as he rigged up his hands-free phone. He updated Turner without delay and sought authority to speak to Stew Grant and visit his house. Sutton was, as ever, absolutely upfront with Turner, making him fully aware of his lifetime friendship with Stew Grant.

Turner was typically direct. He would only consider William as a missing person; there should be no mention whatsoever of him being an informant. He reminded Sutton that he would be sacked if any authorised disclosure was made. That last comment was quite ironic to Sutton; he was one the few people for whom a sacking wouldn't make a great deal difference other than denting his pride.

Sutton discussed with Turner the need for Scenes of Crime Officers attending with him to search William's bedroom but Turner decided against this approach for now. He wanted Sutton to gain as much background as possible about William's life and to keep the Grants updated. In addition, Sutton was to seize a couple of items that might assist in locating the boy, such as his phone or bank card.

Just before the phone call ended, Sutton posed the question, 'What about a toothbrush or comb for DNA?'

'Definitely, yes. Speak later.' Turner put the phone down.

For Sutton, this was a totally different scenario to delivering a death message to a total stranger. He was one of the few people who knew the complete dedication the Grants gave to those in their care. Delivering the death message would have been an easier alternative.

He decided not to ring Stew. The silence, without the car radio, allowed him to concentrate on the job in hand. Stew and Tina were expecting a local uniformed officer to attend, to investigate a report of a missing person. Instead they would be visited by their mate, Geoff Sutton, who Stew knew had been seconded to help with the cop murders. The Grants were no fools. Whilst Sutton could not tell one of his best mates a pack of lies, at the forefront of his mind was the need to glean as much information as he could about William and help to find him safe and well.

He knew the Grants would have similar thoughts.

It took a good forty-minute drive to make the journey back from Holston to the outskirts of Parton. It was yet another route where Sutton was dangerously on automatic pilot. He had four near misses, almost went through a red light, then had an argument with a pedestrian who quite rightly remonstrated with him as he ploughed over a crossing when she had right of way.

Finally, and miraculously, Sutton pulled up outside the palatial house that was the Grants' residence. He didn't even have time to ring the bell before the door opened and he was faced by Tina and Stew.

'What the hell are you doing here, Geoff?' The first

question always sets the tone of any ensuing conversation, Sutton thought to himself.

'Put the bloody kettle on, I'm dying for a cuppa,' instructed Sutton, taking a leaf out of Ron Turner's book.

Stew was straight in, before Sutton even had a chance to remove his Barbour. 'I thought you were up to your neck in the cop murders. That sounds bloody awful. Did you know them?'

'Yep, one of them used to work for me. It's all very, very sad,' Sutton said.

'We're just waiting for one of the lads to pop round to have a chat about William.' Stew went on. 'It's just a bit of a precaution – he's a bit of a handful at the best of times. Goes missing from time to time but even for him this is extended leave.'

'Kettle boiled?' enquired Sutton, looking to move on as Tina glided past into the kitchen.

The conversation halted as Tina made a cafetiere of coffee. There was a prolonged silence; it seemed like an age for Sutton before Tina poured the drinks. He then took control of the conversation.

'We are looking at all incidents reported over the last twenty-four to forty-eight hours that occurred close to the place where the police officers were found to rule out any possible connection between them and the murder enquiry. The missing-person report you made falls into that criteria. I knew you were making the report and I also know you two, so it made sense to kill two birds with one stone and cadge a lovely cup of the best coffee around. That's why I am here.'

He wanted to lighten the mood and also give an explanation that might, or might not, put Stew and Tina's minds at rest.

As he sipped his coffee, he glanced at the expressions on his friends' faces. He knew them well enough to tell that, whilst they were not fully convinced, there was a certain logic to his explanation. For his part, he had not lied; in any major enquiry, personnel would scan local incidents that might have a connection to the murders.

Sutton relaxed to an extent and continued. 'William Carr, is that his correct name?'

'Yes. He was previously known as Julie Carr. He came to us about three months ago from Holston House. We were not made fully aware of the background to the change of name, other than his wish to change sex. I knew that much. He asked us to call him William and, by doing so, we think we offered him both support and help. We also took advice from William's social worker.'

Tina's eyes were trained on her husband.

'William wasn't easy, Geoff,' Stew went on. 'A bit of a nightmare, to be honest, and my personal view would be that he would be our last foster kid.' He looked across at Tina before putting his head in his hands.

Tina nodded. 'I hate to admit it but Stew is right,' she said reluctantly. 'I would never tell this to anyone, particularly social services, but I've been in denial. I don't mind telling you, Geoff, but William was one too many for us in terms of fostering.'

Stew looked up, genuinely surprised at his wife's comments. He immediately walked around and gave her a long hug. They were not a couple known for their open affection, yet Stew's action demonstrated their devotion for each other.

This one action brought home to Sutton the weight of emotion that they must have endured over the years in their combined efforts to provide youngsters with a new environment that was, in all probability, totally foreign to their previously troubled pasts.

'Do you know any background to William? Parents, relatives, etc?' Sutton asked, moving on.

'Nothing. We don't want to, never have done, even after some twenty years fostering. Nearly all our foster children came from Holston House.'

'So you don't know where William hung out? Any friends, acquaintances?' enquired Sutton.

'Afraid not, Geoff. William came back for meals occasionally. We could never pin him down to any structure whatsoever. To be honest, there have been a few times recently, which seemed to be getting more and more frequent, when he was coming home obviously high on this or that. Maybe we should have called the police, but I never thought it was anything other than some soft drugs. Believe it or not, if I'd called you every time one of the kids came home under the influence of drugs over the past years, the police would never have been away from the door.'

'Do you have a contact number for William?' asked Sutton.

'Yep,' said Tina, scrolling through the contacts on her phone. '07881289153. We have tried it repeatedly but got no answer.'

Sutton took another gulp of coffee and looked around the kitchen. The room was adorned, as with the all the other rooms in the house, with pictures of their 'successes', which made their failure with William even more obvious.

As a couple, they were experienced in the frustrations and let-downs that fostering could bring yet they had kept going, buoyed by any positive achievement that they rightly craved and thoroughly deserved. Any success, however minor, was an excuse for celebration.

On more than one occasion Stew, usually pissed, had bought a round of drinks to toast Jimmy, Jane or whoever, as they had moved out and moved on with their lives.

Sutton wrote down the number supplied by Tina. 'Could I have a quick look at William's room?' he asked.

'Crack on, Geoff. God knows what you might find in there. We never go in without William's permission – and then it's usually the cleaner who is brave enough to venture through the door. She hasn't been allowed in by William for a couple of weeks.'

'Thanks, Stew.' Sutton returned briefly to his car, where he located some disposable gloves, evidence bags and a notepad. He knew that Ron Turner would no doubt authorise a small forensic team to search in due course; his brief was action to find anything that might locate William.

Stew and Sutton made their way up the stairs. William's room was the first room that faced them at the top of the landing. The remaining bedrooms and main bathroom were all located on the same floor.

Stew pushed open the door. There was nothing to identify this room as William's from any other on the landing. 'I'll leave you to it,' he said, almost thankfully, turning on his heel and making his way back down the stairs.

Sutton looked around. There was still just enough setting sun beaming through the large window to enable him to complete his task without the need for artificial light but nevertheless he switched on the main bedroom light to provide further assistance.

The room surprised him. It was very tidy and seemed quite organised. He'd expected chaos. There were gleaming, white, fitted wardrobes on the wall to the right of the door, facing a double bed which was neatly made up. Either side of the bed was a matching set of white bedside drawers. Each nest of drawers had a black bedside lamp resting neatly on top.

There were no posters of pop or rock idols adorning the walls. The room was completely bare and, as far as Sutton was concerned, unwelcoming. William had been missing for a few days but the bedroom gave the impression that he hadn't been there for a long time.

Sutton placed the evidence bags and notepad on the bed and donned his disposable gloves. He completed the basic checks, looking under the bed and inside the fitted wardrobes. There had been many a person reported missing when they were actually hiding somewhere in the property.

He rolled back the duvet and checked under both sets

of pillows. He found a phone, placed it in an evidence bag and sealed it, noting exactly where it was found as well as the time and date. He checked each set of drawers, located a bank card and followed the same procedure of bagging and tagging the evidence.

Sutton noticed some NHS correspondence, which he quickly looked over. It confirmed that William had a hospital psychiatric appointment due in the middle of next month. He presumed this was one of the many stages that the boy would have to undertake to undergo a gender reassignment. Sutton took the decision not to seize these documents, although he made a note of the appointment time and date together with the name of the psychiatrist.

Despite the fact that William wished to change sex, there was no doubt the bedroom and furniture had a distinctly feminine feel, remnants of the sad life he wished to leave behind.

Sutton finished checking the drawers on either side of the bed and moved on to the small pink dressing table below the large window. The colour was unusual in that the Grants were so meticulous about furniture – he would have expected the dressing table to be white. Maybe this was an item that William had brought with him.

On the dressing table, Sutton's attention was immediately drawn to a small photograph housed in a silver frame. Whilst he knew William was seventeen years of age, before now he had not seen a photograph of him. There were three people pictured at what looked like a wedding. Sutton estimated that the not-so-blushing bride was well into her forties, with the eldest girl being late twenties. Sutton presumed that the other person in the picture was William, albeit at the time the photograph was taken he was Julie. There was definitely a family likeness between all three females. He seized the photograph. He would ask the Grants on his way out if they recognised the two women with William.

He began to search the dressing-table drawers. There

were three on each side, with a space in the middle to allow for a small stool, which faced a large mirror. The last drawer he searched was the bottom right-hand one. Sutton pulled it open and rummaged through some socks until he discovered a large, white, unsealed A4 envelope. The envelope bore the name and address: *Mr. P Roberson, C/o Holston House, Firston.*

Sutton looked inside and stopped in his tracks when he saw the large bundle of bank notes. He came to an instant decision not to count the notes or proceed any further for risk of compromising any DNA or fingerprint evidence.

The bundle of notes was not a major surprise, given that Sutton knew the large amounts of cash the informant had been paid over the last few months. However, it was the second time today that PCC Peter Roberson had appeared in the course of the investigation. The easy explanation was that the envelope was merely a discarded item, used as a container for the money.

Sutton was concerned that he had seized a large amount of cash without any witnesses present, but leaving it in situ could be risky. However it was more than likely the money would match the informant payments, so he decided to take the money and inform the Grants before he left the house. He would also update Ron Turner without delay on what he'd found.

He again went through the process of bagging and tagging the evidence. In addition he bagged and tagged a hairbrush, as well as an abandoned toothbrush. They could supply DNA. That would do for now. No doubt Turner would proceed with a full forensic search in due course.

Sutton made his way downstairs and walked back into the kitchen. He wasn't surprised that Stew and Tina had no useful information about William's habits or associates. He checked the phone with Tina; it appeared to be one of William's old phones and would probably not show up anything useful.

'This photograph – can you identify the people?' Sutton

asked, showing the picture he had taken from the dressing table.

'The photograph is from William's mother's wedding. I think it was her third! It took place when William was still called Julie. Apparently he was really surprised to be invited. The bride is his mother and we think that the other girl in the picture is his sister. But that's only what William told us and he can be somewhat unreliable,' said Tina.

'Do you know their names?' Sutton asked.

'Sorry, no – but the girl looks very like William,' said Stew.

'She does. Can you confirm it was his sister?' Sutton enquired.

'We can't, I'm afraid. He never really mentioned much at all about his past, although I got the impression – and its only an impression – that he really cared for his sister'

'Just one other thing I need to mention,' Sutton said. 'I found this envelope in the dressing-table drawer. It contains a significant amount of money. Any ideas?'

'I really haven't a clue as to how he would make that sort of money,' Stew said, shocked. 'Possibly drugs. I could think of one or two illegal activities that he could have been involved with. Whose the name is on the envelope?'

'It's Peter Roberson.'

'William must have picked up an envelope from the care home at Holston. Roberson is on the Board there, in fact he's on the Board of a few places. He's your new Police and Crime Commissioner, isn't he?' said Stew.

'Yep, he certainly is,' replied Sutton.

Sutton showed the Grants what he had seized from William's bedroom and told them he would keep them updated with the enquiry. He picked up his green Barbour and went towards the front door. Tina and Stew walked with him as he carried his exhibits out to the car.

Settled in the driver's seat, Sutton turned on the radio. Before he pulled away, he looked back at the doorway to the Grants' house just as Tina's legs buckled. Stew caught her and engulfed her with a massive comforting hug.

10

Dunc Travis

Dunc Travis resided in a small, ordinary-looking town house. It contained some extremely impressive furniture, which reflected his increasingly expensive and modern tastes. He had purchased the property two years previously without a mortgage.

The house was located on the outskirts of the city, about three miles from where he really wanted to be in an East Parton Marina apartment. Travis was a nineties' child and still single – not that the twenty-five year old was short of offers. He just didn't want anyone to divert his attention from his ever-increasing business empire. He drove a very ordinary Black Nissan Juke so as not to attract attention from the police, or anyone else for that matter. That was his way of operating.

Dunc had been brought up by his single mother on the infamous North Leas council estate on the north side of the city, where youngsters roamed the streets from an early age. There were three tower blocks, known locally as The Pines. They were called Sycamore, Chestnut, and Ash. Dunc lived on the fifth floor of Ash. There were another twenty-five floors above their two-bedroomed flat.

His mother, Liz, still lived in the block but had now moved to the ground floor, where the access was a great deal easier. Her arthritis was making her increasingly immobile.

Dunc doted on his mother and visited her on a daily basis. His love for her was undoubtedly due to the sacrifices she had made for him to ensure that he got the very best of what she could give. Her love for 'our Dunc', her only child, was unconditional. He was also lucky that Liz's twin brother Joe, a confirmed bachelor, had played an active role in his upbringing both when he was a child and also as he grew up. Dunc wasn't interested in finding out who his real father was; Uncle Joe was the father he had never had.

When Dunc left the house to go to school in the morning, Shania Twain's 'Feel Like a Woman' would be ringing in his ears, accompanied by his mother's flat singing voice belting out the tune. Sadly for Dunc, that tune was with him for the rest of the day; what made it worse was that when he walked back through the door at home time, his mother was still shouting out her flat chords.

From an early age Dunc knew exactly what he wanted. Unlike many of his peers, he worked hard at school; also unlike many of his peers, he kept out of trouble, was always polite to teachers but was never ingratiating enough to be called a swot.

There was an important incident when he was thirteen years old, in his first term at North Parton High School. A group from the nearby Sycamore block cornered him on his way home from school. He was a target for their cowardly bullying – but they never tried it again. Dunc decked the first one and ran towards the second assailant armed with his Swiss Army knife, a Christmas present from Uncle Joe. The attacker took one look at Dunc and his unfolded weapon and backed off. The other three also turned and ran away. Total cowards, Dunc thought.

He had very few close friends and mainly kept himself to himself. Dunc Travis had to know you very well to allow you to enter into his confidence. That was the way he worked; he never trusted anyone.

He was an academic success and gained eight good GCSEs followed two years later with three A levels, in Spanish, French and Economics. Despite his mother's wishes, Dunc was never going to university; the subjects he had chosen were studied purely because he thought they would be useful in later life.

He was also a talented sportsman, but football and cricket practice at the end of the school day, followed by matches on a Saturday morning, weren't part of his agenda. He spent his spare time down at Uncle Joe's small car-repair business. Uncle Joe was a grafter but had little idea about business. Dunc's duties, for which he was well paid, were to clean the customers' cars after their service or MOT.

It didn't take long for Dunc to invest his money – with additional benefits.

All around The Pines there was constant, low-level drug dealing. Travis was an observer never a participant. Many of the addicts were his own peers, happy to exist from hit to hit with nothing to show for their downtrodden existence. It didn't take long for Dunc to find out who the dealers were. Then he had the foresight to purchase a quantity of drugs himself.

At the beginning, he didn't mind paying over the odds for the product. He could afford it. Once he had sufficient supplies, he started his own organisation of distribution. A couple of school discos, the sixth-form prom, and he was off and running.

The word soon got around.

When he was seventeen years old, he met Stanislav Zenden. Stan had been taken on as a mechanic by Uncle Joe. He had arrived from Poland with his young family. How they got to Parton no one knew but Parton City Council, in their wisdom, placed Stan and his family in The Pines.

Joe had seen Stanislav working on a small old Skoda car and struck up a conversation. Although not particularly business minded, Uncle Joe knew a good mechanic when he saw one. He also recognised something he liked in Stan and wanted to give him an opportunity. It was yet another example of Uncle Joe's generosity; his personality was very similar to his sister Liz's.

Their short conversation gave Stan the opportunity to work two days a week during a sort of probationary period. Then, due to both his work ethic and reliability, and the fact that Joe himself was starting to suffer from the family arthritis, Stan started working full time. Dunc and him connected straight away. He was the first person, apart from Mam and Uncle Joe, that Dunc trusted completely even though Stan was some ten years older. If Uncle Joe was the father Dunc never had then equally Stan was the elder brother he also never had.

When Uncle Joe died suddenly from a heart attack at the garage, it was Stan who attempted to revive him with CPR. Dunc, who was in the sixth form at the time completing his last exam, never went back to school. He took on the garage business immediately, appointing Stan as head mechanic, and opened the hand car wash, making full use of what land was available. Dunc appointed Seb, Stan's brother, as head of his car-wash enterprise. Seb had followed his brother from Poland and arrived at The Pines some two months earlier with his own young family.

The car wash proved an immediate success. Seb recruited keen, hardworking and loyal immigrant staff, willing to be employed on minimum, cash-in-hand wages. Most of his staff were from the Polish community.

The car wash also allowed Dunc's drug-supplying business to prosper. His staff, thanks particularly to Seb, were also able to dig out potentials. Some were sex workers who, when they knew there was a ready and reasonably cheap supply of drugs available, were willing to perform their role and repay their supplier.

Dunc Travis was a real Mr Fix-it, the supplier who always stayed in the background, never at the forefront.

In a short period of time Travis extended the business further, cleverly using the available space to create a small showroom together with a forecourt for second-hand car sales. He called the business Joe's Autos, both in memory of his greatly respected uncle but also because the name would not bring any unwanted attention his way. He tasked some of his girls with a mail drop and employed one of them, who had a degree in IT, on a permanent basis to look after both the website and social media as well as perform the role of office manager.

His prosperous business had taken yet another positive turn when he got Pete Roberson in his back pocket. He had always hoped he might find a celebrity hunting for women on his trading estate but this was even better.

Thanks to Roberson, Travis had made a substantial amount of easy money. His connections had brought new, more vulnerable girls onto his books. It could only continue to grow.

It was so good that he had recently started looking for a new boat, one that would have to be berthed on the sought-after East Parton Marina. His small fishing vessel on the West Marina would go. It was Dunc's ambition to have a boat and one of the much sought-after residential apartments on the Waterside development.

In many ways Travis wanted all the things that Pete Roberson currently possessed. The difference between them was that Dunc had worked bloody hard for his success, rather than being born with a Roberson silver-plated spoon in his mouth.

11

Billy Spitz

It was another bitterly cold February winter night, with yet another severe frost beginning to extend its tentacles. The temperature felt even lower due to one of those County Parton northerly winds that bit into the body like a continual stitch. Sutton didn't know if it was the weather, or due to the day's activities but he felt tired, both physically and emotionally.

He asked himself, not for the first time that day, why on earth he had got himself involved.

It was a thirty-minute drive back to Parton City Centre Police Station from the Grant's residence where he had to deposit his exhibits then attend the evening briefing before finishing work. During the journey, he mused over his knowledge of the investigation to date. He was increasingly concerned about the safety of William Carr. If he wasn't responsible for the murders of Chilter and Wrightson, where on earth could he be? Sutton's past experience suggested that youngsters rarely go too far away. They know their own patch, even though they might go AWOL for a couple of days.

More importantly, as far as Sutton was concerned, at some point his friend Granty and his wife, Tina, were going to know that he hadn't been totally up front with them when he came to their house. He'd only told them part of the story. It was this issue that troubled Sutton most. Stew was a lifelong friend and you did not shit in your own nest. It was an expression that came to mind and had always been sound advice.

Sutton had always kept his work and play completely separate. Not for him the regular socials that ensure police officers become totally inbred and consumed by the organisation. It had even taken some persuading to get him to join the union, the Police Federation.

Sutton much preferred his own friendships as a way of releasing stress and bringing him back down to earth. 'How's the investigation into theft of paper clips?' He chuckled to himself.

It was another journey of near misses for Sutton's Insignia as his mind drifted. He cut someone up at a roundabout, swopping a couple of gestures as a result. It was around 6pm when he parked up and got out of the car. Armed with his exhibits, Sutton went into the station and took the stairway to the basement. It was nearly always the case that the exhibit store was situated deep in the bowels of a police building and Parton City Centre was no exception.

The exhibits officer for this enquiry was Tom Heath, someone Sutton knew well. Vastly experienced in this nightmare role, he had his own office – without any natural light.

Tom Heath looked as though he lived in an underground office and had never ventured outside. The fact he was a keen cyclist amazed Sutton and everyone else who knew Heath. Over the last few years, he had started to look even worse, if that was possible. Being placed in this dungeon of an office did his complexion no favours whatsoever.

Surprisingly given his attachment to two wheels, Heath was an habitual lift user when he needed to update Ron Turner or attend briefings. It was his direct route to the third floor where the station canteen was housed. Despite the austerity measures, the canteen was just about functioning, albeit with reduced opening hours and fewer staff. Much to Tom's frustration, being a confirmed bachelor who hated cooking, it now had a reduced menu. Sadly the writing was on the wall for the canteen and its dedicated staff. Sutton thought that if they ever got rid of the facility it would signal the end of Tom Heath's police career.

Tom's office was littered with items that he was currently booking in through the system. On the table was his exhibits book, his bible that tracked each item and noted whether it could be stored or signed out for potential interviews or forensic examination. His role was pivotal in any major enquiry; if he got it wrong, it would leave the prosecution in chaos when a case came to trial.

Tom excelled as Exhibits Officer, ruthless to the point of being obstructive. Only one person at a time was allowed into his office and they never left his room until each item they had recovered was checked, ensuring the exhibit was correctly labelled and then taken to the property store. Tom then entered the exhibit in his book: time, date and location. Any movement of an item was checked in and out, recorded both in his exhibit book and also on the item's uniquely numbered exhibit label.

It was a rigorous and laborious process that suited Heath down to the ground. He was outwardly miserable but in charge of his own empire. His experiences at Crown Court, the ultimate test, had repeatedly stood the test of time.

Fortunately, there was no queue when Sutton arrived at Tom's office.

'Geoff,' Heath said. 'I saw you this morning at the briefing. Hell, we must be scraping the barrel,' he said, grinning through his full beard which only made him look more unhealthy.

Sutton refused to get involved in this banter; he just wanted to offload his exhibits. He knew for a fact that Heath's try at comedy would more than likely change as quickly as the weather. He would return to his normal miserable self very quickly.

Everything was quickly logged in, apart from the money, which Sutton accepted would need to be counted out in front of Heath and then placed separately in the station safe. It came as no surprise to Sutton that the amount counted represented all the money given out as informant payments, apart from the £2000 authorised for the meeting the previous Saturday. This money was still outstanding, as far as Sutton was aware.

After locking Heath's very own prison cell, namely his office, the two men walked around the corner to the exhibits store, where they placed the items in the cavernous, hangar-like room in an area specially allocated to Operation Trust.

'Going up to the briefing?' Sutton asked Heath.

'Yep, see you up there,' Heath replied, thinking about the lift as he knew Sutton would be doing the stairs.

Sutton left Heath as he reset the alarm of the exhibits store and made his way up the stairs to the briefing.

Ron Turner was shuffling some papers, making final preparations for his audience, similar to a politician taking the stand at a party conference, thought Sutton, as he caught up with Bill Singer. The two exchanged a knowing nod as they knew Turner was about to speak.

Still as smart as a carrot, suited and booted with accompanying waistcoat, Turner meant business.

'Right, today's priority was to trace and eliminate someone we know as Billy Spitz. We have made some progress in that we now know his identity. This is for the room only. Billy Spitz was the pseudonym for the registered police informant initially known and registered as Julie Carr. More recently, Julie was re-registered as William as he is looking to change sex. The main motivation for him becoming a police informant was financial – he wanted to raise enough money to allow this sex change to happen. It would appear that William thought that by changing sex he would put his years of abuse as a girl behind him. Everyone should know and respect that William is an incredibly vulnerable young person.

'He is currently in foster care. Coincidentally, during the course of today, his carers reported him as a missing person. Prior to being in foster care, he was a resident at Holston House. William is a seventeen-year-old juvenile, apparently reporting on the abuse of similarly aged vulnerable people. It is thought that the operation may involve some important local people.'

Turner paused and looked at the assembled officers. 'The important link is that William's handlers were our murdered colleagues, Mike Chilter and Linda Wrightson. We currently have no idea whatsoever of his location. I am right in saying there has been no change, Geoff?'

'That's correct, sir.' Sutton didn't need to call Turner 'sir' but it seemed right and proper, particularly considering there was a large contingent of young and impressionable officers present.

Sutton continued. 'As discussed, I seized some items as a matter of urgency. These included exhibits for potential DNA, a substantial amount of cash, which we have reconciled against the informant payments, together with a photograph of William with what could be his mother and another currently unidentified individual who bears a strong family likeness, very possibly his sister but this is unconfirmed. Not surprisingly, given his lifestyle, the foster parents don't know a lot about either William's associates or habits.'

'What is his lifestyle?' Turner butted in.

'There is little doubt that he is a drug user who has spent most of his life in care. He has a history of dishonesty and has convictions for theft. It was while he was in custody that he turned informant.'

'So why do we trust him?' Turner asked, before anyone else asked the obvious question. 'Believe you me, he was being well paid by the police. He was also being looked after by two of our most experienced and highly trained handlers.

Additionally, his motivation appears absolutely genuine. The fact we have recovered all his payment money bears that out. I repeat what I said this morning, that if he wasn't responsible for the murder of our colleagues then he could well be in significant danger. As an organisation, we have a duty of care. Locating him is still our number one priority. Now, forensics please.' Turner handed over to Detective Sergeant Janice Coombes.

'Thanks, boss. I can confirm that Mike and Linda each had £1000 still in their possession, which would tend to rule out robbery as a motive. From what we have heard now, all the money paid out to the informant we know as Billy Spitz is accounted for. We have rushed through the samples and fingerprints obtained from the van.'

Coombes continued. 'The most important information is that there is nothing forensically in the Bedford van. There's no DNA, fingerprints, etc, that connects Billy Spitz to the crime scene. He was not in that vehicle over the weekend in question or on any other occasion. His previous meetings with his handlers must have been in another vehicle, or by some other means.'

The room was deathly quiet. Sutton looked at Turner. Turner's expression did not change but Sutton knew that his stomach would be churning like a washing machine in full cycle.

Instead of all lines of enquiry pointing directly at Billy Spitz, Turner was now faced with the grave possibility that a vulnerable missing-person enquiry could have a direct involvement in the murder of two constables. What made it worse was that the missing person was a fully-registered juvenile police informant being financed by the Parton Constabulary. It couldn't get much worse from a Senior Investigating Officer's point of view, thought Sutton.

In an ideal world Turner would have traced and located the informant, and forensic examination would have placed him in the back of the van. The icing on the cake would have been blood on William's clothing, a weapon recovered and a full confession. That would have been the ideal scenario: crime solved and job done.

But this was undoubtedly Turner's worst nightmare.

The atmosphere in the room reflected the news. There was total silence, with no one seeking eye contact with anyone else; almost everyone was looking downwards, staring at the floor or their shoes. Sutton bucked the trend and looked around, taking in the bowed heads around the room similar to some religious prayer meeting. After scanning the room he looked forward, only to see the unblinking eyes of Ron Turner returning his gaze.

Turner spoke again. 'Heads up. We have a job to do and it's just become a little more difficult. You are on an enquiry that will be talked about for years. We will be remembered as the people who cracked this case – but the pressure will only increase without arrests and locating the whereabouts of our young informant. Now, let's get going. Jan, the forensics. Please continue.'

It was the closest you would ever get to a motivational speech from Turner. That just wasn't his style.

Janice Coombes spoke. 'We are currently fast-tracking all the other samples, which we will run through for any known matches. No weapon recovered so far from the scene, which is still being searched. We estimate that will continue throughout tomorrow before being complete. Both post-mortems have taken place. Cause of death is multiple stab wounds from sharp instruments. I say sharp instruments because, whilst the pathologist was relatively non-committal, the two murders were slightly different in that two different knives were used. The one that killed Mike Chilter was longer than the one used to attack Linda Wrightson. It is therefore highly likely that there were at least two or more persons involved in the murder of our colleagues.'

Sutton looked around again. It was clear that this detail was proving a step too far for some officers in the room and

DS Jan Coombes was obviously aware that a detailed PM report was not appropriate.

She looked directly at Turner. 'Should you want anything further, sir, I will brief you in private.'

'Thanks, Jan,' said Turner, grateful that she had finished her briefing there and then. 'Right, we finish there. I have a few things to consider overnight, The search and forensic recovery are still ongoing, with a comprehensive trawl of CCTV searching for where our van may have travelled before ending up at the rugby club. Go home, try and sleep and be back here for a 9am briefing. No mention outside of this room of any police informant involvement.'

Again, Turner looked around and searched for eye contact, daring anyone to disobey him. 'The missing person enquiry is now part of our murder investigation and we need to consider our media strategy carefully. Thanks.'

Turner finished, turned and walked from the briefing room, back to the sanctuary of his own office.

Sutton chased after him, seeking a very short conversation. 'Boss, sorry can I have just one quick word?'

Looking back, Turner snapped, 'I've got a bit on, Geoff.' He sighed, stating the bleeding obvious. 'OK, very quickly, then,' he said, as if Sutton's interruption was an annoyance.

Turner sat down and rang though for a coffee without offering Sutton anything. His desk was still incredibly tidy, with only his policy book giving any indication he was in charge of such a major investigation.

Sutton started without being asked. 'This might be absolutely nothing.'

Turner immediately interrupted, 'Then why are we having this discussion? We are having it because it won't be nothing. Something's up. Let me have it.'

'During the course of today's enquiries, I came across the name of the same person on two completely separate occasions. I was in Sue Dalton's office, in which there is absolutely none of this,' Sutton nodded towards the pictures and awards. 'To say it's stark is a complete understatement. But I found a photograph in the slide drawer of her desk where she keeps some stationery. It's of her and Pete Roberson, the Police and Crime Commissioner. The background looks like the Lake District. They were embracing. It certainly looks like they were, and may well still be, in some sort of relationship.'

'Not a crime,' came Turner's predictable reply.

Sutton went on. 'Then, when I searched William's bedroom at the foster parents' address, the informant's money was concealed in an A4 envelope which had Pete Roberson's name and his address, given as Holston House where he is on the management board. There may not be any link, but it is very strange that his name has appeared twice. Could he be in some way connected to the enquiry? It may easily be explained in that William Carr was a previous resident at Holston and Roberson is an associate of the school. William could quite easily have picked up an old envelope. The fact he was involved with Sue Dalton may also be totally incidental.'

'Shit, this is unbelievable. Not only do we have two murdered officers, a missing juvenile police informant, but the only lead appears to be our local PCC. You could write a book on that. Any views yourself, Geoff?'

There were only a handful of instances in the twenty years or so that they had known each other that Ron Turner had called Sutton 'Geoff'. He obviously wanted and needed some reassurance.

'To be honest, boss, I have thought about it constantly since I saw his name on the envelope. I need a little more time to consider my thoughts about Pete Roberson. From what I know about him, he's involved himself in just about every community project going. He is the original Mr Parton.'

'Geoff, let's sleep on this. Investigation of a PCC quite obviously needs the most careful consideration. Get the envelope sent away for DNA comparison. I need to look at the media strategy before going home.'

Sutton picked up his jacket and left Turner to his recently arrived coffee and policy book entries, whilst he made his way out of the office. He felt sure that there would be no formal entry about Pete Roberson at this moment in time although, knowing Turner, he probably would have made some record of their discussion despite the sensitivities. He knew that this aspect of the case would ensure there would be little or no sleep for Turner tonight.

Sutton walked down the stairs back to the basement where he knew that Tom Heath would still be imprisoned. 'Tom, the envelope with the money. Ron Turner has asked it be sent for DNA comparison.'

'Thanks, Geoff. I'll put that down as number 10,003 on my list of things to do tomorrow,' Heath replied sarcastically.

Sutton went out to the car park. His way was illuminated by the starry, cold and clear February sky. He was well and truly knackered and it was all of his own making. He didn't have to be involved in this enquiry. He had made this decision, him alone, so put and shut up. There was no backing out now.

After de-icing the windscreen, Sutton slumped into the driver's seat and put the heater on full blast. Jamie Cullen was playing another folky number on his Radio 2 slot. Let's get home, Sutton thought. Another glass of an Australian number might help me sleep. Or so he hoped.

Fifteen minutes later Sutton pulled up on his driveway. Within a short period of time, he was flicking through the sports channels. Monday night football was showing a live Merseyside derby. He thought he would watch the game till half time then grab another glass of wine to go with his signature dish of scrambled eggs, topped with strips of cheddar cheese and an equally unhealthy splattering of ketchup. He relaxed for the first time in ages, totally oblivious that the enquiry was to take yet another sinister twist for Sutton, Turner and the investigation team.

Drip, drip, drip. Steady dripping. Not raining just bloody cold. William Carr lay bound and cramped in his own attic prison. He must be due some food; he was starving, cold and feeling totally abandoned.

Unable to relieve himself in a toilet, his pants were now soaked in urine, only adding to the cold and discomfort he was experiencing. It was a living nightmare.

He heard the tell-tale noise of the ladders being released to give access to his captors. Thank God, he thought. Some food.

This time he thought he could hear another set of footsteps coming up the steps. Maybe they were sending a bigger meal or some additional clothing. He heard the attic door being slid back. On this occasion it seemed to take more time, probably because there were more people coming in.

Just take this fucking hood off, you bastards, he thought. His breathing quickened against the material of his cloth hood, sucking inwards and then blowing outwards. He could feel his heart pounding against his chest, at first keeping rhythm with his breathing and then overtaking it with a roar that filled his ears, blocking out all other sounds around him.

It seemed like ages before what he believed were three people came towards him. He waited for the glorious moment when his hood would be removed. Stale damp air washing across his face was an absolute pleasure in his present circumstances. But this time the hood was not removed and there was no food.

Somebody unfastened William's urine-soaked jeans. 'Dirty bastard,' he heard one of them say.

It was the first time William had heard a voice that he immediately recognised. It was Dunc Travis. How could he forget Dunc's voice? There was no need for clown masks.

William's stomach churned and his shivering became more intense. Although he'd made more than a few enemies in his short life, he thought that Travis was more than likely behind his kidnapping. The very sound of that voice caused him to convulse and vomit through his small gag and cloth hood, almost choking himself.

Once his trousers had been removed, his body shook not just with the cold but with sheer fright at what could follow. Not still more abuse, he thought.

Instead of producing food from a small Tupperware container, Travis carefully removed a large syringe filled with a lethal concoction of high-purity class A drugs. Travis considered the use of such an expensive resource well worth the money.

Without a word being spoken, Stan took hold of William's legs whilst his brother Seb grabbed William's shoulders. They lay him flat on his back. Stan placed his knee across William's shoulders and pulled William's head to one side, giving Travis easy access to his target.

Travis held the syringe like a javelin thrower and rammed it into William's neck, aiming directly for the carotid artery. His thumb began to push the plunger firmly, down, down, to release the contents of the lethal injection. Travis left the syringe embedded in William's neck, almost like a badge of honour.

William tried to cry out. His hands clenched tightly within the restricted bindings and his toes curled downwards as he went into shock. Crying uncontrollably, his body convulsed again and again. He started choking on his own vomit as the deadly concoction kicked into his already vulnerable system.

Travis, Stan and Seb watched as the life leaked out of William. His death was fully warranted as far as Travis was concerned; nobody worked for him that he couldn't trust.

As for William, an adolescent who'd really had no chance in life, he had been murdered in a manner of horrendous cruelty that reflected his sad, abused life.

Travis, Seb and Stan watched with increasing impatience as the final vestige of life left William's body. They showed no emotion. It was a job done. Shortly afterwards, they removed the body from the attic.

The remote safe house, recently purchased and in a poor state of repair, had been carefully chosen by Dunc; it was one of a couple of properties he had acquired as the money rolled in. It enabled him to offer subsidised accommodation to some of his working girls in return for their efforts.

That was Travis, always one step ahead.

In the pitch-black darkness, they placed William's body in the back of the white van that had been reversed into the driveway. On this occasion, three men made their way out to the Parton West Marina where a few small fishing boats were housed. It was deserted on these long, dark winter nights. With the package on board his small fishing vessel, Travis and his men made their way slowly and surely to the appointed burial ground.

Dunc had made up his mind some time ago about William. There was only one possible outcome once he realised the lad was a police informant.

The opportunity had come the previous Saturday. Dunc had organised Stan, Seb and a couple of other tried-and-tested car washers. The idea was to carry out surveillance on William, but this time Dunc had a crew with him. Should the opportunity present itself, they would kidnap the boy. They were equipped to do so. The opportunity did arrive at another remote location in keeping with informant meetings. As they lifted William, their timings were slightly out. The Confidential Unit van with the two detectives arrived at the scene just at the moment Dunc's team, all in disguises, were grappling with William.

Chilter and Wrightson acted as they had been trained; it was the very reason they had joined the force some years previously. Forgetting their covert role, they tried to save the life of their informant, William Carr. Unarmed and ill-equipped to take on Travis's men, there could be only one tragic outcome for the officers. All members of Travis's gang carried weapons that could all maim or kill.

Chilter and Wrightson fought for their lives, as well as William's, but there could be only one result.

Travis, who nearly always took a back seat on such activities, was very much hands on and led the others. He was equipped with a knife that many people would regard as a machete. The two officers were cut to ribbons and the vulnerable juvenile police informant kidnapped. It was too risky to set the van containing the bodies on fire, thereby attracting attention, and time was of the essence. They needed to leave the area. Travis took the view that, with the bodies left at the scene, the focus of the investigation would immediately turn to the informant meeting and the informant himself. There was nothing else that would raise suspicion. The immediate suspect for the murders would be William. The van being abandoned at a remote location.

Stan did his utmost to leave the scene as forensically clean as possible. He thought that by leaving both money and car keys with the murdered officers at the scene, it might create confusion during the subsequent investigation and further direct the police's attention towards the informant.

It was not often that Dunc Travis thought back over a decision and wondered if he had made the right call, yet this was an instance that kept him awake, if only for one night. He came to the conclusion that he and his men had had little option, therefore it was time to move on. He could see nothing that would lead a police investigation to his enterprise.

Any samples recovered from the van and run through the national databases would reveal nothing about Travis. Stan, Seb and co were all Polish nationals. Whilst Travis couldn't account for their past activities in Poland, he would not tolerate any employee attending court appearances in Parton or elsewhere, so they didn't have records in the UK.

Yet something troubled Travis as the boat made its way slowly out to sea. He drew out his phone and began scrolling through the video section, to the video of Roberson's hit-and-run evening. He played it back once, he played it back twice, looking closely at Nina's face and profile rather than at Roberson's plump, pathetic figure.

There was a likeness in Nina's face to that of the corpse he and his team were carrying out to sea. Putting two and two together, Travis realised that they had been closely related, probably siblings, and he was about to bury William in approximately the same location as his sister.

As the weighted body bag was deposited overboard by Travis and Seb, Dunc thought that Nina and her biological sister, who had once been known as Julie, were united in death after being separated for so many years when they were alive.

Stan remained in the cabin operating the boat's engine as the other two dropped the body overboard. Travis had to shout at him to keep the boat steady as it seemed Stan was more interested on operating his phone than the boat controls.

***

It was another disturbed night for Pete Roberson. Glass of gin and tonic in hand, he looked out across the marina from his apartment window. He thought once again, as he had done on that unforgettable night some months earlier, that he could see a small fishing vessel in the distance, making its way back to its berth in the poorer quarter of the west side.

Little did Roberson know that his blackmailing nemesis was once again returning after completing his dirty work, just as he had done some twelve months earlier. Neither was he aware that whilst he, Roberson, had a direct involvement in Nina's death, he was also indirectly involved in her sister's demise.

Roberson had a flashback; he was back there on the trading estate on that foggy night. He dropped his glass, which hit the floor and smashed into tiny pieces.

***

Ron Turner and Geoff Sutton were sitting in their respective homes, hoping for some semblance of a decent night's sleep, as Travis and his men returned to the deserted Parton West Marina. The two members of Parton Constabulary were totally unaware of yet another murder being added to their investigation.

12

Debbie

Geoff Sutton woke with a start before the alarm went off. It was 6.30 am. He reckoned he had eventually nodded off at about midnight. It wasn't enough sleep for him, but it was the best he could hope for and an early rise would see him having breakfast at The Parlour, coupled with the excitement of seeing Debbie.

He quickly showered and shaved and was in the car by 7am. It took him some time to clear the windscreen. He waited a few moments in the driver's seat, heater on full blast, for the car to warm up before making the short journey to The Parlour. He parked up and walked over the frosted ground to the line of shops opposite.

He decided against a morning paper, he'd have no time to read it. As a result, he was spared Smithy's razor-sharp conversation and wit. He went straight into the cafe.

The Parlour was completely empty at this time of the morning. For some reason Debbie was looking directly at the door when Sutton entered. It was a slightly awkward moment when their eyes met and they didn't speak. It seemed like ages since he'd seen her.

'Twice in two days. Too much of a good thing,' Debbie said and smiled. She was dressed in her usual Parlour pinafore, her hair pinned up, with dark mascara emphasizing her large eyes. 'Menu?' she enquired.

'No, thanks. Just poached eggs on brown toast,' Sutton said, thinking this was probably one of the healthier options available.

Debbie turned around and walked gracefully back towards the counter and kitchen area. Sutton unashamedly followed her walk.

She returned to his table with a mug of tea. 'Enjoy,' she said. 'You must be on that horrible enquiry,' she guessed correctly. It was more of a statement than a question.

'You're right, Debbie.' Sutton didn't look up in the hope that she would not engage further with this particular topic.

Debbie took the hint and returned to the kitchen area.

Sutton's phone buzzed in his pocket. It was a text from Stew enquiring if he had any news on William. Sutton decided to ring Stew on the way to work, knowing that life would hot up once he arrived at Parton City Centre Police Station. He put the phone back in his pocket as Debbie floated towards him carrying a plate of scrambled eggs. Before he could say anything, she pulled out a bottle of brown sauce from the pocket of her pinafore. 'Always be prepared,' she said cheekily then walked away, leaving Sutton to attack his meal.

He finished eating quickly. Debbie returned to his table from the kitchen. 'That was very quick,' she said.

'I was absolutely starving,' Sutton said, trying to avoid a belch at just the wrong moment.

She took the plate and turned away.

'Debbie, would you like to go out for a drink or meal some time?' Sutton could hardly believe he had said the words. His voice didn't seem to come from within his own body, it seemed alien and he was incredibly nervous.

She stopped, and it seemed like an age before she turned around and looked directly at Sutton. 'I thought you would never ask,' she said.

Sutton melted; he felt again like an adolescent.

'If I get a chance, let's do it this weekend. I won't know until closer to the time because of work. Is that OK?' he enquired, growing in confidence.

'Geoff, I can wait. I've waited such a very long time to be asked,' she replied. 'No charge for breakfast. Have a good day and take care. You really have made my day.'

'If that's the case when we go out, the meal is my treat,' Sutton said. The feeling returning to his toes and his stomach settled down.

'It certainly will be, young Sutton. And don't forget you must wear the green Barbour.' Debbie winked and walked back to the kitchen with Sutton's gaze burning through her.

Sutton looked at his green Barbour for a prolonged period, then removed it from the back of his chair. He replaced the chair underneath the table and walked out of The Parlour, into the cold February morning, blowing out small white clouds, as he made his way back to his car.

He was literally walking on air.

***

Debbie sat back in one of the small chairs that she and her staff used when, and if, they had time for a quick cuppa. It was quiet at the moment and she just needed a moment to herself as she reflected on the last five minutes or so.

It had been two years since her violent relationship had ended. Never again, she had decided, and that included all men and all relationships. She had lost count of the number of times Paul had apologised, crying and begging for forgiveness after he had inflicted another violent episode. She had lost count of the number of times she had walked into work heavily made up, disguising not only her obvious beauty but the bruises on her face. She had lost count of the number of times she had cried out both with pain and emotion at yet another beating. She had lost count of the number of times she had decided to leave him. Yet Debbie had loved Paul and she had continued to give everything to the relationship, in the hope that he would change. He never did, he never would.

But it really wasn't her who brought the whole situation to an end, it was her brother Billy.

He had seen enough when he popped next door from his newsagents and saw straight through the make up and Debbie's pain. Without ordering his sandwich, he placed an 'Out to Lunch' sign on the door of his shop and drove out to Debbie's place.

He knew Paul. The lazy bastard would still be in bed, even though it was after twelve noon. He barged in the darkened bedroom, spilling the can of Carlsberg Special Brew on the bedside cabinet. Then Billy, the gentle giant, gave Paul a beating to an inch of his life. For three minutes, Billy totally lost it. He threw Paul out of the house.

Billy knew Paul wouldn't be back, but he also swore that he would never ever lose his temper so badly again. The extent of his anger frightened him.

There was never any likelihood of Paul notifying the police, not with his background and the potential repercussions.

Now Debbie was ready to start again, despite the promises she had made to herself. Time was the greatest healer and for once in her life she had carried out a bit of research on a potential boyfriend. Relying almost totally on her brother, she'd been able to ensure that Geoff Sutton was an alright bloke.

Billy was also a member of Upper Parton RFC. He knew Sutton and his crowd and had, on a couple of occasions, been invited to join the select crew for a few beers at their table.

She wanted so much to ask Sutton to go out, almost as much as Sutton wanted to ask her. She had bottled it, almost as many times as Sutton had done. Finally, she now had the chance. Feeling elated, she stood up as the cafe door's jingle indicated a new customer.

***

Sutton was on cloud nine. He positively skipped back to the car, with all thoughts of his impending day and its associated problems completely abandoned. He thought only of Debbie as he sat back in the driver's seat to recover both his breath and his composure. Why the hell he hadn't asked her out before now seemed absolutely ridiculous considering the reaction he'd received.

His mood changed as he quickly remembered to call Stew Grant, which he did before setting off to the police station for the morning briefing. The call to his mate lasted only for a few minutes; basically Sutton had no information to give Stew.

Neither party to the conversation were aware that thanks to Dunc Travis, the Grants would have a free bedroom. William would not be returning, not now, not ever.

Not for the first time in the last few days, it was a journey during which Sutton showed a complete lack of concentration. He ignored an amber flashing light as an idling pedestrian made her way slowly across the road. Sutton, coming to his senses just in time, swerved to avoid her. He only avoided a collision because, surprisingly, his speed was well within the limit.

He entered the station yard via the sliding gates yet suffered the ignominy of having to get out of his vehicle to use his identity card to activate the keypad, as he had driven up too far away to put his arm out of the window. What made it worse was the queue of cars building up behind him as he completed the embarrassing process.

It was 8.30am and he remained in his car to hear the morning sport headlines, which included Parton Hornets RFC European Cup draw. The first game was a cracker, at home against Munster, one of the competition favourites. Sutton thought that if they could get tickets, which they probably would, it would be some day for him and his mates. Then he wondered fleetingly if Debbie liked rugby. Should he ask for an extra ticket?

Sutton made his way to the briefing room, only to be hijacked in the corridor by Bill Singer.

'Geoff, Turner wants to see us both in his office before the briefing.'

Without replying Sutton accompanied Singer into Turner's sanctuary.

Wearing a different light grey pinstripe suit, matching waistcoat, with a pink shirt and pink and blue striped tie, Turner sat behind his desk. Sutton wondered how long he had been at work. The dark shadows under his eyes were a tell-tale sign about the pressure he was under. Policy book open, yet with no other paper on his desk, Turner was sipping his coffee. He failed to acknowledge the two of them as they sat opposite him.

Neither Sutton nor Singer said anything; experience had taught them to wait for Turner to finish his policy entries. Let him be the first to speak.

Turner took another sip of his coffee. 'Well, gents, any further thoughts about our local good guy, PCC Peter Roberson?'

Sutton and Singer were silent for a moment. Sutton had been thinking about this scenario the previous night but more recently – and wrongly – thoughts of him and Debbie had occupied his time.

Singer took a long breath. 'Boss, I thought about carrying out some surveillance on the guy. Then I thought how on earth are we going to get the necessary authority to do so. It's such a major decision to carry out surveillance on the bloody Police and Crime Commissioner.'

'It's done,' said Turner, matter of factly. 'In order to ensure integrity, I've gone to the Head of CID at our neighbours, Borrington Police Force. They will operate independently, not attend here. Their briefings will be in the Borrington force area. Before you ask, no I haven't told our Chief Constable, or anyone else at his level. From what I've seen, Roberson has the Chief exactly where he wants him and it's highly likely that Mr Conting would either dither or deliberately, possibly mistakenly, inform our PCC that we are looking at him. You two are working on the intelligence background and anything from the surveillance will go directly to me and then to you, no one else. It's my neck on the line, and my decision to take the Roberson lead further. It's really the only one we have.'

There was no response from Sutton and Singer as both took in the magnitude of Turner's decision. It really was going to make or break him. Turner has got some bottle, thought Sutton.

'Another thing, Geoff. I want you to contact the Grants to see if they are willing to have a go at a press appeal for their missing foster child. If they are, we will carry it out at teatime. It's a risk. There will obviously be no mention of his informant background. But I think it's worth the risk to see if there have been any sightings of him or our vehicle.'

There was silence. 'OK, no response so I presume you haven't got any questions,' Turner said. 'Let's go to the briefing.' He emerged from behind his desk and led the way through to the Incident Room.

The briefing was relatively short, with Turner barking out instructions about forensic submissions, informant taskings and enquiries with youth agencies and outreach workers in an attempt to locate William Carr. He made it absolutely clear that there would be no mention whatsoever of William's covert police activities.

There had been a minor breakthrough regarding a CCTV sighting of the white Bedford van used by Chilter and Wrightson when it was on its way to the informant's meeting.

Singer and Sutton were tasked with revisiting Holston House for some further background information on Roberson's involvement. They decided they would arrive unannounced, in the hope of catching Simon Keys unawares.

13

Peter Roberson

Singer and Sutton travelled together in the Insignia, Sutton driving. The decision for Sutton to drive would allow Singer to concentrate on any urgent decisions that needed to be made if the Surveillance Team Leader contacted him. Turner had nominated Bill Singer as his deputy should he be unavailable and if an immediate decision was required. Turner had made that clear to the team Sergeant.

They arrived quickly, after what was for Sutton a surprisingly untroubled and uneventful journey. Entering the grounds and making his way up the driveway, he was aware of a strange, sad feeling, similar to his previous visit. Despite that fact that his last meeting was in the gathering dusk, and today's was in bright winter sunshine, the atmosphere of Holston House was no more welcoming. It was a depressing place. Some people don't get a chance in life, he thought. The pupils were so very, very vulnerable.

After parking up, Singer and Sutton made their way from the visitors' parking bay adjacent to the main building. During the journey to Holston, they had decided that Sutton would take the lead in any conversation with Singer in the background, only contributing when matters grew interesting or if Simon Keys tried to avoid answering questions. It could be important if Sutton missed a crucial question or detail, an inherent problem when there was only one person interviewing.

Sutton's uncomfortable feeling worsened as he heard the abuse emanating from a nearby classroom located on the right as they entered the main Victorian building.

Their timing could not have been better. Keys was emerging from his office, unshaven, still in Nike trainers and denim jeans, with a red-and-white checked shirt bearing the Crew emblem and his identity card hanging limply round his neck.

'Good morning, Mr Keys,' Sutton said. 'Could we have a quick word, please?'

'You have arrived without an appointment and I have a school to run,' replied the hassled head teacher.

'We are investigating not only a vulnerable missing person but also the murder of two police officers,' said Singer firmly.

'Come this way. I have ten minutes maximum,' said Keys reluctantly, ushering them into the disorganised empire which was his office.

Sutton and Singer sat down, after removing a couple of box files in order to do so.

It was Keys who started the conversation. 'Any news of William Carr?' he asked, showing some concern for the youngster.

'No news at this time, I'm sorry to say,' Sutton replied. 'Can I ask about the role that Pete Roberson plays in the school?'

'As I have said before, he is a Trustee on the Board. He also plays an active role, he attends the outings and activities that we run. If I am honest, I think he enjoys the publicity. He is really very popular with the youngsters. He attends all the major functions, particularly those when we have a press presence. He even makes the effort to go with us when we go on out-of-school trips. I thought his time would be more pressing when he became the Police and Crime Commissioner but, to his credit, he seems to have spent even more time with us over the last few months. He is really very popular with the youngsters,' Keys repeated himself.

'Other than his role on the Board, does he have any other key responsibilities within the school?' Singer asked.

'Well, certain Board members have specific tasks and Pete is kindly looking at our missing-person policy. We have youngsters disappearing all the time. Doing a runner, you might say. One of the most difficult decisions we have to make is at what stage do we officially call that person missing and involve the police. As an institution, we could have a Police Constable based here permanently, purely taking missing-person reports if we notified the police every time someone did a runner. It links nicely into Mr Roberson's multi-agency safeguarding work that you always hear about from him in the press.'

Singer continued, looked directly at Keys. 'Do you have any concerns about Mr Roberson?'

'Concerns, what do you mean? He's the Police and Crime Commissioner, for God's sake,' Keys said, looking straight at Singer. 'I've received his Disclosure and Barring Scheme clearance here somewhere. But that would be nothing in comparison with the vetting he's undertaken for his Commissioner role.' Keys looked around the room, glancing at the many pictures depicting school events, more often than not featuring Roberson with a group of pupils.

'I am sure you are absolutely right, Mr Keys,' Singer said, almost apologetically for asking such a stupid question.

'Thanks again, Simon. If there is anything – and I mean anything – you can think of that may assist us in finding William, please give me a ring,' said Sutton, deliberately using the headteacher's Christian name and producing his Parton Constabulary business card as a single point of contact.

They left the headteacher to yet another blast of expletives resonating from the nearby classroom, leaving Sutton to ask himself if there could be a harder job than trying to educate some of these youngsters who came from such difficult backgrounds.

Unusually there was very little conversation between Singer and Sutton on their journey back to Parton. Both of them were having identical thoughts: what on earth was Pete Roberson involved with, because something was definitely not right.

***

Sometime earlier, Detective Sergeant Rory Lomas had started work with his surveillance team out of an industrial unit in East Borrington. He had got a call from his Head of CID the previous night; it was one of the most unusual conversations, albeit there had been some very strange requests since his secondment into the surveillance unit three years previously.

The required surveillance authority was emailed securely through to their office, together with a full intelligence package, including pictures of their target Pete Roberson. The team were briefed and quickly mobilised. Inside a very short time they were on the road, crossing over into Parton Constabulary area and plotted up outside the Waterside Apartments, the home of their target.

Lomas had a team of twelve officers, with six double-crewed cars being deployed. He knew of Pete Roberson, as did most of his team, even though he wasn't 'their Police and Crime Commissioner'. Roberson attracted publicity far outside his local county; that was his intention.

'Its an off, off, off,' said Lomas to his team, as Roberson's distinctive silver Lexus emerged from his underground parking lot with Roberson squeezed into the driver's seat.

Apart from Lomas's team, his Head of CID, Ron Turner, Geoff Sutton and Bill Singer, nobody else had any knowledge whatsoever of this deployment. It was conducted on a purely need-to-know basis.

Turner knew that at some stage he would have to inform Conting of this side of the operation, but not now. If one of the surveillance team cars had an accident, or got an official speeding or parking ticket, he would have some serious explaining to do. He knew full well the ramifications of his decision.

The Lexus made slow progress through the rush-hour traffic, unaware of the six unmarked and unassuming police vehicles following behind.

'Vehicle 4 now has the eyeball. It's a left, left, left towards the council offices,' said one of Lomas's team, broadcasting over the secure airwaves network.

Twenty minutes after leaving the Waterside apartments, Roberson pulled up in a parking bay outside the council offices in Parton City Centre. Intelligence had suggested this was his first engagement of the day where he was attending a multi-agency meeting on adult safeguarding, hosted by Parton Council. This was to be followed by a short press conference and briefing.

There was no doubt that when Roberson appeared before the television cameras and the press, he would naturally be asked a question about the current double-murder enquiry. It continued to dominate the headlines, both locally and nationally. Roberson's stock answer would be about the bravery of the officers who had put their lives on the line in order to protect the good people of Parton. 'Our thoughts are with their families, who continue to suffer greatly. Meanwhile I have every confidence that Parton Constabulary will rise to the challenge and bring those people responsible for this heinous crime to justice. They are currently following up numerous lines of enquiry and I am being regularly updated by the Temporary Chief Constable.'

It was standard stuff, but Roberson knew the police needed a result; the media and the general public would demand that.

The meeting was scheduled to last for an hour or so.

Lomas took the opportunity to ring Ron Turner and update him as a matter of courtesy. As it happened, Turner was otherwise engaged scrutinising the forensic strategy and so, as agreed, it was DI Bill Singer who answered Lomas's call.

After leaving his safeguarding meeting, Roberson made a trip that made Turner's decision to have him surveilled not only courageous but extremely worthwhile. You never knew with surveillance what it might uncover about the target. That was definitely the case with Pete Roberson.

'Its an off, off, off,' one of Lomas's colleagues shouted in, giving the team the message that Roberson had squeezed himself back into his Lexus and was on his way.

The initial journey didn't last long; Roberson stopped off at the nearby Tesco Express quick-food outlet, pocketing a steak bake, slice of pizza and a piece of millionaire's shortcake. It was a typical meal-deal offering, with Roberson ignoring the healthier offerings available. One of the team observed the visit and the purchase to make sure that buying the food was the only reason for his attendance.

After returning to his car, Roberson wasted no time in tucking into his lunch. In a matter of moments, he'd had devoured the savouries. Then, just as he was about to scoff his millionaire's shortcake, he placed it back on the passenger's seat.

Must be for afters, thought Lomas.

'Its a right, right, right.' Another broadcast by the surveillance team.

The plush silver saloon set off, going further out of the city. Lomas knew that Roberson had another civic engagement scheduled for 2.30pm, so now was a good opportunity to observe his lifestyle outside his public persona.

Roberson made a journey of about twenty miles into the more rural area of the county, observed by the team. He stopped without indicating, forcing the surveillance vehicle in immediate pursuit to continue through the small village of Rishope to avoid being spotted.

Lomas quickly deployed himself and another officer on foot. One of them went into the village newsagent's, which also included a small cafe. The officer sat down after purchasing a copy of *The Daily Telegraph* and a skinny latte, easily the most popular drink and newspaper in upmarket Rishope.

Not wishing to engage in any conversation, and choosing a seat not directly behind the window, DC Sally Atwood had an unobscured view of Roberson without bringing unwanted attention to herself. Her partner, DS Lomas, went to one of the three antique and curio shops, for which the village was popular, to provide back up for the other foot officer if required. The officers could contact each other via their covert earpieces and hidden microphones.

Roberson had parked his vehicle in a small layby just inside the 30mph signage and walked past the county award sign for Parton in Bloom – Rishope had achieved a gold standard – that was proudly displayed at the entrance to the village. He then walked forty yards or so to the public pay phone kiosk, the only one in the picturesque hamlet. The pay phone was one of the few still in existence in the county, but it was a necessity for the good people of Rishope as the mobile phone signal was extremely unreliable, an issue of constant protest from the demanding residents. Despite being a small community, Rishope was affluent, housing some important local people. If they had a complaint, their voices were heard. However, the village had no CCTV.

There was something very noticeable about Roberson when he walked; despite his unathletic appearance, he always gave an impression of extreme confidence bordering on arrogance. There was no doubting that the man had presence.

Roberson squeezed into the phone booth and made two calls, punching the digits with his podgy fingers. The first call only lasted a minute or so but the second took some time, lasting a number of minutes before he returned to his vehicle. The PCC no longer displayed his previous arrogant gait; his right hand covered his mouth and chin as if in shock; he was troubled and totally focussed on returning to his car. This significant change in behaviour was observed by members of Lomas's surveillance team and recorded in their log; this policy booklet would be a legal requirement if their deployment became part of the evidence chain.

Once back in his car, Roberson made the return journey back to the outskirts of the city centre, again followed by the surveillance team, which this time was minus a vehicle and two personnel.

Rory Lomas acted without delay. He entered the phone booth and obtained the number of the kiosk, noting the time. Armed with this information, he contacted Ron Turner whose phone went to voicemail. He redialled the other contact given to him and Bill Singer took the message. Not only did Lomas give Singer the relevant number from the payphone, he also informed Singer of the stark change in Roberson's demeanour. 'Boss, whoever the subject spoke to in that second call, it had a profound effect on him. He was a completely different bloke walking back to his vehicle. I can't emphasise that enough.'

***

Just an hour earlier, Roberson had been very happy to leave his safeguarding meeting. He wondered how his comments had been received at the press conference. Now it was time to move on. He needed to speak to Dalton, not about her welfare but to make sure that the murdered cops' investigation had nothing to do with that juvenile informant who had now been reported missing.

He had a couple of hours before his next public engagement and two pressing tasks: one a call to his 'favourite' Detective Inspector, Sue Dalton, and the other to a local escort whom he had found through an online agency. He decided he would make the short drive out to Rishope, where he knew they had a payphone and no CCTV. He didn't want to use his work phone or the pay-as-you-go Dunc Travis hotline for these two calls.

Arriving at Rishope and taking no notice of the pretty little village he made his first call, to a lady who went by the name of Lola. Lola, who worked from home, confirmed she was available for a thirty-minute appointment early in the afternoon.

The second call took longer and caused Roberson major concern.

'Sue, it's Pete. Can I come and see you sometime? Hear you've had a shock,' he said, falsely expressing some compassion.

'Pete, how are you? Please can you come around as soon as possible? Today?' Dalton said, pleading but slightly sluggish, which was no surprise considering the recent events she had experienced and the effect of the sedatives she had been prescribed.

Roberson, interested in only one thing, went straight to his point of the conversation. 'Sue, that awful incident concerning the officers that have been murdered. I was just wondering if that had anything to do with the young informant you were telling me about?' Roberson asked.

'It does, it does,' said Dalton, now crying down the phone. The sight of the staring eyes of both Chilter and Wrightson never left her and were an ever-recurring nightmare. 'Pete, please come around soon. I really need you now,' she pleaded yet again, but her words fell on deaf ears. Roberson had already hung up.

He left the pay phone kiosk, without any thought whatsoever for Sue Dalton. Breathing very deeply, he needed time out to consider his situation; as far as he was concerned, he was the only one that mattered.

Back in the car, he started to consider his options and thought about cancelling the afternoon appointment with

Lola. Then again, he did need a little time to consider his next move, as well as satisfying his constant need for female company. The escort by the name of Lola could satisfy both these needs.

***

Bill Singer actioned the contacts given to him by Rory Lomas without delay. He rang the telecoms unit with the information and directly prioritised this action without compromising the investigation. There was no mention of any names; he wanted a quick answer to one simple question – who were the subscribers of the contact numbers that Roberson had rung from the payphone in Rishope?

Within ten minutes Singer was sitting with Sutton, explaining what had happened with the surveillance team, when he received a call from the telecoms unit. He was completely silent as he took the call and looked directly at Sutton, staring at him wide-eyed.

'The first number he called was to an online escort agency and the second was to Sue Dalton's personal mobile. There must be a reason why he would travel out to somewhere as remote as Rishope to use a pay phone when you can use a mobile in private. He could easily have gone home,' Singer said.

Earlier in the day Sutton had put in a call to Stew Grant about Turner's request for a press conference. He had chosen his words very carefully. He informed Stew that there was nothing further he could tell him at the moment but maybe the press conference would encourage the public to come forward if they had seen William. Stew had never made any mention of Pete Roberson down at the rugby club, but Sutton now knew that both men were on the Board of Trustees at Holston House.

Sutton wasn't sure if that extended to them meeting socially. He didn't need to know anything further at this stage, and certainly he had nothing at all to tell Stew about any developments in the search for William.

The upshot of the conversation with Stew was that he and Tina were more than willing to do anything that would help the police find their foster child. The press conference was arranged for 5pm at Parton Constabulary HQ, the buildings adjacent to the City Centre Police Station. It would feature Stew and Tina Grant, Ron Turner, with the force's media officer in the background. Stew had asked if Sutton could be present, off camera, for some moral support. He wasn't aware that Turner had *ordered* Sutton to be present.

Sutton listened intently to what Singer divulged to him. It certainly didn't seem to make any sense for Roberson to go to such extreme lengths to make a couple of calls, but it raised further concerns and suspicions about the man. And it didn't help Dalton's cause, although her relationship with Roberson was already known.

***

Still under surveillance, Roberson was tracked to Lola's address. He had deliberately chosen her through the agency as she could carry out appointments at a venue on the outskirts of Parton. Whether they were her own premises or rented was neither here nor there, as far as Roberson was concerned. He visited her merely to satisfy a need. It was also highly unlikely, given the area and the way she operated, that she was one of Dunc Travis's girls.

Roberson knew the area well and chose a large car park, not covered by any CCTV cameras or other security measures, approximately one hundred metres from Lola's place. He was fortunate in finding an empty parking bay, a remote corner slot with no one around. He reversed in with the nearside and rear of the Lexus backing onto the two-metre high perimeter wall that surrounded the whole car parking area. This suited his purpose; it was deliberately chosen.

He walked to the back of the vehicle and opened the boot, which gave him further cover. Moments later – and it was only a matter of moments – Roberson emerged, no tie and his shirt now covered by a navy-blue crew-neck sweater along with a black North Face fleece. The biggest change was a scruffy black wig at least an inch longer than his natural hair, a complete change from his previously well-groomed image. Pete Roberson was nobody's fool. There was absolutely nothing sophisticated in his disguise, yet it was a job done.

He had obviously completed this process before and how he wished he'd done so on the night he'd run over that girl. It was the one time his needs had overcome his brains, which he still put down to that extra drink.

Lomas and his team noted everything that Roberson did. From their observation point they were able to take a couple of photographs of the newly-styled Police and Crime Commissioner.

Roberson made his way to the address Lola had given him. It wasn't far, and he walked purposefully. He was in and out of the premises within half an hour. He looked around furtively as soon as he emerged before making his way back to the Lexus. He seemed to have recovered his composure somewhat and his arrogance and confidence were returning. Roberson's time with Lola had been well spent. He returned to the isolated car park and checked around before returning his disguise back to the boot.

Now for the next public engagement.

Back behind the steering wheel, he checked his tie via the rear-view mirror. He took what appeared to be some aftershave or cologne from the glove compartment, splashing the liquid on his hands before applying it liberally to his cheeks and neck in order to remove Lola's scent. Finally, he took a comb from the centre console to ensure that his hair was absolutely perfect; after all Pete Roberson had an image to protect.

Whatever his involvement in the murder and missing person investigation, his target was in serious trouble, thought Rory Lomas, who had made up the ground from Rishope to join the rest of his team. You can't have the Police and Crime Commissioner frequenting local prostitutes. Surely it would only be a matter of time before someone recognised him, despite his efforts at disguise.

Singer stood down the surveillance team. They had traveling time back to their own force area to take into account and with Ron Turner having initially requested them for two shifts, one day shift and one late, they would be back on plot tomorrow afternoon unless otherwise instructed.

14

Tina Grant

Sutton and Singer returned to Parton HQ for the Grant press conference.

Singer turned to Sutton. 'I wonder what Roberson is up to tonight. It's a pity Turner didn't authorise twenty-four-hour surveillance. I know it's bloody costly but Roberson's not right. Disguises for visiting prostitutes – he's supposed to be seeing Sue Dalton! I don't think that Turner will sit on him forever. He's probably got enough to arrest him now.'

Sutton didn't answer immediately but finally said, 'For what? For murder? For the abduction of William Carr? For an association with the missing William Carr? There are no names yet that we have seen from the informant's reporting, so what evidence do we have? The envelope and a couple of calls from a pay phone from the surveillance team? I know it shouldn't make any difference, but we are talking about the bloody Police and Crime Commissioner. Turner's got to level with the Chief at some time and I've got a feeling he's only going to tell him when Roberson is in custody and going absolutely nowhere. Personally, I don't blame him.'

'No, neither do I,' Singer agreed. 'If you were Roberson now and you knew you were in deep shit, what would you do?'

'I would probably want to know if I could how deep that

shit is.'

'I agree, Geoff. I also think he will make a mistake,' said Singer.

Sutton turned in the driver's seat and looked half-heartedly at the road in front of him. 'I've got an idea,' he said, as they pulled up at the sliding gates to HQ. Suddenly there was a tinge of excitement in his voice. 'See you after the Grants' press conference – and tell the wife you will be late back.'

***

It was 4.30pm, thirty minutes before they were due to go live with the press. The Grants both looked splendid.

Sutton introduced Stew and Tina Grant to Ron Turner over a cup of coffee in Turner's office before heading into the press room. He made a mental note that this was the second cup he had consumed in Turner's office, made again by his young apprentice.

The general public might think that the Grants had made a special effort for the cameras, such was their smart appearance, but that couldn't be further from the truth; they dressed like this all the time. Stew was extremely smart in a navy-blue Ralph Lauren suit and light tan shoes; Tina wore one of her favourite Zara numbers. Slightly OTT but this was the Grants.

The room was decorated with large posters of William Carr. There were approximately twenty press members present, a really good turn-out. Tea and coffee were provided at the entrance, courtesy of Parton Constabulary. Whenever it was free, everyone wanted some of the action; apart from those consuming the odd trendy bottle of Evian water, all those present had partaken freely of what was on offer, accompanied by a McVities digestive.

The room was well illuminated, the atmosphere fairly relaxed. The audience all knew each other. The more senior journalists were probably in the pub by now, leaving the juniors to obtain the necessary information then relay it back to the seniors who put their own names to the article.

There was a single microphone on the stage pointing towards Stew, Tina and Ron Turner. Facing the audience was a small plaque with Parton Constabulary's mission statement: 'WE ARE HERE TO PROTECT AND SERVE OUR COMMUNITY'. Sutton thought mission statements were a complete waste of time and money. Every one of the forty or so police forces in England and Wales had a mission statement, yet they all basically said the same, obvious message, that they were just doing the job the public expected them to do.

The press officer had prepared a brief for the Grants, who had decided that Tina would take the lead. They had been coached on some of the more difficult questions and decided that they would talk about their foster child as William Carr, whilst acknowledging that he'd been previously known as Julie. The rationale was that if William was watching the press conference, using that name might further encourage him to contact either his foster parents or the police.

It was exactly 5pm when Ron Turner opened the proceedings. The bright lights created their own heat and even at the back of the room Sutton noticed beads of sweat appearing above Turner's lip. Despite that, he was composed and in charge. Not for the first time Sutton appreciated that Turner had a presence.

He thanked the press for attending as well as William's foster parents, Stew and Tina Grant. He emphasised that the police needed the public's help in locating William. He gave the approximate time and date of when William went missing, and also the contact number to ring should anyone have information that would assist the police in locating the boy. Turner then handed over to Tina.

For a few moments before she recovered her composure Tina Grant, handkerchief in her hand, looked like a rabbit staring into the headlights of an oncoming car.

She began with the trauma of coming to terms with the fact that as a couple couldn't have children of their own and how they came to love fostering. 'It isn't easy and there's a lot of frustration, but success does happen and when it does it's the most rewarding feeling in the world.'

She told the press how many children they had fostered. She also stated that William wasn't the easiest, but he got exactly the same amount of love and attention as the others. 'We want him back. Most importantly, we need to know he's safe and well.'

She touched on the fact that William had suffered a difficult life and had been a resident at Holston House. 'Like a lot of foster children, he came and went unannounced and in many ways used the house as a hotel, for his food and sleep, like many children of his age. We tried so very hard with William. Stew and I have thought about him constantly since we sought the help of the police.'

Tina looked directly into the cameras. 'Please come back, William. Stew and I want you back safe and well.' She then reverted to the prepared script. 'If anyone out there has any knowledge of William's whereabouts, please, please contact the police on the number provided.'

Tina grabbed another tissue. She had done remarkably well holding it all together. It was an honest and a heartfelt plea.

Ron Turner took over. 'Any questions?'

A voice came from the rear of the room. 'Is there any connection between William going missing and the murder of the two police officers?'

This was Turner's field; he was in control. The plea for help in locating William was not going to be hijacked by the press looking at another angle on the police murders. He knew that many of the journalists present would be covering both stories. He knew about the connection but to give that to the press at this stage could deflect the importance of finding William. It could also make for some very awkward questions about the link between the two murdered officers and missing person that Turner wanted to avoid.

'As a matter of course, we review incidents in and around the area of a crime scene. This has raised the issue of a vulnerable missing person. Quite rightly we need to locate William and, until we do, we are not in any position to disclose or discuss any potential connection.'

'Detective Chief Superintendent, can you categorically state there is no link between the two incidents?'

Turner looked directly at the member of the press who'd had the temerity to ask the question he had already answered. 'I've answered that question,' he replied disdainfully.

'Why is William also known as Julie? Does it have any impact upon his disappearance?' came an expected query.

'He prefers to be called William,' said Tina helpfully.

'We don't know at this stage if the change of name has anything to do with him going missing,' said Turner helpfully.

He now wished to bring the press briefing to a close. He knew from past experience that press conferences go two ways: they were either extremely helpful for both parties, or turned into a barrage of questions, with people calling out over each other, achieving absolutely nothing.

He thanked the press yet again for their time and assistance, packed up his briefcase and pulled back Stew and Tina's chairs as they rose from behind the desk. It gave those present the strongest indication that the show was over. Then, in a moment of natural tenderness and respect, Stew took Tina in his arms and hugged her lovingly in full view of the assembled crowd.

That moment made everyone pause whatever they were doing. They stopped, turned and stared at this open show of affection in such a public arena. It mirrored a minute's silence at a Remembrance Day parade.

Turner, whose mind was just moving on to his next major problem, openly stared at the couple before following them as they left the stage.

A few miles away Dunc Travis, alone in his small office, watched the press conference on his iPhone. He took a large swig of coffee and chuckled to himself.

Hand in hand, Stew and Tina returned to Turner's office. Tina's mascara was slightly smudged. Stew's face was drawn due to a lack of sleep and the emotion of the past couple of days.

Sutton embraced them both. 'You were terrific. I am proud of you both,' he said.

The couple sat down in Turner's office, still holding hands. There was complete silence before Stew Grant grunted, 'Is this not the time when the people who make the press appeal get arrested?' He lifted the hand that was holding Tina's, loosened his cuff links, rolled up his sleeves and offered his bare wrists to Sutton and Turner.

Turner offered an unconvincing smile.

It was Stew's poor attempt at a joke to relieve the tension of last fifteen minutes or so. The comment referred to the many times that media coverage of a press conference had ended somewhere down the line in the successful prosecutions of those actually making the appeal. In hindsight, Stew wasn't convinced his comments had hit the right note.

'Thanks to you both,' said Turner, after what seemed an age. 'I hope you didn't find it too much of an ordeal. Now let's hope we are successful.'

Due to the unique circumstances of the enquiry, Turner thought it better for Sutton to act as a liaison for the family. He had already allocated Family Liaison Officers to Mike Chilter and Linda Wrightson's nearest and dearest. The close relationship between Sutton and the Grants could have put Sutton in an invidious position but Turner trusted Sutton implicitly.

***

Fifteen minutes later, Sutton and Singer were back in front of Turner's desk like two naughty schoolchildren in front of the headmaster. It came as no surprise at all to Sutton that Turner was sipping a cup of coffee without any consideration whatsoever for the needs of his colleagues.

'Sir, Bill and I have a suggestion. We don't know the extent of Roberson's involvement in all this but we do know that he is currently in a relationship with Sue Dalton and he is our only lead. From Roberson's perspective, he doesn't seem to be particularly bothered about Sue – he's more interested in visiting prostitutes than seeing his so-called girlfriend. She might see the relationship in a different light and Roberson could be the love of her life. We just don't know.'

'Why don't Bill and I pay Sue a visit? She's now fit enough to take phone calls and she must know she's in some deep shit. We need her on side, wired up and speaking to Roberson to get an indication of his involvement – or not. It would also allow us the opportunity to get some concrete evidence.'

'Concrete evidence with a listening device planted to covertly record a conversation on our Police and Crime Commissioner?' said Turner, staring first at Sutton then at Singer.

'Well, it's only slightly more intrusive than surveillance,' said Sutton, offering a certain amount of logic, together with a lot of bottle. 'I know that Sue has had exemplary career. I know she's a really good operator – but it looks as though she could be head over heels in love with our PCC. He may not feel the same way about her but at some stage he will make contact. Not out of compassion but maybe to obtain some information. It's a knocking bet he will visit her at some time.'

'I agree with Geoff,' said Singer. 'We could arrest Roberson now but we need more on him. Once he's in custody, we need to ensure that he is going nowhere, despite whichever expensive solicitor he chooses.'

Turner placed both hands under his chin, his elbows on the desk helping to support the weight of his head, which suddenly seemed heavier. His steely eyes never lost focus. The PCC's arrest was becoming increasingly inevitable. He also knew that any subsequent conversation with the Temporary Chief Constable, Alan Conting, would be memorable. He smiled at the thought, lifted his hands away from underneath his chin and placed them flat on his desk.

'In for a bloody penny, in for a bloody pound.' Turner ended the interminable silence. 'Visit her, make a pitch, and I will research the authorities. Before you go, have you considered your actions if Roberson arrives at Dalton's place when the pair of you are present?' This occurrence was more than a distinct possibility and was the exact reason why they had considered this course of action.

There was complete silence from both Sutton and Singer. They had never considered this scenario, although they knew Roberson had another civic engagement first thing tomorrow morning.

Turner continued. 'Bill, arrest him on suspicion of William's abduction. It's tenuous but his name appears on the envelope in our mispers bedroom and we suspect that Dalton and him have talked about William's information.'

Sutton and Singer walked out of Turner's office. Unbelievable. Un-bloody-believable they heard him muttering out loud.

15

Sue Dalton

Since her attendance at the crime scene two days previously, Dalton had been prescribed sedatives by her own doctor and received a home visit from the force's occupational health unit. It was anticipated that, when the time came, she would receive appropriate counselling to assist in her recovery.

It was early evening and she had made herself cheese on toast. It was her second meal of the day. She did feel slightly better, mostly because she had heard from Pete that afternoon, albeit it wasn't the best of conversations and had ended abruptly. She dearly hoped he would pop round to see her; she needed him.

Just hearing his voice had an immediate impact on her health and well-being. Whilst the cheese on toast was her second meal of the day, the two empty bottles of Chenin Blanc, together with a remaining half bottle of gin, told a different story about Dalton's recent dietary habits.

She felt well enough to open the backlog of two-days' post. She immediately chucked out the annoying advertising flyers, which made up most of the correspondence she currently received. There were two letters that caught her attention. She opened the first, which was a get-well card from one of the administration staff at the Confidential Unit. The sender would be one of the very few who knew she was in deep trouble.

Her hands trembled with excitement at the thought of what the second letter contained. She grabbed it, ripping it open like a child on Christmas morning going from one present to another. Hands shaking, she removed the two tickets she had purchased online only last week. Two of the very best and most expensive tickets in the house for a Springsteen concert on his latest tour, at the Etihad Stadium, Manchester City's ground.

She felt elated. It was her birthday present to herself. Could she persuade Pete to join her?

***

Sutton and Singer made the twenty-minute trip from Parton Police Headquarters. Sutton was fully focused on the traffic. There was no need now for the Ted Baker sunglasses, and the green Barbour was slumped on the back seat. Sutton wondered whether there was ever a season when his jacket was not required; at this moment, nothing came to mind.

The pair of them knew that ringing ahead, or going through the OHU, might be the proper process but it had to be an unannounced visit if their plan had any chance of success. Circumstances dictated that this would probably be their best – and only – opportunity..

They both knew Dalton well; she had worked for them over a period of years. She had a reputation as a good officer and a good operator. Neither of them knew her outside the job, but there was an element of sadness for them both now that Sue Dalton had found herself in this mess. What had been a successful career, with further promotions in the offing, had been instantly derailed through her complete lack of judgement.

As far as Parton Constabulary was concerned, her actions were unforgivable. Her involvement in the investigation had not yet been fully determined. Whilst neither Geoff nor Bill could control her ultimate destiny, they might be able to offer an arrangement where she could recover some ground.

Sutton was finally able to reverse the Insignia into a free parking space fifty metres away from Dalton's upstairs flat. They made a quick check of the surrounding area to ensure there was no sign of Roberson's Lexus.

'It must be a nightmare living here and trying to park a car,' said Singer as they made their way to the flat.

Dalton just about heard the front doorbell ring above the sound of the music she was playing. She turned the CD down momentarily and waited, wondering if she had misheard.

Waiting on the doorstep, Singer took over from Sutton, pressed his finger on the buzzer and let it remain there for a couple of comments.

Dalton wasn't expecting visitors. She wondered if Pete Roberson had, for the first time in their relationship, actually done as she had requested and arrived to see her. She almost skipped down the stairs in anticipation and opened the door, after releasing the deadlock and the upper Yale.

'Hi, Sue. Can we come in, please?' asked Sutton politely.

The sight of her colleagues, two people she only knew from the workplace, confused Dalton. She immediately suffered a short flashback to the staring eyes of DCs Chilter and Wrightson. She also suffered extreme disappointment because her visitors were two members of Parton Constabulary and not her beloved Pete Roberson.

She recovered. 'Geoff, Bill,' she stuttered. 'Please come in.' She walked upstairs, allowing them both to follow.

They made their way through the tiny hallway into the kitchen-diner. Sutton immediately noticed the empty bottles of alcohol. Other than that, and knowing Sue Dalton's personality, the room was exactly as he expected: very clean and tidy, bordering on minimalistic. The only surprising aspect was the array of items of Springsteen memorabilia. Despite knowing Dalton for a considerable period of time, she had very much kept herself to herself. That was absolutely fine; it wasn't an offence.

What really stood out in the room was the large framed photograph of her and Pete Roberson. Due to the room's design it was difficult to have a focal point, yet this photograph seemed to occupy the most prominent position and attracted their attention. It was a significant statement of the relationship and made the ensuing conversation that much more difficult.

'Cup of tea, coffee?' Sue offered quietly.

'Coffee, milk no sugar,' they said, almost in unison.

Sutton started gently. 'I'm so sorry, Sue. Is there anything you need, or that the organisation can assist with? How are you doing?' Three questions, all in one statement, in an empathetic tone. He felt he had to ask these questions if only to make himself feel better.

Sue set about making the drinks in the kitchen area, set back from the dining section in the open-plan design. She was using a noisy, modern stainless-steel coffee machine. Sutton thought such things were a complete waste of money as they took ages to make a drink and the coffee was normally cold and tasteless.

The flat doorbell rang, unheard by Dalton due to the background noise of both the coffee machine and Springsteen's vocals. Sutton and Singer looked at each other, both thinking the same: Roberson had arrived. They immediately raced downstairs, Singer with his right hand curled around his handcuffs.

Opening the door, Sutton and Singer faced the occupant of the downstairs flat. 'Internet delivery for Sue. Bye now,' he said, and handed the small Amazon parcel to Singer. Dalton's neighbour turned quickly on his heel and disappeared next door.

'Just a minute, guys,' Sue said firmly, still busy with the machine. It seemed an eternity before she returned to them with three lukewarm mugs of Americano and after eventually reducing the volume on her CD player.

By this time Sutton and Singer had already arrived back in the diner and placed the small parcel on the table. Dalton hadn't even noticed either their short disappearance act or her recent delivery. She seemed to recall Sutton's questions. 'I'm OK, thanks. Definitely better than I was forty-eight hours ago. I guess this is not just a polite enquiry into my welfare, gentlemen. How is the investigation going?' It was a genuine question, which required an appropriate response.

'Well, we know the identity of Billy Spitz. As you know, his real name is William Carr and he's been reported missing from his foster home. Before being fostered, he lived at Holston House. Nothing has been confirmed to suggest that the informant's meeting actually took place. Mike and Linda still had the money and the informant's slip with them when their bodies were found. Other than that, we have CCTV of the van, but it's at a garage not that far from the police station.' Singer gave a limited update. He cleverly failed to mention Pete Roberson.

Singer now took the initiative. 'Sue, the purpose of this visit is to see if you can help us.'

Dalton's eyes opened wide. 'Me? Help? I'm in the shit, and you boys well know it. The payment wasn't supervised and I failed to ensure Mike and Linda were back after the meeting, safe and secure. They are back now – murdered, stabbed to death, and found twenty-four hours later. Where the hell does that leave me?'

Dalton spoke with venom, summing up her position extremely well. She rose from her kitchen stool, walked towards the dining area, grabbed a tissue and wiped her eyes. Those last words had caused another flashback. Singer and Sutton knew that whatever her errors of judgement, her grief was utterly genuine.

'You are in trouble but so are we,' Singer said. 'There are very few worthwhile leads so far. Not only have we two murdered colleagues but we have a missing, vulnerable juvenile, a police-registered informant who may or may not be involved.'

Sutton looked directly at Sue Dalton with a stare that Turner would have been proud of. 'Pete Roberson's name has come up as being of interest. He has connections with Holston House. We found an envelope with his name and address in the informant's bedroom. Could Roberson have been aware of any intelligence that the informant was providing to Chilter and Wrightson?'

Dalton looked at Sutton then swung her eyes away. It was a significant enough sign for Sutton to know the answer to his question. She stood up and walked towards the dining-room table. She sat down and put her head in her hands. Not a word was spoken by anyone present.

Sutton followed her and, in a moment of compassion, sat next to her and placed his arm around her shoulders. She sank into his arms, sobbing loudly. 'I'm exhausted, Geoff. Totally exhausted.'

For a moment Sutton was confused. Was she referring to her physical state or the circumstances surrounding her involvement in the investigation?

'I told Pete that we had an operation that involved the abuse of vulnerable youngsters from a care home, and that the informant was a juvenile. He knows that the disappearance has something to do with Mike and Linda's murder. He asked me. He's the PCC – if I can't trust him, I can't trust anybody,' she said, justifying her actions and removing her head from Sutton's shoulder.

'Sue, we are not clear about his involvement in all this but there has to *be* an involvement and he needs to be eliminated. We need you to inform him, to allow him to open up, and we need to record that conversation. Depending on what is or isn't said, it may become evidence.'

'You want to covertly record the PCC? It's Pete, he's my partner! You must be joking,' Dalton said defiantly.

'It's Pete, the guy who was with an escort girl this afternoon,' came Sutton's immediate response. He said it almost without thinking.

'No, he wasn't! He wouldn't, that's not him.' Dalton shook her head.

'Sue, I could get you the photographs if you like or you could just ring the Surveillance Detective Sergeant,' Singer chipped in. His comment was quick, almost to the point of being cruel, even though it was the truth. He continued, 'Sue, there are two things to consider. Firstly your position – as you rightly say, you are in deep trouble with work. But by agreeing to what we are proposing you may recover some ground.'

'By informing on my partner?' Dalton now looked directly at Sutton and Singer. She knew them both well enough; the comments about the surveillance team and her beloved Pete with the escort would be absolutely true. They would not be bluffing.

Sutton stood up and looked down at her. 'What choice have you got?'

'Think of yourself, Sue,' said Singer.

Dalton was stunned. The escort – how could he? Not him. What had she done wrong? Okay, she'd given information on an operation but it wasn't as though he would compromise matters.

'Speak tomorrow,' she said. 'But bring round the kit.' She was referring to the listening devices that would be required should their plan receive her blessing.

Sutton and Singer drained their mugs of cold coffee and left Dalton dazed and even more confused after their twenty-minute visit. They were more than happy to leave.

***

It was just after 9pm when Sutton got home. Singer had updated Turner on their conversation with Dalton on the way back to the station to collect his own car. Turner had obtained the necessary authority, although neither Singer nor Sutton had a clue where from. Due to Turner's distrust and lack of respect for his current Temporary Chief Constable, he had obviously gone elsewhere. Another favour called in by his mate from the neighbouring force was the conclusion that came to mind. Turner was sorting out the listening devices with the Head of Technical Support. The fewer people who knew about this the better. It was definitely a need-to-know basis.

Just the one glass of Australian red for his nightcap. Sutton was really tired but excited. Adrenaline was coursing through his veins. They had, after what seemed an eternity, made some progress. His initial misgivings about the investigation had been banished. Circumstances had dictated that he was playing a crucial role and he was loving being back in the limelight.

He had another fitful night's sleep but probably better than Sue Dalton's. He awoke at 7am when the alarm roused him. He discovered that he'd missed a call sometime yesterday from Maggie. There was no voicemail, which indicated that it wasn't urgent. Nevertheless, he must ring her – he always did as soon as possible. He also needed to ring Stew and update him and Tina, after checking to see if the press release had thrown up any leads.

Time was tight. He was meeting the Head of Technical Support, Harry Temple, at Dalton's place at 8.30am. He needed a quick chat with Harry, one of the few people he didn't know in the organisation, before they went to install the equipment.

16

Dillon's

Despite the tight timescale, Sutton was desperate to see Debbie at The Parlour. It was slightly warmer today, no need to scrape the ice off the car, yet still bright and clear.

He didn't turn the radio on for his short trip to The Parlour. He made the smallest of detours into Dillon's Newsagents, for a copy of *The Times*. He wasn't sure he would have the time to read it, but he wanted some semblance of normality in his life and the paper was part of his daily routine.

He held the door open to allow a customer to exit. As soon as he entered the shop Smithy, with no one else to serve, was in his element. 'So you asked her at last, Geoff,' he said, smiling.

Sutton ignored him, picked up his paper and took the money from his pocket, placing it on the counter.

'And a good morning to you as well, Mr Sutton,' continued Smithy.

Again no answer; there was no need. Sutton just looked Smithy in the eye, gave him a wink and a smile and walked out. He turned right and entered The Parlour.

'Bacon and mushroom to take out please, a bit of a rush this morning,' Sutton said to no one. The place was empty.

Debbie appeared from the kitchen area, smiling with those gorgeous eyes. Geoff again became that pathetic adolescent as she acknowledged his appearance. 'Coming up.' She turned on her heels, appreciating Sutton's haste, and returned a few moments later after placing the bacon and mushrooms in the pan. She came towards him and, without any warning, kissed his cheek. She stepped back. 'How are we doing today?' she enquired.

Sutton was initially stunned by both the intimacy and tenderness of her action. 'Well, I'm getting better all the time.' He smiled but thought his answer was really cheesy.

Debbie returned to check the food before returning a couple of minutes later and handing over a white bag containing his sandwich. 'Hope we can make it at the weekend, Geoff,' she said.

'So do I, Debbie. I really do,' he said sincerely.

For the second time in two days, Sutton skipped out of The Parlour and back to the Insignia. He was feeling a warm glow; whether it was the temperature indicating that winter might finally be on its way out or from his recent meeting with Debbie, he didn't know.

He was just about to replace his sunglasses before setting off when his phone rang. It was Harry Temple. They arranged a meeting point where they could have a quick chat about two hundred yards away from Dalton's address.

It wasn't long before Sutton was sitting in the front passenger seat of Temple's work's van. It was clear that Temple knew very little about the investigation. He didn't need to. He didn't know DI Sue Dalton either, which made life easier.

'Geoff, I just need to check, to ensure the authority has come through. It hadn't when I left the office.' Temple scrolled down his phone, checking his latest emails.

Sutton wondered if Turner was having second thoughts or hadn't been able to get the operation sanctioned.

'It's here. Just checking through the form,' Temple said. He was being thorough.

Sutton had only met the guy five minutes earlier but

liked the way he operated. Temple wasn't asking unwanted questions but rightly ensuring that the necessary paperwork and authority were in place rather than dangerously relying on word of mouth.

Harry Temple collected the two recording devices from the rear of his van and put them in his pocket before the two of them made their way to Dalton's flat. They needed to ring the bell twice. Sutton hoped that Dalton wasn't pissed or drugged up and was still willing to have the devices fitted.

She eventually opened the door and they followed her up the stairs to the flat. She looked rough – there were no other words to describe her appearance. She had smudged black rings around her eyes, probably from a mixture of lack of sleep and tears. He looked around for some tell-tale signs and saw that yesterday's half-empty gin bottle was no longer half full. There was a stale smell of alcohol in the kitchen-diner. The flat, usually spotless, was also showing signs of neglect with unwashed glasses keeping company with the smear marks on worktops.

Yesterday's Amazon parcel remained on the dining table.

'Sue,' Sutton said, 'this is Harry Temple, Head of Technical Support. I don't think you two have met.'

The two shook hands and Harry smiled in a friendly manner.

'Can Harry carry on and install the devices?' Sutton asked.

'I don't have a choice,' Dalton said curtly. 'I don't suppose Pete will pop round anyway. Just do it and leave me alone.' She walked out of the room, not wishing to engage any further with Temple or Sutton.

There was no sign of warmth from her. The full impact of her predicament had been disclosed to her during last night's visit. She had failed to exercise the normal duty of care required to ensure that her officers were safe. Not only that, she had unknowingly supplied information to her lover who could well be implicated in their murders.

For the first time in her life, Dalton had found someone

with whom she was totally infatuated. She had seen no wrong in her beloved Pete. She loved him, it was as simple as that. Yet her Pete, Police and Crime Commissioner, used prostitutes. That information alone was enough. The thought of his involvement in the murder of her two colleagues was just too much to deal with.

Dalton was in a mess. Sutton and Singer had known that yesterday and exploited her circumstances to their operational advantage.

Temple took ten minutes to install the two devices, one in the kitchen and the other in the dining area. That was as much as the authorities would sanction. He checked, then rechecked to ensure they were operating correctly.

Dalton only returned to the room when they were about to leave. She was dressed in denim jeans and a maroon crew-neck sweater. She said nothing and Sutton struggled to engage with her. 'Please give me a ring if he pays you a visit,' he said. She already knew his mobile number. Out of kindness and concern he went to give her a hug but she saw him coming and backed off.

Sutton turned around, embarrassed. He looked at Temple, who was already making his way down the stairs. The two men walked back to the car in silence.

Sutton turned to Temple as they got to the Insignia. 'Would you trust her?' he asked.

'That's your area of expertise,' Temple responded. 'She's between a rock and a hard place.'

'She certainly is, Harry. She certainly is. Thanks again for your help.' With that, Sutton opened his car door and Temple went back to his works van.

Geoff had missed the day's briefing. He decided to report back to Bill Singer for an update before ringing Stew Grant.

17

Harry Temple

Pete Roberson had just finished another public engagement at the council offices in Parton city centre. He had a couple of hours free before a meeting with Simon Keys at Holston House to discuss the progress of the missing persons' policy.

His mind drifted to Lola and the excitement of the previous afternoon. He wondered if she was free, then he reminded himself that he had already made an appointment with her for the following evening. Too much of a good thing, he smiled to himself. Unusually he decided on exercise and walked the hundred yards or so to Tesco Express, as opposed to driving.

Roberson ordered another steak bake, pizza slice and this time a Belgian biscuit. Back at the car, he squeezed behind the wheel. He decided it was time to visit his Detective Inspector. He knew that she really wanted to see him and she was the only way he could keep track of the investigation. He was also desperate to know about the connection between the murdered police officers and the missing William Carr, who Roberson knew from Holston House activities. The down side of the visit was that he would no doubt have to endure a weeping, wailing woman. Nevertheless, he could use his charm and comfort her – and you never knew where that might lead.

Driving the Lexus through suburban Parton to Sue Dalton's flat, Roberson stopped for petrol. After filling up, he went to the forecourt shop to pay, passing a black bucket containing bunches of flowers. Roberson paused, his attention drawn to a bunch of roses with a price of £5.50. He took his time looking at the prices before deciding on some rather bedraggled carnations for £2.50. That was more like it, he thought.

A few minutes later, armed with his flowers, Roberson rang Dalton's doorbell.

Her second visitors of the day. Dalton thought it might be staff from the Occupational Health Unit coming early. She descended the stairs after having the first sip of the gin and tonic she had just poured. It was shortly after 10am.

She opened the door and immediately threw her arms around Roberson before he had time to protect himself. He could smell the alcohol on her breath and half-heartedly put his arms around her. It certainly wasn't a reciprocal embrace. He stood back in the doorway and produced the cheap bunch of carnations.

'Thanks Pete, they're lovely,' she said, although they clearly weren't. Roberson knew that for a fact and that was why he'd made the purchase.

He took in Dalton's appearance. She looked awful: little or no make up, denim jeans and a scruffy sweater. He thought that her hair hadn't seen a comb in days. He looked at her disdainfully. There would be no comforting from him.

He followed her up the stairs without asking how she was doing and sat on one of the stools beside the kitchen island. Roberson noticing the greasy marks and the smell of alcohol. He had always been impressed by the way she looked after her flat. It was always spotless and tidy, even though the amount of Springsteen memorabilia around the place was definitely not to his taste.

He was direct. 'Sue, you said on the phone that the missing boy was linked with the murdered officers. What did you mean?'

Dalton answered without any thought to the listening devices. She was mesmerised by Roberson's presence. He had come to see her; he *did* care. 'He was the informant. He was reporting on people using and abusing vulnerable youngsters. The boy was one of them. He used to be a girl, you know, but now he's known as William Carr.'

Roberson was stunned but maintained his composure, allowing Dalton to continue.

'He is still missing and two of my staff are dead – murdered, stabbed, butchered,' she cried.

'Chilter and Wrightson were meeting the informant on the day they died.' She started to weep. 'Pete what are we going to do?' She looked at him, imploring him for help, begging him to hold her, to tell her everything would work out, to provide a solution, to use his influence. To do something, anything, to help her.

We, thought Roberson. Her predicament had nothing to do with him yet his worst fears had been realised.

He didn't answer or move a muscle. The last thing to cross his mind was to give her some comfort. All he wanted to do was to get out of the flat and get away from her. She wasn't any assistance to him while she was in this state. She probably wouldn't be any use to him ever again. She was now no more than a hindrance.

Roberson made to get off the stool. Dalton looked directly at him. Surely he wasn't going? He'd only just got through the door. He must want to stay, to be with her. He hadn't even had a drink or a cup of coffee, nothing.

He wanted out and it had taken her this long to realise it.

She took a long, steady swig of her gin and tonic and composed herself. 'Pete, what did you do with what I told you? About what the informant was saying?'

Roberson stood completely still. He was staring and speechless.

Dalton focused, her eyes never leaving his. 'What is your

involvement in this?' The words now came so naturally to the Detective Inspector.

Roberson, mouth open as if to speak but with no words forthcoming, reached out with his left hand. He picked up the bread knife, abandoned on the kitchen worktop among some crumbs from a half-cut loaf. His fingers curled tightly around its black handle.

'Come on, kill me, Roberson. Kill me. Will it make you feel better? I've nothing worth living for. Come on,' Dalton said in a calm monotone.

Roberson walked towards her, eyes not leaving hers, knife held tightly. At that moment his mobile rang from the inside pocket of his suit but at first he ignored it. However, the continued ringing distracted him from the knife, from Sue Dalton and from killing her.

It was Travis on his phone. The tell-tale, distinctive ringtone had saved Dalton from death. As had become the norm over recent months, when Travis rang Roberson answered. Travis had ultimate control and Roberson had to react immediately. Without a word, he dropped the knife, descending the stairs in haste before slamming the door. He reached for his Travis phone as he walked back to the Lexus.

Dalton collapsed on a chair in the dining area, head in hands, crying and breathing deeply. She felt a release, like floating. Reaching for a bottle – and not the gin – she opened the top of her sedatives. Time for sleep, she said to herself, as she emptied the contents of the bottle on to the table. The scattered gleaming white tablets looked so appealing.

She walked around to where she had placed her gin and tonic, returned to her seat and the tablets. With her right hand, she picked up her drink; with her left, she placed a pill between her lips. A swig and a swallow. Then she did it again … and again…

Half an hour later, Sutton was sitting with Bill Singer receiving an update of the morning's briefing. He'd already checked the response to the previous day's media appeal for

William. It had been poor and he had rung Stew to update him, whilst trying to stay as upbeat as possible.

His phone rang. It was Dalton, slurred and incomprehensible. Sutton shouted down the phone, 'Stay awake, Sue. Walk, walk!' He ended the call almost as soon as it started.

Inspector Cheryl Connor was the Control-Room Supervisor on duty, sitting in an elevated position, headset on, looking at the screen of ongoing incidents with the staff facing her doing likewise. It was like a scene from the original sixties' TV series *Star Trek*, with the supervisor as Captain Kirk on the bridge on the Starship Enterprise.

Connor answered Sutton's call via her headset.

'Inspector, it's Geoff Sutton from Operation Trust. This is an urgent call concerning an officer, Detective Inspector Sue Dalton. She may have taken an overdose.' He gave Dalton's address.

Connor, calm and efficient, replied. 'Incident created. We will contact the ambulance service and ask for a forced entry,' she informed Sutton, whilst tapping away on her screen.

Sutton grabbed his coat and, together with Bill Singer, ran out of the office door. The pair of them set off to Dalton's flat. This time they took an unmarked works' car, a Skoda Octavia that wove its way gracefully through the traffic. Singer spoke briefly to Ron Turner on the phone and provided him with an update. Turner requested further contact as soon as Dalton's condition was known. Typically he also requested that the listening devices be seized immediately, rightly believing that Roberson's visit had precipitated Dalton's actions.

There was no magnetic blue light in the car to alert other road users and cut their travelling time, but Singer still made good progress. They arrived at Dalton's upstairs flat, The entrance door hadn't just been forced, it had been destroyed; only remnants of wood were sticking to the frame. The stairs that rose up to the living area were visible from the pavement. The road was partially blocked off by the emergency vehicles, one ambulance, two marked panda cars and Singer's Octavia.

Two uniformed officers were stationed at the entrance. The paramedics were already inside, attending to Dalton.

Sutton and Singer waited outside for what seemed like hours before Dalton finally appeared, comatose on a stretcher. She looked peaceful, her eyes closed but surrounded by smudged mascara and dried tears. Her body was covered in a red woollen blanket and there was an intravenous drip on the inside of her left elbow.

As she was being placed in the ambulance, Sutton made a polite enquiry to the green-uniformed staff. 'How's she doing?'

'Too soon to say. I've got her medication,' came the abrupt reply. The paramedic produced an empty tablet container. His tone brokered no further conversation; what he was really saying was, 'Shut up, we are busy, let us get on with our job.' Time was an essence, due to Dalton's condition.

The driver illuminated the blue lights and activated the siren. They set off at speed to Parton General Hospital.

Singer produced his warrant card and asked the two officers at the entrance to Dalton's building to arrange some repairs to the door. He then asked them to visit a few of the premises either side of Dalton's flat to complete some basic house-to-house enquiries and to ask if anyone had CCTV that might help. At that time, no one knew the events that had occurred an hour or so earlier and both Singer and Sutton were experienced enough not to rely totally on technical evidence.

They climbed the stairs to the kitchen-diner. Sutton knew exactly where Temple had placed the devices some three hours earlier. He removed them without a problem and rang him. 'Harry, we've had an incident at Dalton's flat. Not sure if our man arrived or not, but she's on her way to hospital. We need this to be transcribed immediately.'

'Just bring it over, no problem,' came the immediate reply.

The two uniformed officers knocked on a few doors

as part of the house-to-house enquiries but didn't get any information. Many of the houses were currently empty, which was hardly surprising as due to the time of day most people would be at work. The area was popular with young professionals. The same officers would return later, before the end of their shift, and contact the Incident Room if they had any success.

Singer drove back to Parton HQ to get the transcription completed and also to brief Turner. All of a sudden, after a couple of days slow slog, the investigation was increasing in pace.

Before going in to see Temple, Sutton obtained the necessary exhibit number from Tom Heath who was still imprisoned in his cell-like office.

Temple was as good as his word. 'Grab a cup of coffee,' he said, pointing at the kettle. 'I'll get one of the techs on to this immediately. Three copies OK?'

'Cheers, Harry,' said Sutton.

Within five minutes, the designated tech officer came through from the workroom. He possessed the biggest and bushiest beard Sutton had ever seen. He looked as though he hadn't seen daylight for six months, let alone spoken to someone. He produced one of the listening devices and said to Temple, 'This one was only working intermittently. There's nothing at all to transcribe for some reason.'

'Shit! It was bloody working when I installed it. I checked it twice.' Temple swore to himself.

'I'll try the other one.' The Brian Blessed lookalike went back into the bowels of the workshop, like a hedgehog who'd just been woken up from hibernation and decided it was still far too cold.

Singer and Sutton couldn't look at each other. If the other device was also buggered, the whole plan had been a waste of time – and what was worse was that Dalton had overdosed.

There was a good twenty minutes of tension before the tech officer returned carrying three pieces of paper. 'Bingo.'

He smiled, a couple of teeth just about visible from the undergrowth that surrounded his mouth.

Without reading the transcript, Sutton led the way with Singer following. Turner's door was open. Bravely, and without asking, they walked straight in and sat down. Turner was making a landline call. Sutton placed the third copy of the transcript on his desk.

Turner replaced the receiver, cutting off in mid-sentence, and then took his time to study the A4 document. Eventually he spoke. 'He nearly killed her, the bastard. The shit bottled it.'

'Why didn't he finish it?' asked Sutton. 'Why did he answer the phone? What was so very important? It doesn't make sense.'

Singer remained silent, still taking in the contents of the transcript. Then he looked directly at Turner. 'Boss, he has got to come in. The bloke's unhinged and dangerous. We need to arrest him as soon as possible.'

'Give me thirty minutes,' Turner said. 'I need to update our Temporary Chief Constable at some stage about Roberson's involvement. The best way of doing so would be if Roberson was either arrested or in custody. I can then try and justify why I've gone behind his back. Once we've got Roberson in custody, we need to be in a position that whatever he comes up with during interview he's still going on a charge sheet.'

Sutton was still poring over the papers and their contents. He looked up. 'He's disclosed very little to Dalton that implicates him in the murders of Mike and Linda, or in William's disappearance. So, apart from the assault on Dalton taking her to the brink, that's it. No visual, just Sue's words. Depending on Sue's condition it would be a matter of interpretation if he was responsible.'

'You're right, Geoff,' Turner agreed. 'There is also the issue of how far we have gone along the lines of entrapping him and how that may, or may not, stand up in court. That was last night's dream. Go to the hospital. I need to know what

Dalton can give us. More importantly, of course, what's the update on her condition?'

Sutton and Singer left a subdued Turner in his office. It was a strange atmosphere after a high-risk strategy that had so nearly paid off. However, Dalton had been pushed to the edge, of that there was no doubt. Sutton took some comfort from the fact that he hadn't forced Roberson to visit, and that at some stage Roberson and Dalton's meeting was inevitable. The outcome was always going to be unknown and unpredictable.

Singer drove again; they were still in the Octavia. This time no haste was required.

He broke the silence. 'Turner's got to level with Conting, no matter what he thinks about him and his relationship with Roberson. I think Roberson will crack when he's in custody, I really do. Plus, he's unpredictable at the moment and potentially dangerous.'

They pulled up at Accident and Emergency at Parton Hospital. The hospital was a new build, opened just before the annual winter rush of patients in late November of the previous year. It was a huge complex, like a massive spaceship that had just landed in the middle of nowhere. Located on the outskirts of Parton, its situation made it accessible to the arterial road links that avoided the city centre.

Similar to most hospitals, there appeared to be a distinct lack of parking facilities for the general public even though the place was surrounded by barren fields. No doubt this area wouldn't be earmarked for more car parking but for a housing development in the near future .

Driving into the hospital, there were signs everywhere for wards and departments but the most distinctive, written in bright red, warned of clamping should you park illegally.

As this wasn't an emergency and they were in an unmarked car, Singer drove round and round until he finally spotted a vehicle moving out from a pay-and-display parking bay. The driver stopped and, as he passed the Octavia, wound down the window. 'There's thirty minutes left on this ticket,' the elderly man offered. Singer took the ticket gratefully. The driver's gesture was both thoughtful and considerate, a welcome change to the selfishness and greed that often motivated many of the serious crimes they investigated.

Singer led the way, following the signs to Accident and Emergency. He had his Parton Constabulary folder; should Dalton be in a position to talk, at least he could record a written account. They made their way through a maze of corridors, uniformed staff, trolleys, and signs upon signs to the main emergency reception point.

Singer produced his warrant card and showed it to the kindly looking, but obviously highly stressed, middle-aged female receptionist.

'We are colleagues of Sue Dalton. Is there any chance we can see her? If not, can we have a very quick word with the doctor who is looking after her? She came in about an hour or so ago,' Singer asked politely.

The receptionist looked at her computer screen, reaching for her glasses from the desk as she did so. 'Have you got a date of birth?' she enquired.

'Sorry, no. I would guess she is in her mid-forties,' Singer said.

'Please take a seat. Someone will come out and see you.' She removed her glasses and returned them to her desk then rubbed her eyes. Sutton thought she must be on a series of early shifts; she looked extremely tired.

They sat in the large reception area alongside a large queue of patients, some on trolleys, some in wheelchairs. Most of the people waiting were elderly. For many, the reason for their visit was patently obvious.

The sign stating how long your projected wait would be to see a doctor was located in a place where everyone could view it. It seemed that, for some reason, your attention was continually drawn to that point.

Sutton's concentration on the sign was lost momentarily

when his eyes were drawn to an elderly man in a wheelchair, shoes and socks removed to show an obviously broken ankle. Although he was desperately trying to control the pain, the poor man's groans brought him an unwelcome audience. Fortunately a passing nurse spotted him. 'I think we will take you through for some pain relief,' she said kindly. 'Your name?'

'Wilf,' came the reply, through gritted teeth.

After what seemed an age but was no more than ten minutes a white-coated male, stethoscope swinging around his neck, entered their waiting area from the swing doors facing them. 'Mr Singer?' the young voice enquired politely.

'Yep,' replied Singer.

'Please come this way.'

Sutton followed them, making use of the hand-gel machine on the nearby wall. They moved through the swing doors. Sutton glanced around the open-plan facility in front of him, with its curtains giving some semblance of privacy when examinations took place. There was the buzz of machines, intermixed with mostly hushed conversations between nurses, doctors, porters and paramedics. He had been to many A&E departments and the organised chaos he observed there never ceased to amaze him.

His scrutiny was short lived as both he and Singer were escorted into a small office, with one examination couch and a desk supporting a laptop.

'Please take a seat, gentlemen. I'm Doctor Radcliffe. May I ask what relation you are to Sue Dalton?'

'We're not relatives, we're work colleagues. Is it possible to have a quick word with Sue? It could be time-critical as part of a serious investigation,' Sutton said, emphasising the need to talk with her.

'I'm afraid not. Sue passed away some ten minutes or so ago. We did everything to save her but the mixture of the alcohol and the drugs she had consumed caused irreparable brain damage and organ failure. The post-mortem will be give us the full picture. I am very sorry,' Dr Tony Radcliffe explained sincerely.

An awful silence followed. Neither Singer nor Sutton could look at each other. They had both known Sue over a period of years, not as a close friend but as a respected colleague. She had undoubtedly messed up and her career was finished, but the more they investigated the tragic deaths of her two officers, the more they thought that Sue's relationship with Roberson had been her undoing.

Singer looked blankly at the bare ceiling as Sutton, elbows on his knees supporting his head, hands supporting his head, looked down at his dark-brown shoes. Another waste of a life, he thought. And we still haven't a clue about the whereabouts of William Carr. Everything points to Roberson.

Dr Radcliffe broke their silence. 'Do you know who is her next of kin?'

Singer answered quickly, his voice breaking as he spoke. 'I believe she has a sister who lives down south. We'll make a few enquires and I'll get someone to give you a ring. Thanks for your help, doctor. Come on, Geoff, heads up. We have work to do.'

He patted Sutton on the shoulder, a moment of tenderness and concern between the two colleagues.

18

Ron Turner

Sutton and Singer made the long walk back to the car through many corridors that all looked the same. They didn't speak or acknowledge anyone on their return journey. They had no wish to communicate with anyone.

Sutton was still carrying his folder. What a waste of life, he thought again.

He always thought the world should stop when a death or other tragedy occurred but it never did. They passed nurses, patients, porters, doctors and cleaners, all hurrying around the hospital, ignorant of their recent loss.

'I hope they have bloody clamped you,' Sutton said to Singer in an effort to lighten the mood as they left the main building and arrived at the car park.

'So it's me and not us who is in danger of being clamped,' replied Singer.

The two of them chuckled, relieved at being able to share some emotion. To their surprise they hadn't been clamped. Climbing into the car, Singer rang the OHU and informed them of Sue Dalton's death, as well as the need to contact the hospital and inform them of the next of kin.

Sutton rang Turner's mobile. For once it was answered. 'We need to speak, boss. Are you available?'

'Yep, available for the next hour. I've got an appointment

with the Chief later.'

Sutton and Singer made their way back to Parton HQ. After a while they had a general conversation about Dalton's excellent career, which had been totally ruined over the past week. Sutton thought that her life would never have been the same. She would have faced criminal proceedings and, whatever the outcome of that scenario, she would have been disciplined and would undoubtedly have been sacked. Yet, knowing Sue, it would be the knowledge that her actions and her relationship had been responsible for the deaths of her officers that would have haunted her forever.

Not for the first time over the past few days, Sutton and Singer sat facing the increasingly troubled Head of Parton CID, Ron Turner. Sutton noticed a subtle change in that Turner's desk was moderately untidy. It wasn't in the Simon Keys' class but there were more items occupying the space.

'Well, guys, some good news, please,' said Turner, not looking at his colleagues.

Sutton replied immediately. 'Dalton died in hospital about an hour ago. Very sad.'

'Shit, it just goes from bad to worse,' Turner said resignedly. He gazed out from behind his desk around his fine office. The accolades that had followed him were evidence of his excellent and rewarding career that was nearing its end. What on earth had he done to deserve this investigation? It was the worst the force had ever seen. And now it had just taken another turn, and not for the better.

'I'm seeing our beloved Alan Conting within the next hour. Whatever else I tell him, I need to inform him of Sue Dalton's death. I can tell him truthfully that it was an overdose. I am not going to speak to him about Roberson's involvement. I'll do that tomorrow morning, when Roberson is arrested and in custody. I will take the flak. Conting will probably go berserk and he has good grounds for doing so, given the circumstances.'

He looked around his office again, no steely-eyed stare

now.

He continued, 'My only hope is that we get a result from Roberson's arrest. Either he rolls over and talks, or we get something back from searching his car and apartment. God knows what Conting's responsibilities are when his PCC is locked up. Contact the Home Office? I can also inform him of ACC Harries breach of force procedure when he authorised the payment to William without a senior officer present, although that seems to be a relatively minor issue at this time,' he said, for once musing over someone else's problem.

Turner went on, 'Roberson's arrest, tomorrow morning first thing. I want you parked up outside the Waterside. He is due back at County Hall for some committee meeting at 9am. I've spoken to the area commander and a marked panda car will be made available for you, with two uniformed officers. They will not be given the name of the suspect. Roberson's not going to kick off, it will be a low-key stop. Bill, you will arrest him for conspiracy to murder and bring him into Parton City police station. There will be a team waiting to search his home. When he's arrested we must secure his phones – he's got at least two. Geoff, don't forget to record any significant statement he makes when he's arrested. When you've got him secure, ring me. Then, and only then, will I inform Conting.' He paused for a second, 'Any questions?'

Neither Singer nor Sutton said a word.

'Right, I have an investigation update to give to Conting, and the only news I can give him, is the death of yet another serving officer. Speak tomorrow, gentlemen.' Turner rose from his chair, shuffled his papers and left his office before Sutton and Singer could move.

19

Robes

Roberson was back from Holston House after another highly unproductive meeting with the incredibly scruffy Simon Keys. He became concerned when Keys mentioned the police visits to the home. Keys was somewhat evasive when Roberson asked him direct questions about the purpose of those visits. His response was that they were making background enquiries in the missing person investigation of William Carr, a former resident at Holston.

Earlier, when he left Dalton's flat, Roberson had rung the Travis hotline. He was exceptionally glad he was out of that situation. He had lost it big time with Dalton, and when he had time to reflect back, it worried him that he had been so irrational. Thankfully Travis's intervention, his phone call, had saved both him and Dalton. Or so he thought.

What an end to a relationship. He wouldn't see her again. How right he was in that assumption.

Now, back at his apartment in the Waterside, Roberson poured himself an early gin and tonic. His conversation with Dunc Travis was characteristically short. Travis wanted to meet with him at 6.30pm that evening on his, Roberson's, boat. Since the night when Roberson had run over that girl and the blackmailing had started, he had never met Travis. Travis had called the meeting for 'a catch up'.

It was 5.30pm when Sutton pulled up outside the Grants' residence. He noted that the nights were getting lighter; it was still just about daylight when he rang the bell.

He thought he would take the opportunity of speaking to them personally. He hadn't a lot to impart but he didn't want to go straight home alone and thought he might be able to cadge a drink with good, loyal company.

Tina opened the door. For her, she was dressed casually in a pair of top-of-the-range black denim jeans with a crisp white blouse. Her eyes gave the impression she had been crying.

'Come on in, Geoff. Have you found William?' she asked anxiously.

Sutton didn't answer and Tina stopped in her tracks. Her hands shot to her face, palms on her cheeks. 'He's dead,' she said in a quiet, controlled voice.

'No. Sorry, Tina, I have no real news of any significance. The response to the press appeal has been disappointing, to say the least. Can I have a drink?' Sutton asked.

'Tea, coffee?'

'No, gin and tonic, if possible, Tina,' Sutton said firmly as they joined Stew, who was sitting at the kitchen island playing on his iPad.

'Make that two, darling,' said Stew.

'Tell you what, let's make it three.' Tina reached into the drinks cabinet.

For the next half hour, Sutton was able to relax. They talked about everything bar William and the ongoing investigation. There was nothing worthwhile for Sutton to impart. The conversation moved from who would fill the full-back slot at Upper Parton RFC after an injury crisis to the planned garden patio to go with last year's purchases of a conservatory and summer house.

Finally Sutton drained his glass, picked up his Barbour

and headed out to his car. He hoped that tomorrow he could give the Grants some answers as to the whereabouts of their missing foster child. It really was the very least they deserved.

***

At the same moment, Roberson was leaving the Grebe apartment. He was fortified not only by two large gin and tonics but also by a small weapon, a sharp kitchen knife, concealed in the inside pocket of his long black overcoat. It was the second time in one day that he had armed himself with a knife.

It would take only five minutes for him to leave the apartment, walk along the decking to the prime position where his boat *Robes* was berthed. It was a cool evening but luckily there was no biting frost and his footing was secure as he walked purposefully to his destination.

Dunc Travis and Stanislav Zenden had done their reconnaissance in daylight and taken up a position to observe Roberson and his journey to the rendezvous. Travis loved this area and, more importantly to him, the trappings that went with it. He had called the meeting not because he desperately wanted to see Roberson but because he needed to ensure he was on track and it was business as usual after the recent unwanted attention. In addition, he had a business proposition to put to him and Travis, for his own entertainment, wanted to see Roberson's reaction.

Roberson was nervous as he approached his boat. He had no control over the situation, other than the knife he'd taken from the kitchen.

He approached *Robes*, glancing nervously around. At this time of night and time of year the place was quiet. No one was out for an evening stroll, jealously looking and dreaming of what might have been, enviously looking at the boats berthed in the East Marina. It was early enough for those with reservations in the restaurants along the Waterside not to have taken their seats. It was probably the quietest time of year for the busy night-time economy of Parton.

Roberson climbed over the ropes that secured his pristine white vessel. It gleamed, reflecting the moonlight and lapping water. The boat looked beautiful, but for him it was the status of *Robes* that mattered as opposed to any lifelong ambition to sail the ocean blue.

Due in part to his size and also his lack of fitness, Roberson almost lost his balance as he clambered on board onto the Sessa C35. He had purchased it from a dealer on the south coast costing him nearly £200,000. He walked forward to the cockpit, which contained a mass of instruments and dials, and sank down on the white foam-covered captain's seat capable of swivelling a full 360 degrees. He purposefully had his back to the sea and was looking towards the boardwalk, the restaurants and the relatively empty bars.

Dunc and Stan had observed Roberson from their observation point located in a nearby bar, laughing quietly as he literally tripped onto the boat. Travis left Stan to watch and record the meeting with his phone and made his own way to speak to Roberson. Stan, being the professional operative, saw his boss meet up with Roberson then took up a covert position on the deck of a neighbouring vessel. He guessed it might not be an uneventful encounter; not only was he in a better position to record the meeting, he could also react if necessary. He knew full well Roberson's attention would be fully focussed on meeting Travis.

Roberson saw Travis emerge from the darkness and walk along the boardwalk from about thirty yards away. His eyes trained on him and he naturally failed to notice Stan's movements, moments later, as he positioned himself on board a neighbouring vessel. Roberson reached inside his coat, seeking comfort from the knife handle.

Travis skipped over the landing ropes, arriving on the deck in one swift, graceful movement. He stood facing Roberson a couple of yards away on the deck area with a confident smirk across his face.

As it was the first time that Roberson had ever seen Travis in the flesh he was surprised by his appearance. Travis was not a portly, late middle-aged business man but a smart, fit and casually dressed young professional. He exuded confidence and arrogance. Roberson recognised the similarities in himself.

Roberson was aching within; he had never felt such loathing for a person in his life. His tormentor stood in front of him, grinning from ear to ear.

'How's it going Pete?' Travis asked with mock concern.

Roberson couldn't answer; he needed composure now, more than ever.

'Come on, Pete, just asking how you are. It's a welfare check from a concerned boss.'

'Bloody fine, bloody fine.' Roberson just about spat out the words, hands deep in the pockets of his overcoat .

'Just checking it's business as usual, Pete, after your run of recent bad luck. I'm here to make sure my most valuable asset is OK.' The smirk reappeared on Travis's face as he finished the sentence.

'I'm here, I'm fucking here, shithole,' spat Roberson.

'That's good, Pete. Got a bit of a proposition for you. I'm taking the boat, your boat, as a reward for the bit of extra overtime I've incurred recently.' He waved his phone at Roberson, a boastful reminder of the Nina video. His eyes never left Roberson, who met his gaze with increasing anger.

Roberson reached across with his right hand to the inside left-hand pocket of his overcoat with surprising swiftness. The weapon emerged immediately, the blade glinting against the moonlight. He lunged forward, not at Travis but at Stanislav Zenden, who had already anticipated that Roberson was probably armed and had acted immediately, having previously stopped his phone recording in anticipation of the action. Zenden swiftly and expertly arrived onto the deck of *Robes*, threw himself forward and pushed Travis aside. Roberson lunged forward, knife in hand and met with fresh air. Stan was a highly trained operative, Roberson a total amateur. Zenden had seen him coming and merely stepped aside, kicking out at Roberson who was now unbalanced. Stan hit his target, the inside of Roberson's right knee. Mr Parton, the Police and Crime Commissioner, sprawled pathetically across the white decking area of the boat he had owned only moments previously.

Travis walked forward, picked up the knife and threw it overboard. 'Not your best move, Pete. I'll be in touch soon to collect the keys to the boat,' he said nonchalantly, as both he and Stan climbed neatly out of *Robes* and started walking away along the boardwalk.

From his prone and embarrassing position, Roberson was sure he could hear them laughing. He looked pathetic and he knew it.

He managed to drag himself to his feet. There was no one about – he would have been surprised if there had been. With his right hand on the landing rope, he managed to lever himself out of the boat. He walked back to the Waterside block and his top-floor apartment. His eyes were full of tears. Travis had broken him and taking his boat was the ultimate humiliation. There must be some way out of this bloody mess, he thought.

Once inside the splendour of Glebe, Roberson threw down his coat and poured himself the largest and strongest gin and tonic he had ever had the opportunity to drink. He placed his half-pint glass under the ice machine in the fridge door and rubbed the tears from his eyes. He gazed out across the East Parton Marina; not only had he been totally humiliated and lost control, he had now lost his bloody boat.

The ice clattered into the glass. Roberson took a huge gulp of his drink, feeling the alcohol oozing down the back of his throat. There had to be a way out because he faced ruin. Another gulp of gin and tonic. His only thought at this time was the timely death of Travis and his mind started to play games on the best way of eradicating his blackmailer.

Two more drinks followed. Roberson's thoughts were in overdrive. Maybe he could sabotage *Robes* before it became another of Travis's assets. Maybe he could hire a private detective to find some dirt on Travis, so that he could play him at his own game.

There wouldn't be much sleep for Roberson tonight.

***

That was also the case for Geoff Sutton, Bill Singer and Ron Turner. All three were at home contemplating the following day's events, Sutton with his usual glass of red wine, Turner with a Glenmorangie with ice, and teetotaller Singer with a glass of Schweppes bitter lemon.

20

Bill Singer

Sutton's alarm pinged at 6am the following morning. He showered and changed then consumed a large mug of tea. He had neither the time nor the inclination for food this morning. The arrangement was that Singer would pick him up at 6.45, giving them ample time to liaise with the uniformed staff who, unbeknown to them, had been detailed to carry out the stop on Roberson's Lexus.

Sutton looked outside as he waited for Singer to arrive. He was both nervous and excited. He really wanted this to work out, not just for himself but because hopefully it would shed some light on William's disappearance and provide some answers for Stew and Tina.

Suddenly, from absolutely nowhere, Sutton was full of emotion. Not for the first time in the last few days he felt tearful. He was tired but adrenaline was driving him on. He had enjoyed the excitement for a short time but a big part of him wished for some semblance of normality to return. He had the date with Debbie to look forward to and missed meeting her this morning. Tears started appearing as he waited in the privacy of his own home and thought about his murdered colleagues. He was brought back to reality when Singer pulled up outside his house.

Here we go, he thought. Nervous anticipation started to

replace his melancholy state.

'Morning, Geoff, fit and well?' came the polite enquiry from Singer.

'Fine and bloody dandy. Bring it on, Billy boy, bring it on.' Sutton smiled, his recent emotions already a distant memory.

Turner had given Sutton a mobile number for the Uniform Inspector covering their operation. Inspector Harrison answered Sutton's call. 'Bill Harrison, how can I help?'

'Bill, it's Geoff Sutton from Operation Trust,' Sutton said.

'Geoff, how you doing? Haven't seen you for years.'

Sutton recognised the voice. 'Bloody hell, it's Barnacle Bill!' he said, referring to Harrison's well-known nickname that resulted from his love for fishing.

'Not much fishing at the moment, pal. Problems with the back. Anyway, how can we help? You need a couple of uniforms from 8am, so my boss tells me. He didn't tell me anything else.'

'Yes please, Bill. Can we meet them at about 7.45, in the car park of St Oswald's Methodist Church?'

'Not a problem. Take care, Geoff. Good to speak to you.' Harrison rang off.

St. Oswald's Methodist Church car park was about half a mile from Roberson's Waterside apartment. It was a quiet, out of the way setting, ideal for a quick briefing for Harrison's staff.

Singer pulled the Octavia into the car park. It was empty, as they had both expected. Having said that, neither Sutton nor Singer would have been aware of any daily services; the only time they had ventured into church recently was to attend funerals.

Sadly a few more were about to take place in the immediate future.

Sutton and Singer had been in place for approximately five minutes when the marked panda car arrived at their location. There was a polite shaking of hands. P.C. 1342 Jim

Atkins and his colleague PC 873 Ian Urwin were on their first early shift of three and were suitability enthusiastic at being designated for a job that no one knew anything about. It also allowed them to be excused from their monthly self-defence training. They looked athletic and keen, wearing their high-viz kit, with all the necessary equipment hanging from their utility belts.

Just the ticket, thought Sutton. He didn't know either officer personally but he estimated that they probably had about eight years combined service.

The four of them sat in the Octavia, Singer and Sutton up front and the two uniformed officers in the rear. Bill conducted the briefing. 'Gents, this is a straightforward stop and detain. I will then arrest the subject. We need to secure any phones that he will probably have in his possession at the time of the stop – we believe he has two. He will be driving a Silver Lexus, registration number BC18TLX, and leaving the Waterside Apartments anytime from about 8.30am. We will give you the off, as soon as he leaves the underground car park. Then you take up a mobile position behind him and perform the stop in a safe place of your choice. It's as simple and straightforward as that. There are no warning markers against the subject and we are not expecting any trouble.'

The usual 'Any questions?' was greeted with the usual silence. The officers didn't even ask the name of the subject. They were going to get a hell of a shock, smiled Sutton to himself.

The time was 8.00am. Sutton and Singer went to a drive-through Costa coffee then parked up outside the Waterside Apartments, sipped their coffee and waited.

***

Unsurprisingly, Roberson had a disturbed night. He woke soon after 6am and roamed his apartment, like a lion stalking his prey. His mind raced continually but he needed composure and a little time to consider his move on Travis.

Breakfast was a huge bowl of granola, washed down with an extra-strong espresso. He dressed in a black suit, a crisp, white, open-neck shirt and brown brogues. It was after the 8.30am news headlines when he left the apartment, grabbing his two mobiles on the way out. He took the lift rather than the stairs down to the basement. His silver Lexus, sparkling clean, seemed to smile at him and raised his spirits. He opened the car from twenty metres away by activating the key fob. The vehicle's hazard warning lights flashed and moments later Roberson squeezed himself into the driver's seat.

He reversed out of the bay and onto the street. It was a dull day but milder than recently as the car emerged, like a dolphin rising above the waves, onto a mini-roundabout then the main thoroughfare, Gull Lane.

Sutton shouted into his radio, 'Its an off, off, off. Right onto Gull Lane, travelling east towards the A325.'

'Yes. Yes, 1342 received,' came the immediate response from Jim Atkins.

Singer pulled out onto Gull Lane and followed Roberson at a safe distance. The marked police vehicle soon overtook them with PC Ian Urwin in the driver's seat and Jim Atkins his front-seat passenger.

Sutton saw the blue lights being illuminated some way ahead. The journey was over in a couple of minutes as the Lexus slowed immediately in front of the police vehicle and then pulled in to a small designated layby, coming to a halt and parking up safely.

Roberson had been driving along with the Travis issue monopolising his thoughts. In his rear-view mirror, he saw a marked police vehicle immediately behind. Moments later, its flashing blue lights were activated. He rechecked his mirror and saw the front-seat passenger indicating for him to pull over. What the hell did they want, he wondered, as he indicated his intention to comply with their request. It wouldn't take long, he thought, once they realised who he was.

PCs Urwin and Atkins pulled up behind Roberson, with Sutton and Singer slightly further back. Roberson slowly extricated himself from behind the driver's wheel. His suit jacket flapped in the breeze as he walked back towards the two officers sitting in their vehicle.

Urwin and Atkins immediately recognised their Police and Crime Commissioner, Pete Roberson. Atkins, who had also got out of his vehicle, met him halfway.

'Can I help, officer?' Roberson said, in total control.

'Would you like to take a seat in the car, sir? There are just a couple of questions we would like to ask,' Atkins said with a slight tremor in his voice.

'Do you know who I am, officer?' was the predictable reply. Roberson's tone was dismissive.

Singer quickly arrived on the scene, much to the relief of the two uniformed officers.

'Mr Roberson, my name is Detective Inspector Bill Singer and I am arresting you for conspiracy to murder,' Singer said it with absolute confidence. He continued, 'You do not have to say anything but it may harm your defence if you do not mention when questioned something which you later rely on in court. Anything you do say may be given in evidence.'

As Singer spoke, Roberson's knees buckled and he started to sweat profusely.

'Do you understand the words of the caution, Mr Roberson?' Singer finished, as PC Jim Urwin secured the handcuffs around the wrists of his most famous prisoner to date.

Roberson was speechless. Sutton thought how pointless it was trying to record a statement from a prisoner who couldn't actually speak. The PCC looked as though he'd been shot.

Singer took hold of his arm and walked with him to the marked police vehicle. He had to assist him in doing so.

Singer said, 'Mr Roberson, we have the power to search you for both evidence of an offence or to prevent harm to both yourself and us.'

PC Urwin quickly and discreetly searched his prisoner and recovered two phones, which Roberson had placed in the two inside pockets of his jacket. He immediately handed them both over to Sutton, who had the evidence bags ready and waiting.

'Why have you got two phones, Mr Roberson?' Sutton asked firmly.

Roberson's mouth opened and closed but he didn't utter word. Sutton wondered if he really wanted to speak but was in so much shock that he was unable to do so.

The uniformed officers placed Roberson in the rear of the Octavia. Accompanied by Sutton, Singer drove the short distance to the central custody suite at Parton City Centre Police Station.

Still not a word was spoken.

Sutton, from his position in the rear of the vehicle, glanced across to his right towards Roberson. The PCC's eyes were staring forward, his brow breaking out in beads of perspiration. Sutton recognised the obvious signs. Roberson was in total shock.

The car pulled up in a secure area enclosed by a high metal fence, out of view from the general public. From now on all events would be recorded by the high-tech CCTV system that was required in all custody suites to ensure both the integrity of due process and the safety of everyone who visited or worked in this high-risk environment.

Singer pulled at Roberson's arm. Roberson's size and immobility, coupled with his handcuffs, caused him some discomfort as he left the vehicle, but neither Singer nor Sutton cared.

Sutton took out his phone, whilst Singer pressed the buzzer that informed the Custody Officer of the arrival of yet another guest. When he was out of Roberson's earshot, he rang Ron Turner and informed him of the arrest and the recovery of the two phones. Turner had secured John Seaton's technical support services to interrogate the phones as soon as Roberson was booked in. The flat was secure and the two uniform officers were at the scene, awaiting the arrival of a search team.

Turner now had to deal with Alan Conting.

A sharp knock on the door of the best office in the building allowed Turner to gain access to the Chief Constable's domain. It was located in the building that doubled up as the county's headquarters, adjoining Parton City Centre Police Station,.

Turner was no stranger to the Chief's empire. He had, over the years, been a fairly frequent visitor for promotion boards, crime and intelligence updates. He believed he had seen it all before – but he could never in a million years have anticipated this particular meeting.

Once inside Conting's office, Turner took a deep breath and composed himself as the current leader of Parton Constabulary finished off a phone call. Turner was going to take control of the situation, despite their difference in rank. He had known Conting for a lengthy period of time and didn't rate him. Turner's feelings were not lost on Conting, who avoided his Head of CID as much as conceivably possible.

Turner looked around the room whilst Conting completed his call. It reflected Conting with its fancy art landscapes scattered around the walls that had absolutely no obvious connection to police work. Every picture tells a story, thought Turner.

Conting put the phone down. 'Ron, you wanted to see me about Operation Trust. You have a development?'

'Yes, sir, we have made an arrest.'

'That's excellent, Ron! Who?' asked Conting, already anticipating a triumphant press conference. 'I'll inform the Police and Crime Commissioner. Brilliant news.'

'He already knows,' said Turner. He couldn't help himself. 'He is the suspect. He's in custody downstairs.'

'What? You've arrested the PCC? On what evidence?' Conting grabbed a glass on his desk and gulped down water. He then refilled his glass from the expensive water fountain located in the corner of his office.

In for a penny, in for a pound, thought Turner. 'He's been involved in a relationship with the late Sue Dalton. She was giving him information on the informant reports made by our missing person, William Carr. An envelope was recovered from William's bedroom containing the informant's money. The envelope was addressed to Pete Roberson. We carried out surveillance when Roberson made a phone call to Dalton, before disguising himself and visiting an escort – although that is a side issue. We detained him this morning, secured his two phones, and we're about to search his apartment,' Turner finished.

'Who authorised the surveillance, the conversation between him and Dalton? And why was I not informed, Turner?' Conting was seething, immediately dropping 'Ron' from his address.

'The authority came via a colleague of mine from a neighbouring force with the required rank. I didn't inform you because I didn't want you to feel compromised by your close relationship with the PCC,' said Turner, growing in confidence.

'You didn't trust me, did you?' Conting snarled.

'No, I didn't,' Turner said simply and honestly. It was a comment made by someone who knew he was due to retire in the not too distant future. 'I have to go, sir. Operational necessity. But I have updated you.' He turned around and walked out, feeling better already and not giving the stunned Temporary Chief Constable any opportunity to respond further.

In the custody area of the adjacent building Singer, his hand firmly on Roberson's left elbow, guided the PCC along the bare, white-walled corridor. A ten-yard walk took him into the working environment of the custody suite itself that for this particular shift belonged to Sergeant Quinn, an officer with twenty-years' service, the last five of which he had spent working in this domain. Quinn relished the role and responsibility; this was his gig and he was in charge. He sat in an elevated position, looking slightly down on the prisoners.

He had three computer screens in front of him to record prisoner details, circumstances of arrest and any special, individual requirements to ensure the safety of all concerned. Behind him hung a very large whiteboard showing the prisoners' surnames, the offences under investigation, their detention time and any subsequent reviews, together with their allocated cell numbers.

Quinn had four experienced detention officers to help him in his duties, all of whom were ex-cops and knew the job inside out. His expression did not change at all as Roberson stood in front of him, accompanied by Bill Singer with Sutton bringing up the rear.

'Inspector, what's this gentlemen been arrested for?' he enquired, going through the booking-in process.

Bill supplied the circumstances whilst Sutton observed Roberson. It had been a complete turnaround, Sutton thought to himself; Roberson had been cocky and arrogant as he approached the police car after being stopped. Then he'd gone into total shock as his wrists were placed in cuffs and his phones seized. Now, as he stood in front of Ed Quinn, Roberson was back to his self-assured best.

'Please remove his handcuffs,' Quinn requested his detention officers. He turned to Roberson. 'Remove your belt and any jewellery and valuable items. You will then be searched.'

Quinn had a significant presence; you needed it to perform his role. There were very few, other than the obnoxious drunks, who talked back at him when he was diligently carrying out his duties.

'Sergeant, do you know who I am?' Roberson asked with both arrogance and disdain. His comments were almost humorous as, without his belt, he was having to use both hands to stop his trousers dropping around his ankles.

Quinn, fully aware of the visual and audio custody-suite recording facility, replied politely. 'Sir, I don't know, nor do I care, who you are. I am here as Custody Sergeant. I am not involved in the investigation but have responsibility for you during your time in custody. Do you understand?'

He spoke firmly and politely. Ed Quinn was one of the few people around Parton who didn't know Pete Roberson. His life focused on Parton Rovers FC. He had taken their recent struggles personally as they continued their demise with another relegation likely in the next couple of months. Continuing with the custody process, Quinn paused only momentarily when he noted Roberson's occupation.

Details obtained, Roberson requested a solicitor and also asked for the Temporary Chief Constable Alan Conting to be informed of his arrest.

'He already knows, Ed,' Sutton said quietly to Quinn. 'Ron Turner has just briefed him.'

'Take him down and put him in Male Cell One.' Quinn gestured to one of his detention officers.

Almost immediately Harry Temple was waiting to be buzzed through to the custody suite. It was not an environment he was familiar with – but when the Head of CID requested, the Head of CID got what he wanted, particularly if that individual was Ron Turner.

Temple rarely got tasked with a visit to the custody suite, for which he was extremely grateful. He absorbed the lights and sounds of a place with which he did not feel altogether comfortable. He was happy to see a couple of familiar faces in Sutton and Singer.

Sutton produced the evidence bag containing the two phones seized from Roberson. Temple was more than happy to carry them away back to his office, leaving the custody suite as quickly as he possibly could.

21

Stanislav Zenden

Some two hours earlier, PC 8558 Steve Barker had arrived at Parton East police station for the morning parade. It was only a few days since that fateful late shift when he and Sergeant Ged Graham attended the scene of his murdered colleagues. After a couple days off, and with some Occupational Health Unit counselling, he was back to work on a set of early shifts from 7am to 5pm.

As soon as he walked back into the parade room, Barker felt at home. The place was both dirty and scruffy; it always was, but he enjoyed the atmosphere. The walls, covered in white paint that was flaking in parts, were filled with posters from numerous agencies offering support and welfare for vulnerable persons. There were also police force performance statistics. Barker noticed an internal A4 poster advertising a new European database available via a control-room extension. He made a mental note of it. He was a keen traveller, particularly in Europe, and his journeys had helped to develop his knowledge. His degree from St Andrews University was in East European Cultures.

After the parade, when officers were given their respective deployments, Sergeant Graham asked to see him.

Barker knocked on the door of the Sergeant's office. 'Sarge, you wanted to see me before I go out?'

'Yep, come in Steve.' Ged liked the probationer; he was conscientious, intelligent and able to speak to people in the right way.

'How's things, Steve? Counselling worthwhile?'

'I'm good, Sarge. Thanks. And yes, I did find it was worthwhile, I have a further follow-up appointment in a fortnight,' Barker replied politely.

'Look, we need to sign off everything to complete your probation at the end of the month. I was just checking your work record. It's very good and I have no complaints whatsoever but I notice it's slightly unbalanced in terms of crime as opposed to road traffic. If the opportunity presents itself, and only then, a summons or two wouldn't go amiss – but not to the extent of alienating our general public,' said Graham.

'Fully understand, Sergeant,' Barker replied.

He returned to the parade room, finished his mug of tea and collected the panda keys for his vehicle. He'd been allocated to the Alpha beat. He smiled to himself as he placed his empty mug by the sink, where it joined the six others belonging to members of his shift. No doubt he would be expected to wash them all at the end of his tour of duty.

Barker headed out onto mobile patrol via the locker room where he picked up his utility belt, containing CS spray, a baton and cuffs. He had been well trained; he checked his vehicle thoroughly to ensure that no one from the night shift had left him with some unreported damage that he would have to justify at a later stage. He carried out a quick airwaves radio check with the Control Room, then set off. His first stop was Walter's Cafe, a greasy-spoon establishment, where he got his favourite early dayshift meal, an egg and mushroom roll bathed in brown sauce.

The cafe was a meeting place for many of the shift when they were working the early turn, providing there were no urgent jobs outstanding or a 999 shout. Barker usually had a quick chat with his colleagues if he hadn't made contact with them during the parade briefing. Most of the chat in the cafe this morning was still about their fallen colleagues. It was something that would remain with PC Barker forever.

Steve took up his position during the rush hour traffic. He remembered Sergeant Graham's instructions. He was on the lookout for a worthwhile stop.

***

Stanislav Zenden had been at work for some time. One of Uncle Joe's former best friends had arrived with a brake problem just as he was locking up last night. Like every other customer, he needed his car back as soon as possible; they all did and Joe's Autos had no facility to provide courtesy vehicles.

Unusually, Stan had had a poor night's sleep. He'd collected his children from the child-minder, whilst his wife completed her late shift at the Tree Tops Residential Care Home. His nine-year-old son, Filip, and seven-year-old daughter, Lena, ran out of their child-minder's house to greet him as he made his way up the garden path.

Stan loved this time, this short walk back home and tea with his beloved children, time to talk through their day at school before his wife returned. It was *his* time with the children.

The UK had been good to him and his family and he knew it.

On their way home that evening, they had crossed the small play area adjacent to their block of flats. Two drug addicts, who had obviously recently scored, were literally bouncing off the swings, roundabouts and other play facilities. Their behaviour had shocked Filip and Lena. Once safely back in the flat, the questions from the children started. No matter how hard he tried, Stan could not deflect his children from what they had seen. Even when their mother came home, the topic remained the same.

Worse was to come. Lena was awake most of the night after a nightmare about the play area, a place she had always associated with happiness and joy. So Stan was not in the best frame of mind for work but, in the interests of customer service, he'd foregone his breakfast with the people who meant the most to him, his wife and family, and tried to put last night's drugs episode and the effect on his children to the back of his mind.

It took him two hours' labour to replace the brake discs and pads. He worked alone, before anyone arrived and the phones started ringing. The car-washing franchise opened soon after 9am.

He had Radio Parton playing loudly in the workshop. He stopped work after an hour for a mug of English tea and quick call home to his wife and children. He wished them a lovely day at school and told them to behave and do what their teacher asked of them before saying goodbye in Polish. Unfortunately Lena was still asking questions about their walk home through the park last night. It troubled Stan.

After finishing the job, he decided to take the vehicle on a short test drive before ringing the customer and telling him that his car was ready. The possibility of another decent tip for the skilled mechanic was also a significant factor in his decision, and you could never be over cautious when it came to brakes.

It was shortly after 9am and the car-wash team were rolling in when he took the Astra out on the road. Stan rarely drove in the UK, never mind taking customers' vehicles out, but this was one of their best customers and someone he knew would be very generous when his car was returned, repaired and in double-quick time. Because of the brakes, he needed to give it a test drive.

Turning right out of the garage, Stan knew he hadn't spent sufficient time familiarising himself with the Astra's controls. He made his way onto the main road that gave him access to the roundabout that would then facilitate his return to the garage. A three to four mile journey taking five minutes max, he thought.

As he approached the roundabout he activated the wrong indicator. His intention was to turn right but his nearside indicator was illuminated for all to see.

Eagle-eyed PC Steve Barker responded immediately. He didn't activate his blue lights but manoeuvred his vehicle behind the Astra, allowing it to safely clear the roundabout before he discreetly flashed his headlights to attract the driver's attention and ask him to pull over.

Stan saw the flashing headlights and immediately complied with the request, pulling into a bus stand layby. He remained in his vehicle as Barker approached; remember your training, the former Polish Intelligence Agent said to himself. He looked for the instrument to activate the driver's window so he could focus on the officer's instructions.

'Morning, sir. Could you please take a seat in my car,' Barker said, friendly but firmly.

'Lovely morning, officer,' said Stan in his best English accent, although it didn't take a language graduate to work out he was Eastern European. He was soon sitting in the rear of the police vehicle. Remember your training, he repeated to himself.

'Your name, sir?' enquired Barker.

Stan thought for a moment, a fact immediately spotted by Barker. 'Alex Zenden, date of birth the twentieth of December 1978,' he replied.

Stan, as ever, had already planned for this type of scenario. He had no current UK driving licence. His previous occupation in Poland, as well as the problems he had left behind, meant any brush with officialdom could present serious immigration problems. They were problems he needed to avoid.

Barker told him that the manner of his driving and the incorrect use of his indicators were the reason he had been stopped.

'I am sorry, officer,' Stan said, as meekly as he possibly could. He needed to get out of this situation without undue hassle. 'Here, would you like to see my driving licence?' He produced his wife Alexsandra's UK licence. It gave all the correct details, apart from the Christian name.

Stan had been able to create a passing forgery because of the poor picture that appeared on the official document. He and his wife both had classical Eastern European features; he was always clean shaven with short dark hair, similar to his wife's. Although Alexsandra was a Polish girl's name, Stan thought that by using the shortened Alex the chances of him being caught out were minimal.

Barker, thorough as ever, checked out his name and address. Zenden wasn't recorded on any criminal systems. The voters' check came back with an Alexsandra residing at the address Stan had given.

Barker knew from his studies and travelling that Alexsandra was a Polish girl's name. He looked more closely at the small, pink, hologrammed card. The photograph didn't look genuine.

'Have you got any other identification, Alex?' Barker asked, knowing that there would only be one way of sorting this out and proving beyond doubt that this person was, or wasn't, whom he claimed to be.

'No, officer,' Stan replied. Whilst Barker was distracted, jotting down a couple of notes, he slipped his sports centre pass and a Polish identity card in the name of Stanislav Zenden out from his trouser pocket onto the floor of the panda car, moving the protective mats over the documents with his feet.

He was concentrating so hard on what he was doing that he was oblivious to the officer, who was radioing for back up.

Barker read out the caution and explained the grounds for his detention. 'Well, Alex, we can't prove who you are and therefore where you live. We need to go to the police station to verify that in order to issue a summons. In addition, I am not satisfied with your driving licence which I believe could well be stolen.'

For Stan this was the worst possible scenario.

Another traffic car with a double crew arrived alongside them to assist in transporting the prisoner. Stan was handcuffed, in accordance with force protocol, and placed in the rear of the traffic car. Barker followed them in his own police vehicle. It was a timely traffic summons and maybe something else with a little more investigation. That would impress Sergeant Graham.

Barker arrived at the Parton City Centre Custody Suite. Diligently, and practising one of the first aspects of his basic training, he checked the rear of his vehicle where his prisoner had been sitting. Under the protective mats he discovered two items in the name of Stanislav Zenden, obviously discarded by the prisoner whom he'd just arrested. This traffic stop was getting more interesting by the minute.

After entering the Custody Suite, his prisoner was housed in the secure holding area, waiting to be called up by Sergeant Ed Quinn, who was just checking in another recently arrived guest.

Barker, as with many of his colleagues, held Quinn in the highest regard. It was respect bordering on fear; standing in front of him and relaying the grounds of the arrest, the young constable wondered if one day he would be a Custody Sergeant. He had learned so much from Quinn during his probation – the way he dealt with prisoners, staff, solicitors and procedure. Quinn was never fazed, whether he had ten prisoners fighting drunk all arriving at the same time to be processed, or dealing with a very vulnerable sex offender.

'Sergeant, the prisoner was driving in an erratic manner. He produced a driving licence in the name of Alexsandra Zenden, a Polish girl's name. In addition, we have recovered a Polish identity card and sports centre pass in the name of Stanislav Zenden from underneath the dustmats of the police vehicle where he was initially detained.'

Stan looked down, angry with himself. He feared the worst.

Quinn informed him that his detention was authorised in order to ascertain his correct identity and establish who was the rightful owner of the licence. Then Stan was searched by Quinn's detention officers and his mobile phone, wallet and house keys placed in a locker.

'Male Cell Three, please,' Quinn ordered one of the detention officers. 'Good arrest, Steve.'

Praise indeed from Quinn, thought Barker.

Stanislav Zenden was angry. He had let himself and others down – and he wasn't thinking about Dunc Travis, or their valuable customer. He was thinking about his wife and young family.

Unknown to him, Pete Roberson was housed in a nearby cell in the very same Custody Suite.

22

Ed Quinn

Sutton's phone rang. It was Harry Temple. 'Geoff, you need to see this quickly.' Although Sutton had only met Temple on a couple of occasions, he recognised the urgency in his voice. Five minutes later he and Singer were sitting with Temple in his office, Roberson's two mobiles on the desk in front of them.

Temple gave them an overview of the text messages. 'I'm no detective but it's obvious from the recorded messages that Roberson has been subject of blackmail over the past ten months or so. In addition you need to have a look at this.'

Temple played them the video clip, clearly showing a black Lexus colliding with a young girl, Roberson getting out of the car, looking around and then leaving. From the time and date on the clip, it appears that the blackmailing texts started soon after the incident.

Singer and Sutton looked at each other. Who was that girl? It was no one they recognised. Where did it happen? For all they knew, that girl could still be alive.

Sutton put in a call to Turner, informing him of the discovery. The line went quiet and Sutton knew that Turner was considering the next course of action.

'Geoff, an urgent interview. I will authorise it on the basis that if the girl is alive, albeit that is doubtful from what you tell me of the recording, Roberson is the only person who can provide us with a potential lead.'

'Thanks, boss.' Sutton thought that was an excellent call by Turner. Who knew what Roberson's reaction might be? He was already traumatised by being arrested. As he informed Bill Singer of Turner's decision, adrenaline surged through Sutton. How the hell would Roberson react to this?

'Thanks, Harry,' Singer said, as he and Sutton hastily left Temple's office armed with Roberson's phones.

'Any time,' said Temple to a closing door.

Returning to the Custody Suite, Sutton outlined the circumstances to Ed Quinn, who recorded the authorisation after confirming it with Ron Turner. 'It's been an interesting morning, Geoff,' said Quinn.

'Let's hope there is more to come,' Sutton said.

Roberson was brought back into the holding area; ironically, he passed Stanislav Zenden's cell door on his way.

'Mr Roberson, I have the power and now the authority to request you go with these officers for an urgent interview. They have some evidence that they wish to show you, which might assist with our enquiries,' Quinn said.

'I'm not saying anything without my solicitor,' Roberson replied, disdainfully. 'When am I going to be released?'

'Go with the officers,' said Quinn firmly.

The three men walked into the interview room, Sutton carrying a small evidence bag with the two mobile phones.

'Please have a seat, Mr Roberson,' Singer said politely. 'There's a cup of water here if you need it.'

Roberson rolled his eyes and ignored the plastic cup.

Sutton and Singer sat opposite him, separated by a bolted-down table. Singer operated the technical video and audio equipment before stating the time and date and reminding Roberson that he was still under caution. Then he took a mobile phone from the exhibit bag and introduced the evidence from the recording. 'Mr Roberson, could you please have a look at this,' he asked and started the video clip.

Roberson looked, squinted, looked away. 'No! No, don't! Don't,' he shouted.

'Mr Roberson, look,' Sutton said firmly. 'Look.'

Roberson forced himself to look at the phone again then started crying. Rocking on his chair, head in hands, he dragged his eyes away then slowly and deliberately placed his head on the grey surface of the desk. He was sobbing loudly.

Sutton reached for the plastic cup of water. 'Mr Roberson, is there anything you would like to tell us?'

'Yes, I killed her! I killed her.' Roberson groaned. 'And I've suffered. Let's get this out. I'm living the nightmare. I don't want a solicitor, I just want to talk! Please, just let me talk.' He raised his head and looked at Sutton and Singer, who were left in no doubt that whatever Roberson was going to impart, he had suffered.

'Please go ahead, Mr Roberson, but I have to remind you that you're still under caution,' said Sutton quietly.

Roberson relayed his story, starting with the leisure-centre function and striking up a conversation with Detective Inspector Sue Dalton. A drink too many, a visit to the trading estate frequented by prostitutes. He described the accidental death of a girl whose identity he didn't know, and leaving the scene. He told them about the subsequent video clip, a graphic reminder of his actions that he retained as a personal torture, and the blackmailing texts from Dunc Travis. They should all be on his other phone. His role was to supply vulnerable youngsters to Travis, who were given drugs in return for sexual favours.

Roberson told them that he'd been so hounded by guilt that he'd gone to turn himself in at East Parton Police station but changed his mind at the last minute. He talked through his sad relationship with Sue Dalton, from whom he'd obtained information linking the missing William Carr with the murdered police officers. He was brutally frank about his relationship with Dalton; he had used her.

'Sue Dalton died of an overdose yesterday,' Sutton said when Roberson paused.

'I nearly killed her,' said Roberson without feeling. His composure was returning.

Sutton thought how cold and evil Roberson's attitude was towards Dalton. He couldn't give a damn when she was alive or now that she was dead. The fact that he had played a significant part in her death seemed to pass him by.

The confession brought Roberson immediately relief; he felt instantly better, without a thought of what the future might hold. This had been a tortured few months that had changed his life. It was only later, when he faced serious charges, that he realised how dire his situation was. His life and ambitions were in tatters.

Pete Roberson, the disgraced former Police and Crime Commissioner.

Pete who?

Roberson was placed back in his cell, whilst Sutton and Singer went to meet with Ron Turner. He needed an update and also to consider Dunc Travis's arrest.

***

Ed Quinn was typing up Roberson's custody record. This was a shift he wouldn't forget in a hurry. The buzzing from Male Cell Three, Steve Barker's arrest, disturbed his concentration.

'Steve, go and see what your man wants, please,' Ed said to Barker.

Stanislav Zenden's mind was in overdrive. He'd been caught out and he knew it; he'd forgotten his training. He had a past, which could come back to haunt him and have implications for his family. It was more than likely that the police would search the flat and interview his wife. They could even arrest her.

His children. The effect on them of last night's experience with the drug addicts in the play area still played on his mind.

Through his ever-deeper involvement with Dunc Travis, he had been complicit in supplying drugs and the subsequent deaths of more than one person.

Barker was away a couple of minutes before returning to his Custody Sergeant. 'He wants to speak to my supervisor. He won't tell me anything else.'

'Well, give Ged a call and in the meantime get his fingerprints scanned. It may help to prove his identity,' Quinn requested.

Fingerprints obtained, Sergeant Ged Graham was sitting in an interview room together with PC Barker and Stanislav Zenden. Barker, as thorough as ever and remembering the parade room notice, had rung through Zenden's details to the Control Room extension for a check on the newly available European database. They were awaiting a response.

Stan started. 'No tape. Just please listen to me. It is very important. My family are everything to me and I need to ensure they are safe and protected. No one matters more to me, than them. We are settled. Things have gone so well for us in England. They are happy here.

'Your checks will show I am Stanislav Zenden. I am a former member of the Polish Intelligence Agency but when I left the agency things went badly for me and I committed a robbery on a general store in the outskirts of Warsaw. I am wanted back in Poland for that offence. I also have information on my boss, Dunc Travis, who took the leading part in the murder of your two officers. He disposed of another two bodies, both of people who were working for him in return for his drugs supply. One was the missing boy, William Carr. I also played a role in these crimes and I'll face the consequences, but I need to ensure that my family will be allowed to stay in this country.'

Both officer's listened intently. Steve Barker couldn't believe what he was hearing.

Ged Graham took the initiative. 'How can you prove it?' he asked Zenden.

'Bring my phone,' Zenden replied.

Barker shook his head as he left the room, as if to clear the haze. He returned a couple of minutes later.

Unknown to his boss, Zenden had secretly recorded Travis's actions. He had been detailed to remain in the cabin when the disposal of the bodies took place after they had taken Nina and William out to sea. It was all neatly recorded on his phone.

Stan knew full well he was also delivering evidence of the part he'd played in these crimes. He'd also implicated his brother Seb but that didn't matter to Stan; his wife and children came first, above anything else, even his brother. He had never fully forgiven Seb for getting him involved in that robbery on the general store back in Poland.

In addition, he played them clips from some of the conversations he'd had with Travis over the past few months. Neither officer said a word.

Stan told them that Travis kept his 'special knife' strapped under his desk in his office at the garage.

'Never trust anyone,' said Zenden, almost as a prophecy. 'Please, my family. I will take my punishment.' He remembered the conversation he'd had with his children.

There was knock on the interview room and Ed Quinn poked his head round the door. 'Stanislav Zenden, wanted for robbery in Poland. The Control Room has just been on the phone. Fingerprint scan also confirms Stanislav Zenden.'

'Ed, Stanislav needs to go back down to his cell – without the phone,' Ged Graham said to his colleague.

Five minutes later, Graham was sitting with Sutton and Singer in Ron Turner's office, talking about the information they'd obtained from Zenden's phone. It was time to go after Travis but this needed to be carefully planned and co-ordinated. Travis seemed like a cool customer but he had a propensity for violence. In many ways, Turner wanted a reaction from Travis when he was arrested. Turner wanted behaviour that would be in keeping with a serial murderer, as well as providing good evidence.

He ordered the copies of Stan's recording of disposing the bodies and organised a specially trained search-and-arrest team to accompany Singer and Sutton when they went to Uncle Joe's Garage.

***

It was approximately twelve noon the same day when Sergeant Ben Linton's team of six uniformed officers appeared in their personnel carrier. They had arranged to meet Sutton and Singer in the same church car park they had used earlier that day prior to Roberson's arrest.

Linton's team were two staff down from their full quota because of sickness and annual leave. His team of constables were one of two that provided Parton Constabulary with a response to outbreaks of major disorder. They also policed high-profile events and could carry out specialist searches. Bill Singer knew Ben from a couple of jobs that he had coordinated.

Leaving their vehicle in the church car park, Sutton and Singer joined Linton and his staff inside the personnel carrier. It was an interesting environment, to say the least, as they squatted between the riot shields and equipment for breaking down doors. All the constables were wearing their stab-proof vests, as were Sutton and Singer. Linton and his team were armed with CS gas and batons.

The plan was that Sutton and Singer would go to Travis's office with Linton and two of his team. The remainder would go to the car-wash franchise to detain Seb Zenden.

Parking at the entrance, and equipped with a copy of the phone recordings supplied by Stan, Singer led the way. Thanks to Stan's information, they knew the exact location of Dunc Travis's office. Without knocking they went in, deliberately leaving the door slightly ajar so that Linton and his two trusty constables could partially observe, and hear, any conversation.

'Mr Travis, you do not have to say anything…' Singer gave the caution, finishing with the line, 'I am arresting you on suspicion of murder.' At that point, Sutton pointed the phone directly in his face from across his desk and switched on the recorded messages.

Travis had his feet up on his desk when they entered his office. He kept them there when Singer was giving the caution and informing of his arrest. Mr Cool. However, when he heard the first few words of the phone recording, his feet came down to the floor. Linton and his colleagues entered the room. Travis, with his hands searching under his desk, was lifted off his feet as Linton pushed the desk forward, jamming Travis's arms against the back wall of his office. He was pinned and helpless. Linton's constables moved round the sides of the desk and took hold of him.

Linton barked instructions to Travis. He had his hand on his CS gas canister, just in case. 'Your right arm first, very slowly. Now your left.'

Within seconds Travis was handcuffed and being led out of the office. Over at the car wash, Seb had identified himself to the officers and come very quietly. Transport had already been called for both prisoners.

Singer crawled into the space beneath Travis's desk. Looking up, he saw a large machete-type knife wedged underneath it. He left it there. Other officers were arriving and the scene would be secured. He needed forensics to photograph the item in situ before bagging and tagging it as evidence.

Singer hoped that they had recovered the murder weapon that had been used on his two colleagues. Despite how clever Dunc Travis thought he was, he might well have a sad and perverse connection with the weapon and be keeping it as some sort of badge of honour. He obviously thought he was untouchable and there was a strong likelihood he would have used it again.

The prisoners were taken to a different custody suite although Turner thought mischievously that putting them in the same cell complex with Roberson and Stan could prove entertaining. He knew that they had the main men, although there would be others involved in the murder of Chilter and Wrightson. He was satisfied that, with Stan Zenden's assistance, they would be easily identified.

The hard work would now start to secure convictions, particularly against the instigator Dunc Travis, who had no motive to confess.

He sat behind his desk with Sutton and Singer in attendance.

'That European arrest warrant will remain with us and not be executed at this time. Stan is going through our courts, our justice system, no matter how much assistance he gives from now on. He murdered our colleagues and two extremely vulnerable people,' Turner said to the assembled throng. 'Don't pursue his false document and driving offences at this time. We will not upset, or cause issue, with his family. We don't need to. Now, gentlemen, I'm going to have a chat with our Temporary Chief Constable.' His tone was full of disdain.

As Turner stood up to leave the office, Sutton's mobile rang. It was Simon Keys from Holston House. 'Just a minute, sir,' Sutton said to Turner. 'Mind if I take this? It could be important.' Unusually, Turner nodded his agreement. He was a man not prone to being interrupted.

'Mr Sutton, it's Simon Keys here from Holston House. Sorry to trouble you but are you alright to speak? This could be of some importance to your investigation.'

'Yes, Simon, please go ahead,' Sutton replied immediately. There was an urgency to Sutton's voice that gripped the attention of both Singer and Turner.

'I've just had the Matron here and we have had a disclosure from one of our older residents regarding her being abused on numerous occasions by two men, one believed to be a police officer by the name of Bob Harries, the other by a previous foster carer.'

Sutton's heart sank. 'Who is the foster carer? Anyone we know?' Sutton sought the answer with increasing concern.

'Someone by the name of Jones, not from the Parton area at all. I certainly have not heard his name nor met him,' said Keys.

Sutton breathed a huge sigh of relief; for one moment, one single moment, a doubt had passed through his mind. Not Stew Grant, a man he knew so well, trusted, respected, admired and yes, loved. Sutton was disgusted with himself for letting that thought pass even fleetingly through his mind.

He immediately scolded himself for ever doubting one of his very best friends.

He had always considered trust to be the most important aspect in any relationship.

'Simon, I will have an officer attend from the investigation team as soon as possible. In the meantime, if the Matron can remain with the girl and keep a note of any relevant comments I would be much obliged,' Sutton said respectfully.

'That is not a problem,' replied Keys.

Sutton faced his audience who had listening keenly to the one-sided conversation.

'Boss, you will recall that the original reporting by Billy Spitz suggested abuse by some important local people. Well, it looks like the first important person is one of our own. There has been a disclosure made by a resident that she has been abused by a police officer by the name of Bob Harries. Whilst it still to be confirmed at this stage, I am not aware of anyone else in the organisation called Bob Harries other than our Assistant Chief Constable. No wonder he authorised an informant's payment without a senior officer present. Yet another matter to bring before Mr Conting.'

Turner, who had got up to leave, sat down again. 'I need another coffee before I brief Conting. Sadly, gentlemen,

Parton Constabulary will take some considerable time to recover from Operation Trust,' he said with absolute sincerity.

He then proceeded to ignore his coffee that he had only just requested and left the room, followed by Sutton and Singer.

23

Geoff Sutton

It was after 5pm when Sutton left the Incident Room. The place was buzzing. Trained interview teams were just going into what in all probability would be a second 'no comment' interview with Dunc Travis. The teams assigned to Stan Zenden and Pete Roberson had obtained a full picture of events, which had been confirmed by outside enquiries. The forensic samples from all the detainees had been fast tracked and initial reports had placed Travis and both Zendens at the murder scenes.

Ron Turner, back from updating the Temporary Chief Constable, had a smile larger than both East and West Parton Marinas spread across his face. He authorised the diving team to take Stan Zenden out on one of their vessels to see if he could identify approximately where the bodies of Nina and William had been dumped. An oceanographer would look at tidal movements to help them. In addition, there was now only one owner of *Robes*: it was seized by Parton Constabulary as part of the investigation.

Given the amount of time that had passed, finding Nina was an extremely long shot but there was hope of recovering some of her brother William's remains.

Sutton knew that his role would diminish over the next few days, as it rightly should. He would be back to 'projects' within a very short time. He was knackered, both physically and mentally. Barbour over his arm, he trudged across the car park and back to his car. He perched the Ted Baker sunglasses on his nose; even if he didn't need them they really did look the part. That's what matters, he thought.

He had an important job to do on his way home.

Some twenty minutes later, he pulled up outside the Grants' house, walked up the driveway and rang the bell. Stew came to the door, immaculate as ever.

'Come in, you bugger. I'm sick of seeing you, Geoff,' his mate greeted him.

'You can't get too much of a good thing,' Sutton replied and followed Granty through to the kitchen where Tina, fresh from a gym session, was waiting.

Without being offered, Sutton said, 'Large gin and tonic, please.'

'Coming up.' Tina went to the cupboard.

When they all had drinks in front of them, Sutton continued. 'Tina, Stew, I have some sad news. We strongly believe that William is dead. I am so sorry.'

Stew immediately went to his wife, who collapsed in his arms. For the next ten minutes Sutton slowly took the Grants through the day's events, divulging as much information as he could given that further interviews were taking place and people were in custody.

Sutton rightly gave the caveat that it had not been fully corroborated but they believed that William had been murdered and his body deposited out to sea. They were hopeful that his remains could be recovered but there were no guarantees.

'He had an awful life, Geoff,' said Stew. In some small way he was relieved that they could now have some closure. He still had hold of Tina.

'I knew William was dead. Call it intuition,' Tina sobbed. She took a deep breath in an effort to compose herself. 'Thanks, Geoff, for everything.' She stood up and embraced him.

Sutton felt himself crumbling from both fatigue and emotion, and also from Tina's spontaneous action. He hugged her close, head on her shoulder, both in gratitude and to prevent her seeing his tears.

'Look, I'm heading off. You need some time on your own. See you Saturday, Stew. The normal golf and rugby.'

'Can't wait, Geoff. Now bugger off. We need some gin left,' Stew said, trying to smile through his tears.

Sutton showed himself out and walked back down to the driveway to his car. He found his mobile and tapped in Debbie's number.

'Hello, you,' said that lovely voice.

'Italian, Friday night, Debbie?' he asked hopefully.

'Can't wait, Geoff,' she replied eagerly.

Epilogue

The April sunshine filtered around the most scenic rugby ground in the country, according to the learned thoughts of Geoff Sutton, Stew Grant, Roger Strong and Pete McIntyre. Sutton, sunglasses perched on his nose, was trying to look a twenty something, although that ambition was dashed as he was still wearing his Barbour.

The weather was good, the sun at last gave a promise of some heat after what had seemed to be a very long winter. The trees that provide the backdrop to the rugby club were waking up to show the earliest sprouting of spring blossom. The clocks, having gone forward an hour, ensured that at least there was still daylight as the game drew to a close.

That morning had seen another Texas scramble golf match and the lads were still in with a chance until the dreaded seventeenth hole. This time it was Roger Strong's right-handed slice that took the ball at a forty-five-degree angle straight into the back garden of one of the grand homes that backed onto Parton Golf Club.

Sutton was the first to pluck up courage to communicate with Strong, some way down the eighteenth fairway. 'Unlucky, Rog. You've been playing so well,' he said, sympathising with his mate.

'Piss off, Geoff,' came the response, replicating Sutton's own retort in similar circumstances a couple of months earlier.

The lads were now back at their usual Saturday afternoon spot behind the posts, furthest away from the changing rooms. It was the final home game of the season and the players were putting on a good display, coasting to a 43–5 point victory against already relegated Fretton RFC.

'Go on, son, pin your ears back,' McIntyre shouted to Upper Parton's left winger, as he made for the corner only to be tackled in touch just as he was about to dive for the line.

The referee blew for full time. The four men, instead of walking down the pitch towards the welcoming clubhouse for a cup of tea, pork and stuffing sandwich before a pint or three, decided to make a diversion.

Sutton, Strong, McIntyre and Grant, turned to their right and walked slowly in silence towards the layby near the picnic area that gave access to the woodland walks. As they drew closer, their attention was drawn to a new, brightly varnished garden seat surrounded with floral tributes, some now past their best, that had been placed at the scene.

The plaque affixed to the seat bore the words: *To DC Mike Chilter and DC Linda Wrightson, who died whilst doing their job and protecting others, from their friends and colleagues at Parton Constabulary.*

There had been a thought to include Sue Dalton's name on the plaque, to recognise her contribution to the force. However, this tentative proposal had been thrown out after strong representations from the family and friends of Chilter and Wrightson, once they were aware of the full facts.

They reached the layby and Stew Grant took a small red rose from inside his overcoat. He crouched down and placed it at the very spot where Geoff Sutton had seen the Confidential Unit van parked up only a couple of months previously. Nobody said a word; they didn't need to. The rose, wrapped in cellophane, had a small note attached.

To William,
Please be peaceful.
All our love, as ever,
And forever.
Lots of love
Stew and Tina X

Stew said, 'Be peaceful, William. You had a crap time. Love you. Tina is coming down to see you tomorrow and probably every day. Take care.' He wiped away a tear and looked back at his mates. They all looked down, ashamed to admit to their own tears. Then, in a moment of emotion and for the first time ever, they all embraced before making their way, again in silence, down to the first-team pitch.

They had reached the halfway line when Sutton spouted off. 'It was still a shit shot this morning, Rog. Your round for the tea and sarnies, no pickle in mine.'

'Bollocks,' said Roger. He knew full well he would spend idle time queuing and then suffer the abuse when they started to complain about salt, pepper and sauce.

It was a good hour later. All four were sitting around their table, perched on their high chairs like disgruntled toddlers. Each chair had its own nameplate, or in some cases nickname plate, securely fastened to its seat.

The atmosphere was good; it was always better after a win, and they were now supping their third pint. Unfortunately for Roger, it was his round again. 'Like the Gobi desert around here,' said Pete impatiently.

Stew, proudly wearing his Upper Parton Rugby Club waistcoat, drained his glass. 'Kalahari,' he said.

Roger's shoulders dropped, as he walked slowly to the bar.

'Stand by your beds,' Pete advised, as he glanced over to the entrance doors. Unbeknown to Sutton, Debbie had walked into the club.

Sutton followed his gaze and saw the new woman in his life sway towards him. 'A pint of what you're having, Geoff,' she said as she pecked him on the cheek, signifying a discreet intimacy between the two of them. Sutton went to the bar and asked Roger to buy the extra drink.

Roger, Stew and Pete knew of the emerging relationship and were delighted for their mate. Debbie's confident appearance in the rugby club had taken their relationship to a different level.

Roger returned from the bar.

'No bloody crisps,' Stew said.

'Bugger off,' Roger retorted. 'Sorry, Debbie'

Stew continued. 'A toast – to William.'

'To William,' they replied in unison.

It was at that point that Sutton's phone rang. It was Ron Turner. 'Excuse me, I need to take this.' He made his way outside the clubhouse.

'Geoff.' Turner didn't wait for Sutton to introduce himself. 'I've been promoted to Assistant Chief Constable.'

'Well, congratulations, sir. I thought you were retiring,' said Sutton, surprised.

Turner continued. 'I'll come straight to the point. I have a proposition to make. Continue on your current contract on the understanding that if, and when, we have another major enquiry you will be seconded to work as an unofficial assistant to the Senior Investigating Officer. We need you, Geoff. I want you there.'

Sutton looked through the window and saw Debbie waving at him. 'Boss, I appreciate the call and the offer. I really enjoyed working with you again on Operation Trust. Can I give it some thought and come back to you?' he said, stalling for time.

'Not a problem. Speak soon, I will make myself available for your call on Monday.'

Typical Turner thought Sutton as the call ended.